BOOK ONE OF THE [illegible] JUSTICE SERIES

Opal Fire

(It is highly recommended that this series be read in order.)

BOOK ONE OF THE STACY JUSTICE SERIES

Barbra Annino

The characters and events portrayed in this book are fictitious. Any similarity to real persons, living or dead, is coincidental and not intended by the author.

Printed in the United States of America.

Published by Thomas & Mercer
P.O. Box 400818
Las Vegas, NV 89140

ISBN-13: 9781612186122
ISBN-10: 1612186122

For George,

who never stopped believing.

Chapter I

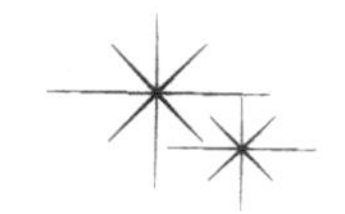

You might say everything was fine until the fire.

I was back in my hometown and living in my grandmother's guest cottage. I had a steady boyfriend, a steady job, and a sturdy dog.

Right now, my main concern was the dog.

"Stacy!" Cinnamon yelled through the haze of hot smoke. "Are you still in here?" The panic in her voice matched the fear pumping through my veins.

"I can't find Thor!" I coughed back.

"He'll be fine. Just get out!" Cinnamon was about to step forward when a beam whistled, then cracked and plunged into the floorboards. A wave of sparks shot into the air, barricading her in the back room of the bar.

I sure hoped that exit wasn't locked, and if it was, I prayed Cinnamon had the keys with her.

"Cin," I choked. I couldn't see my cousin anymore through the thick fog and debris, so I stepped forward.

A wave of fire licked the air—too close to my eyebrows for comfort. It forced me to lunge backward into a beer barrel. I lost my footing, scrambling for anything to sustain a landing. My arm caught the edge of the brass foot rail as I went down—the searing pain instant and vicious.

Then I saw him.

My recently adopted Great Dane was wedged between the keg that toppled me and another, set close to the bar. We hadn't had a chance to hook them up before the fire erupted.

"Thor! Come!" The desperation in my voice shook me to the core.

His rear end was wiggling while the kegs blocked him like linebackers. I couldn't figure out what was holding him there. My eyes flashed to the front entrance of the bar. The flames hadn't reached it yet, but I was certain we had minutes, maybe only seconds, to escape.

Sirens screamed not far off.

I flopped on my belly and skidded quickly to Thor, ignoring the burn. I managed to get my head around the first keg. The dog's eyes met mine, pleading with me not to leave him there. Not to let him die as waves of heat threatened his long, tan tail.

The ornamental footrest that trailed the bar was intricately carved, and Thor's tag had locked onto one of the decorative loops.

"Hang on, buddy." I heard another whistling sound and looked up. A second beam had caught a spark.

Thor whimpered.

My fingers crawled around the keg to grab the tag, but my arm wasn't long enough.

Thor yanked his head back, the muscles in his huge neck bulging as if they would burst right through his fur. The tag bent beneath his force, but he didn't have enough leverage to move his head, or I was sure that collar would have broken apart. It wouldn't have been the first one that couldn't contain Thor.

I sure hoped it wouldn't be the last.

With one good arm, I shoved at the first keg, hoping for enough room to free him.

It wouldn't budge.

The sirens screeched closer.

Or was that Thor wailing?

The bottle opener! It was in my back pocket, and it might get me just enough length to lift that stupid tag over the brass.

Just as an ugly orange flame crept closer to Thor, I heard a familiar voice.

"Stacy!" Leo yelled, and a bottle burst.

Then another.

I kicked my foot. "Down here! Help me get Thor!"

Leo covered me with a tarp and yanked me back by my ankles as Thor howled like a wolf beneath a full moon.

"Get out!" Leo yelled and grabbed his utility knife. To cut the nylon collar, I guessed. There was no time for that.

I grabbed the gun from his holster and fired three shots into the far keg. Beer shot up, then showered down on the bar, my dog, and the floor. It was enough liquid to set the flames at bay.

Leo shoved the first keg out of the way and cut the collar off Thor. The three of us sprinted from the Black Opal, spilling onto the street where a crowd had already gathered.

Leo grabbed his gun from my hand and guided me through the red, white, and blue lights—a rare sight in the tiny tourist town where we lived. Firefighters zigzagged across Main Street, hosing down the nineteenth-century building as volunteers ran around asking how they could help.

It was late afternoon in February, but I wasn't cold. We headed to Leo's police cruiser, and I leaned against it, coughing out a sigh as he handed me a towel to wipe my face.

We stood there for a moment in silence, and I felt a lecture coming on.

"Are you crazy?" he finally asked.

I looked at him, pointedly. "Don't call me crazy. You know that drives me nuts."

Leo set his incredibly sexy, always-stubbly jawline.

"You could have been killed," he said in a low voice.

"But I wasn't, so let it go." I was too pumped with adrenaline to let my guard down. Had I stopped and thought about what might have happened…I shivered at the possibilities.

Leo ran his fingers through his thick black hair and sighed. He pulled me into him and rubbed my shoulders. I flinched as my arm met his leather jacket, and he stood back to examine it. He snapped his fingers, and an EMT promptly said, "Sure, Chief," and shoved an oxygen mask in my face.

Leo is my boyfriend and the chief of police of Amethyst, Illinois, where the pie is homemade, the pump is full-service, and *quirky* is a compliment. He has a Mediterranean look about him and a slight temper to match. Mostly when I put myself in life-threatening situations. Which is hardly ever.

"Look at that burn too," Leo said to the EMT.

"Nah, it's fine," I said. "The aunts and Birdie will take care of it." No co-pay when you live with witches.

Thor was leaning against me, licking the beer off his backside, and I began to towel him off with my tarp.

Leo said, "You two get in the car and stay warm. Give me a minute to straighten out this mess, and then you can tell me what happened."

I looked over at the crowd. It had developed its own heartbeat.

"I need to find Cinnamon, Leo."

Leo pulled out his radio and called to Gus, his right-hand man. He opened the door to the backseat, and Thor and I slid in.

A few minutes later, he knocked on the window.

"She's fine. Not a scratch. Now, sit tight so I can ask you some questions before the mayor has a coronary and I have to explain why my girlfriend is always caught up in the chaos that surrounds this town like *The Twilight Zone* on steroids."

He shut the door again, and a firefighter approached him.

I drank in the scene around me. Some people were directing traffic, some were throwing buckets full of water on the flames (the whole bucket too, not just the contents), some were snapping photos, and one guy, who I recognized as a regular of the Black Opal—Scully—was clutching a stool and crying.

It was like the bleacher seats at a Cubs game when the beer gets cut off, but how was that my fault?

Before Leo turned back toward the car, a small group of men, all dressed in purple polo shirts with plastic badges, approached him.

"Chief, where did ya want me?" a man asked.

"I can close off the streets," another offered.

"Hey, I called that," said a third.

I rolled down the window. "Leo, what's this?" I asked as the three men neared the squad car.

Leo turned back and said in a low voice. "Remember I told you we were hosting a citizens' academy class?"

I nodded.

"Today was graduation."

I winced. In a matter of seconds, the rent-a-cops swarmed Leo like a group of bees in a bed of sunflowers. Actually, they weren't even rent-a-cops. They were rent-a-cop wannabes. It was disturbing.

While Leo fought them off, I seized the opportunity to slip away. Thor and I sneaked out the other side of the car and headed down the street.

I needed to find my cousin. See her. Touch her.

We made it about a block when I noticed, displaced from the crowd, a pimply-faced teenager with hair like a Brillo pad staring at me, an oddly satisfied look on his face.

I stopped and stared back. He smiled wildly. Then he bolted like a cat attached to a firecracker.

And a chill rumbled through my veins.

Chapter 2

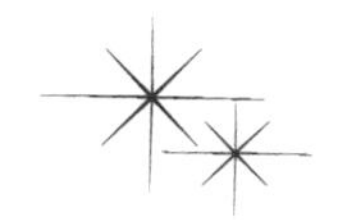

I wasn't in the habit of chasing after men half my age, but the circumstances seemed to call for it.

The kid gave me the heebie-jeebies.

My new cross-trainers, which had been white about thirty minutes ago, were getting quite a workout as I pumped my legs and sprinted through the thick crowd, the blanket falling from my shoulders. Thor was having a ball playing chase, not certain what we were running toward and not caring. His huge lips flapped in the cold air, as if he were smiling, happy to be alive. I couldn't blame him.

The smoke I had inhaled inside the building was catching up with me, and the kid was getting farther away. Why he even ran in the first place was a mystery, but I was determined to find out.

"Hey, stop!" I yelled.

He was a block ahead of me. He turned and flipped me the bird, which I found completely unnecessary and more than a little irritating.

I tapped Thor on the behind. "Get him," I said and pointed to the little snot. Thor paused, uncertain what I was asking, but when the kid bolted again, he had his target. He took off at full speed, and I followed close behind.

Brillo-Head turned a corner, and Thor made a wide left turn the way a semi would, all four paws kicking up slush and salt behind him, looking like a mountain lion on the hunt.

That was all I saw before I smacked face-first into something bulky and cold. The hit catapulted me through the air and into a snow bank. It wasn't that soft, fluffy snow that kids sled through in December. This was midwinter, been-plowed-into-a-rock-formation snow.

"Damn, lady, where's the fire?" said a voice I didn't recognize.

If the wind hadn't been knocked out of me, I would have punched the idiot who just said that.

"Ehh..." was all I could squeak out.

"Holy hell! Stacy?" Cinnamon this time. Thank goddess. She tried to help me to my feet, but I raised a hand to stop her. I was pretty sure my left lung had deflated.

"Stacy? You Stacy Justice? Damn, girl, you're finer than your picture." Okay, who was the weirdo? Granted, I had on my size-six skinny jeans, which had been blue before the fire, and a tight sweater that brought the ladies to attention, but I was pretty sure my mascara had melted all over my face, and the best I could hope for my hair was that it smelled more like beer than barbecued dog tail.

"Who the hell are you?" asked Cinnamon.

That's my cousin, direct and to the point. I imagined her hands were parked on her ample hips and her jaw was set to "pissed off."

"Sorry, I'm Derek Meyers. I'm the new photographer at the paper. Just started today. Mr. Parker sent me down here to make sure Stacy was okay and to ask her to cover the story. Thought I'd bring my gear and maybe snap a few photos while I was at it." His voice was chipper. Cinnamon hated chipper. She wrapped Chipper up in duct tape, pounded nails into it, and used it to beat the crap out of Perky.

"Oh, really? Well, Derek, I've already snapped a few photos myself and put them on my website," said my cousin.

I knew where she was headed with this, so I tried to stop her. "Eh, eh, Cin, don't."

"You did?" Derek sounded incredulous.

"Sure did. It's called shoveitupyourass-dot-com."

I tried to close my eyes at that point, but the lashes were glued to my eyelids.

"Hey, that's uncool! Who are you, anyway?" Derek asked.

My lungs had inflated during this little tête-à-tête, and I attempted to right myself. Both Cinnamon and Derek reached out to help me. Cin slapped Derek away and hoisted me to my feet.

"Leave her alone, you ass! Don't you have a brain in that bobble-doll head of yours? We just escaped a burning building, and now, thanks to you, my cousin is a Popsicle," Cinnamon said.

I wasn't cold until she said that. Now, in between breaths, my teeth chattered, but the throbbing burn felt better.

"You two are related?" Derek asked, completely missing the point Cinnamon was trying to make. "I don't believe it."

Cin and I looked at each other.

It was true we didn't seem to sprout from the same family tree. Birdie (our grandmother) and I take after the Irish side of the family with red hair and green eyes. I'm a few years older and a few inches taller than Cinnamon at five foot eight. She's a couple pounds heavier and a couple cup sizes bigger than me at "don't squeeze the melons." But her olive skin, mahogany hair, and chocolate eyes are all Italian, thanks to her mother, Angelica, whom my uncle imported from Sicily.

"You saying I'm lying?" Cin jabbed Derek with her finger.

Which side the feisty temper comes from is still up for debate.

I stepped in between Cinnamon and Derek and assessed him for the first time. He was in his twenties, dark skinned, a bit taller than me. Ski jacket, blue jeans, enormous camera bag, which I assumed was what knocked me on my rump.

"Hi, D-d-d-erek. Yes-s-s, I'm S-t-t-acy and this-s-s is my overprotec-c-c-tive c-c-c-ousin, Cin-n-n-a-m-m-m-on P-p-p-a-n-z-a-n-o.

"Hey, I'm really sorry about running into you. I didn't see you." Derek extended his hand, and I shook it; then he offered it to Cin, who feigned a hangnail.

The cold air bit through my sweater, and I felt like I was forgetting something.

"You must be freezing, honey. I'll get a blanket from a fireman," Cin said.

Derek didn't need another hint. He dropped his camera bag and had his coat around me in a flash.

"Th-th-anks," I said.

"Humph," Cinnamon said, and Derek was forgiven.

Iris Merriweather, the owner of Muddy Waters Coffee Shop, approached us then with three paper cups of coffee. Iris wrote a gossip column for the paper, which often entailed week-old stories because folks tightened their lips around her. She was in her sixties, with light hair grown frizzy from forty years of using Clairol.

"Here you go, kids. Maybe this will warm you up," she said.

We all thanked Iris and sipped the coffee.

"I'm so glad you girls are okay. I saw the flames from across the street and called the fire department lickety-split."

"I'm okay, Iris, but Stacy here refused to leave that damn dog." Cin turned to me. "Leo said you got a nasty burn. Did you let the EMT treat it?"

"It's fine, Cin. And he was your damn dog first." Through a series of circumstances I still don't understand, Thor decided he wanted to adopt me. Cinnamon, recently back with her ex-husband Tony, agreed to the arrangement.

"A burn? Lemme see, honey," Iris asked.

"Really, it's okay," I said.

"Stacy, where is Thor?" asked Cinnamon.

Crap! The kid.

"Oh my God. Don't tell me…" Cin said.

I shook my head and laid a palm on her shoulder. "He's fine. We were…" I stopped. If Iris knew I sicced a 180-pound Great Dane on a high school kid, the phones at the paper would light up like a marquee.

I nodded toward Derek. "Iris, have you met our newest recruit for the paper?"

"Why, no, I sure haven't. I'm Iris." She smiled at Derek.

"Pleasure to meet you," said Derek.

"And what is your position at our fine paper?"

Guess the camera around his neck didn't tip her off. Before Derek could answer, Iris launched into her welcome speech.

I grabbed Cin's hand, left Derek's jacket near his camera bag, and rushed down the street to find Thor.

"Hey, wait. Don't we have a story to do?" Derek called.

I waved behind my head. "Not me. Not tonight. Tell Parker to get someone else."

"You want to clue me in?" Cinnamon asked. She was out of breath as we wove our way through the crowd in the direction Thor had gone. Cinnamon's version of exercise was pumping the gas pedal on her vintage Trans Am. "Why are we rushing away from Main Street, anyway?"

"I have to find Thor. Then I'll explain," I said. I peered down the alley the kid had taken. No sign of him or the dog. I knew Thor wouldn't run away, but he would stand guard over anyone who meant to harm me—or anyone I told him to, for that matter.

"Thor!" Cinnamon yelled.

In two seconds, the dog came prancing up to us.

"Dammit, Cin."

"What?"

"He was after something. I wanted to see if he caught it."

Cin tapped her foot. "Stacy, I love you like a sister, but I swear to God I am losing patience."

I looked at her. Geez, the girl just escaped a fire. I had no idea how much damage had been done, but at the very least, she was going to lose thousands in sales while the building was repaired. Thousands I was sure she couldn't afford.

She was all brick and mortar on the outside with a mouth like a truck driver. The only time I ever saw her cry was when her dad, my uncle, died a few years ago. But on the inside, she was a marshmallow.

I hugged my cousin. "Are you okay?"

She squeezed me back and said, "Don't forget who you're talking to. I'm a pretty tough nut." True. I once witnessed her single-handedly bounce three drunk bikers from her bar without breaking a nail. Or a sweat.

Thor pawed at my knee, and I broke from Cin. "Hey, buddy." A shred of clothing dangled from his jaw.

I cupped my hand and said, "Drop."

Thor deposited what appeared to be the back pocket of a pair of Levi's. I knuckled his ear and said, "Good boy, Thor." He sat down, tongue draped over the side of his jaw, proud as a peacock.

"Stacy, what did you do?" asked Cin.

"Nothing." I shook my head.

"Stace..." Cin crossed her arms.

Even before I said it out loud, I knew it would sound juvenile and stupid. But maybe Cin would understand since she's an expert on impulsive behavior.

I took a deep breath. "There was a high school kid outside in the crowd, and when he saw me, he took off like a bullet. It seemed strange, so I chased him. But then Derek got in the way, so my boy, Thor, kept up the pursuit." I fingered the patch and held it up, smiling. "Brought me a souvenir too." I winked at Thor.

Thor roared, then barked and did a little happy dance. Cin glared at him, and he stopped short, then lowered his head in a pout.

"Stacy, all high school kids run when they see a Geraghty Girl."

"I am not a Geraghty Girl. I'm a Justice woman."

Cin waved her hand. "Doesn't matter. You've got the bloodline, the hair, the cape."

"Hey, the cape was a gift, and my hair is more blonde than red. Besides, you have the bloodline too." I shivered again, and Cin handed over her jacket. "Thanks," I said and stuffed my arms through the sleeves.

Cin sighed. "Look, you haven't been back that long, so I'll clue you in on a little secret. Kids are petrified of witches. Sure they'll tease, play jokes, tell stories, but when it comes down to it, they buy into all that flying-on-a-broom bull and sacrificing-small-rodents nonsense. It's a game."

I could not believe my ears. She was calling me one of them! I pride myself on not being one of them. Hey, you can't choose your family. Just because Birdie and the aunts believe in abracadabra, hocus-pocus, doesn't mean I do.

"I am not a witch." I stuffed the torn pocket in my jeans and glared at Cin.

She raised one eyebrow. "Are you or are you not practicing magic?"

"Only to keep Birdie off my back, you know that. She forces me to join her little hex circle whenever the mood strikes. Or the sun is in Venus, or a spider crawls down her chimney, or whatever the hell else sets her in motion." I looked at Cinnamon. "Come to think of it, ever since I was a kid, she's had it in her head I was the one to be her protégée. Just be lucky it's not you."

"Ah," Cinnamon said in a phony European accent, "but you are the sensitive one, dear cousin."

"Sensitive to what?" I asked.

"I couldn't tell ya."

I laughed. "Come on. Let's go find Leo and Tony."

Thor sidled beside us, and Cin slung an arm around my shoulder as we strolled down the middle of the street, back toward the Black Opal.

After a moment, Cinnamon said, "It must just be your destiny, Ms. Justice Seeker." That was a term Birdie had pinned on me. Cin thought it was hilarious to repeat it and watch my skin crawl.

"Shut up," I said. Then I cocked my head and asked, "Why don't they run from you? The kids, I mean."

Cin smiled, still looking ahead. "Oh, they do. Just for different reasons."

It was true what Cin had said. I had picked up a wand again since I had moved back to town a few months ago, but only to appease my grandmother. Birdie was named after the great Goddess Brighid of Ireland. The name means "exalted one," and if she had purchased the title at Witches 'R' Us, she couldn't have chosen a better one.

Birdie has a book of theology that holds my maternal family history, which spans back to an ancient Celtic tribe from Kildare. The book is filled with laws, spells, symbols, beliefs, and even predictions for future generations.

Which is where I come in. My great-grandmother had scribbled something about a third-generation child of the New World in the Blessed Book…blah, blah, blah…and poof! I was now dubbed the Seeker of Justice. I pointed out that it was just a coincidence, since that happened to be my father's last name, but Birdie didn't buy it. I am the one, she is sure of it. So while Cinnamon was off catching fireflies, skateboarding, and flashing crossing guards, I was learning about the properties of herbs, crystal power, and how to position a scrying mirror beneath the full moon.

Not that it's done me any freaking good.

The scene back near the bar wasn't any less hectic than when we'd left. The fire was still smoldering, an eerie orange glow illuminating the building. The brick seemed to pulsate beneath the force of the water pressure, like the walls were breathing a sigh of relief. We just stood there for a moment, mesmerized, and I still had that feeling I was forgetting something.

"Damn shame," I heard behind me. I turned to see Mr. Huckleberry puffing away on a stogie.

Mr. Huckleberry is a longtime family friend. He used to play poker with Cin's dad, and he sold Cinnamon the bar when he retired a few years ago.

"Hi, Mr. Huckleberry," I said.

"Hey, Huck," said Cinnamon.

He nodded toward us. "Girls. You okay?" He looked like Santa Claus with his white beard and protruding belly.

"Uh-huh," we said.

"Huck," said Cin, "I'm so sorry this happened. I know how much you love the place."

"Sweetheart, these things happen." He puffed the cigar, the burning tobacco mirroring the flame from the fire. "Old buildings with old wiring plus a bunch of numb nuts that don't know their ass from a hole in the ground inspecting them. Bound to be trouble sooner or later." He patted Cin on the back. "You take care, sweetheart."

Mr. Huckleberry ambled away, and Gus Dorsey came up to us then. Gus had a basset-hound face and floppy ears that were too big for his frame. I was sure he had yet to shop in the men's department.

"Hey, Stacy. Hi, Cinnamon. You okay? Can I get you something? You cold? You thirsty or something?" This was all directed at Cinnamon, whom Gus has been in love with forever. He hadn't quite grasped the fact that she was back with her ex-husband, and even if she weren't, he was a used Volvo kind of guy, where Cinnamon was a muscle car woman.

"Gus, get Stacy a blanket, would you?" Cin said.

"Sure, sure. Oh, I almost forgot. Stacy, the chief wants to talk to you right away," Gus said and scampered off.

"I feel another lecture coming on," I mumbled. I returned Cin's coat and rubbed my arms.

Derek was talking to a fireman and snapping photos a few yards away. He and Iris were jotting down notes. I guess Parker didn't send anyone else to the scene. Odd.

I turned to Cin to tell her I was going to find Leo and that I'd meet up with her later, but before I could say a word, a meaty hand smacked her upside the head.

"Ow, Mama!" Cin cried. Aunt Angelica. Famous for her cannoli and right hook.

Thor ducked behind my legs.

"This is what I get, hah? I have to hear 'bout a fire on the radio? Not from my daughter. My flesh and blood. I raised you better!" She lifted her other hand and realized she was still holding a spatula. She calculated if that would border on abuse, then tried to swing it anyway before Tony caught the interception.

"Mama Angelica, please. Cinnamon has been through enough," he said. He wasn't as tall as she, but what he lacked in height, he made up for in charm and personality.

Angelica flashed Tony a look of betrayal, then softened. "Oh, my baby!" She pulled Cinnamon to her huge chest and sobbed. Cin flailed her arms.

"Mama, stop."

"Hi, Auntie," I said, hoping to deflect some of the heat from Cin.

Angelica faced me, still wearing her bakery apron smeared with frosting and sprinkles, her dark hair streaked with flour. Thor snaked around and stole a lick from the spatula Tony was holding. I said a little prayer for her not to notice.

"Oh, Stacy, my beautiful niece." She pulled me in for a bear hug, then stood back and said, "What's wrong with you, hah? That one"—she pointed to Cin—"that one I know is trouble. But you a good girl. You should call when things happen, hah?"

I nodded. "But the bakery is only a block away."

Angelica leaned forward and waved her finger. "You getting smart?"

I shook my head. "No."

"You come for dinner tomorrow, hah?" she said.

"I will."

In the distance, I spotted three women who seemed to claim the street as their own, walking in tandem. Confidence radiated from them like the brilliant colors of the bright capes they wore. One red, one yellow, one green. The Geraghty Girls.

Crapbasket! Who knew the fire would be the highlight of my day?

I whirled around to Cinnamon. "What are they doing here dressed like that?"

"Don't you remember what day it is?" Cin whispered.

I flipped through my mental calendar and drew a blank. "Thursday."

Cin rolled her eyes at me. "Imbolc."

I slapped my forehead. In all the excitement, the holiday had slipped away from me.

The pagan calendar consists of eight major celebrations. Imbolc occurs between the Winter Solstice and Spring Equinox. It's one of the three Celtic feasts of fire, and in Ireland, it is known as Brighid's Day.

In Amethyst, that translates to Birdie's Day.

"What, they figured there's already a fire, so let's have the ceremony here?"

"Hey, you try telling them what they can and cannot do," said Cinnamon.

The crowd was thinning out, giving Birdie and the aunts space.

"Stacy, I have to go find my insurance papers and give my agent a call. I'm sure he'll want to assess the damage right away. Maybe it isn't so bad," she said, but her face showed that she thought it was bad. "I'll call you when I'm done, okay?" She kissed me on the cheek, and she, Tony, and Aunt Angelica headed in the opposite direction, toward the bakery.

"Okay," I said. But what I meant was, *Thanks for feeding me to the wolves.*

As I watched the Geraghty Girls approach, Gus draped a blanket over me and said, "Hey, Stacy, no kidding, you need to come with me."

"Not now, Gus," I hissed.

They drifted closer. Streetlamps shined on each strand of red hair that poked through their hoods, the smoke creating a billowy backdrop. I felt like I was about to become the first victim in a Wes Craven film.

"Cripes, Stacy, please. He gets real mad when I don't follow orders. Cinnamon already gave her account." He said that like it would prompt me to follow suit.

"Gus, I have no idea what happened. I was behind the bar one minute, setting up for Cin, and the next thing I knew, smoke filtered up through the back stairs and the beams were on fire. That's all I got. Type it up."

I watched as Birdie paused to whisper into a fireman's ear. He was taking a load off on the side of the truck. He bounced up immediately and started to roll the hose that lay across their path. Another fireman paused to whistle at my great-aunt Fiona. She winked back.

Gus followed my gaze, perked up, and said, "Hey, it's your granny." Gus and Birdie have a strange friendship that developed through her occasional bouts with the law.

"Anastasia," my grandmother said and clasped my hands. She refuses to call me by the name on my birth certificate, which is simply *Stacy*. Something about bad luck naming a female child after her father.

"Hey, Birdie," piped Gus, "how about another round of Dungeons and Dragons?"

Her eyes slid toward him, and she smiled as if he were a child asking for a lollipop. Then she tilted her head and raised her manicured eyebrows.

"Oh, sure, you want to catch up. Maybe later," Gus said and darted off.

And then there was me.

I waited for my grandmother to say something. Why her eyes were fierce, I didn't know. I glanced at my great-aunt Lolly, who despite being a few letters short of a full alphabet always dresses like it's Oscar night. This occasion proved no different. Her purple-silk ball gown was fluffed out by a hoop skirt, and her face looked like a paint-by-number. Her eyebrows were shaved smooth, then penciled in. With an actual No. 2 pencil, it appeared. Lolly grinned and waved. She had pink lipstick all over her teeth.

Fiona, the middle sister of the three, smiled softly at me. She's one of those women you just know was a pinup girl and probably still could be.

"Birdie, what the hell are you doing walking around town like this?" I finally asked when no one else spoke.

Their beliefs weren't a secret, but I mean, come on.

Birdie straightened. "Like what, dear?"

"Stacy, honey, we didn't mean to embarrass you," Fiona chimed in. "But we were preparing for the Imbolc when we heard about the fire. And then it happened."

Well, sure, that about cleared it up.

"You mean you were preparing for the Imbolc when the fire happened."

"No, dear. Something else," said Birdie.

"Something else? You have got to be kidding me. Your granddaughters nearly die in a fire, and there was something more important than that? Weren't you worried about me? About Cin?"

Birdie didn't even bother to look surprised. "Cinnamon can care for herself, and you were wearing the amethyst when you left," said Birdie.

"Plus your familiar was with you," said Fiona, patting Thor on the head. He licked her hand in return. Fiona is loved by all four-legged creatures—and two-legged ones, for that matter.

"What do you mean, my familiar?" I asked.

Birdie sighed and looked at her watch. "Your witch's familiar."

"I'm not even familiar with being a witch, and stop calling me that!" I said.

"A familiar is an animal totem, dear, who protects you," said Fiona.

Lolly barked.

"Protects me? But he…" I glanced at Thor. "I mean, I…oh, forget it." It was true. Thor was my guardian angel of sorts.

Thor plopped on my feet and belched.

I wagged my head to shake out the loose screws and continued. "Okay, so what else happened, then?"

Lolly yanked the blanket off me and worked a winter-white velvet cape around my shoulders. I tried to slap her hand away.

"The bat, dear," said Fiona.

Birdie folded her arms and pursed her lips.

"Big bat," said Lolly, who finished strapping me into the cape from behind.

Fiona's eyes grew wide, and she nodded.

A bat in February? I was speechless.

They stood patiently waiting for me to come by some sort of epiphany.

I had nothing.

Fiona tilted her head toward Birdie and quietly said, "She hasn't been practicing that long since she returned. She needs more time."

"Nonsense," Birdie said. "The child learned everything she ever needed to know by the time she was thirteen."

It was true that Birdie had molded me from birth to practice under her wing. A point my mother fought her on constantly. But after my father died—after the dream showed me he would die and my warning didn't save him as I had hoped, but instead put him in the path of a tractor-trailer—I had no more use for magic.

"But she blocked it out after," said Fiona.

After. She meant after my father died, after my mother left with no forwarding address. My whole life could be divided into "before" and "after." Before I killed my father. After my mother disappeared.

"She was born with more talent than we could ever teach her," said Birdie.

"Yes, but she still has so much to learn," Fiona pointed out.

"Would you two quit talking about me like I'm not here!" *Wait, what happened to the other one?* "Where's Lolly?" I asked.

We all scanned the street, and I spotted Thor hitched to a lamppost while Lolly worked a cape and fresh collar around his neck. He had the look of a man whose wife just sent him out to buy tampons.

"Lolly!" I hissed.

"I'll handle it, dear." Fiona patted my arm and rushed off. I winced from the sting.

Birdie's forehead creased, and she lifted my cape. Her eyes locked with mine after she examined the burn. "We have work to do," she said.

Chapter 3

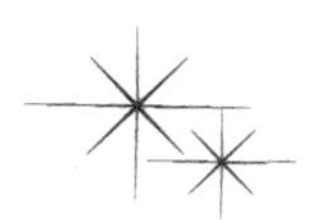

There are moments in my life I am not proud of. Like the Christmas Eve I replaced the Virgin Mary with the Goddess Diana on our neighbor's lawn because she refused Aunt Lolly's cookies. Or the time I inhaled a little too much wine and flashed a tour bus—and, well, this one.

We were standing in the back parking lot of the Black Opal, where Fiona had applied a mixture of lavender oil, comfrey, and chamomile to my arm. Thor sat near the Dumpster, on the lookout. A tiger's eye dangled from the tassels of his cape, and he kept trying to eat it.

"Birdie, I am begging you to take this somewhere else. You cannot have an Imbolc ceremony here right now," I said.

"And why not? What better way to honor the great goddess than at the scene of a fire?"

I felt a migraine coming on.

"Because, for one thing, they don't need any more uncontrolled blazes." I nodded toward Lolly, who liked to play fast and loose with the matches. She was chugging the ceremonial wine, and I was thankful because, for some reason, alcohol sharpened her senses.

"Don't be ridiculous. We're not going to light a bonfire," Birdie said.

Whew. That's a relief. Then I heard the distinct sound of a lighter flicking.

Lolly was snapping a lighter beneath what appeared to be a homemade cigar.

"Lolly, stop that," I said with a wave of my good arm. Fiona was still patching me up.

"You just said no fires," I said to my grandmother, louder than I should have.

Birdie paused and lifted her shoulders. "A smudge stick of sage, dear, for cleansing. Lolly, let's get on with it."

Lolly fumbled around inside her cape and produced a bottle of milk, a poppy-seed cake, and a bouquet of heather and myrrh. She set everything at the back entrance.

My mouth fell open. She was like Batman, except female, much older, and less lucid.

"We always come prepared, dear," Lolly said.

"But how—"

"Fiona, is she ready?" Birdie interrupted, her voice authoritative.

No, I am not.

"Yes, all better," sang Fiona.

"Lolly, the cross," said Birdie. Lolly hung what I recognized as Brighid's cross on the doorknob.

"Now, the stones."

She opened her cape again, and I tried to peek in, but I didn't see any pockets or purses. She pulled out four gemstones: an amethyst for protection, a bloodstone to banish evil, hematite to purify smoke, and a fire opal to release the demons of the past. She placed the stones on the threshold.

This is nothing like the Imbolc ceremonies of my childhood.

Birdie waved the sage cigar all around the doorway and chanted. Then she removed the caution tape and stepped inside.

I turned to Fiona. "What's going on?"

"What do you mean, dear?" She had taken her place to face the north wind. Lolly picked up the cue and found her place to the east and grabbed my hand. They both bowed their heads.

"Okay, if we're doing a spell to heal the business from the harm of the blaze, shouldn't Cinnamon be here?"

"This isn't for the business, Anastasia." Birdie returned behind me, prompting me to jump out of my skin. She is excellent at undetected entrances. This is why I rarely misbehaved as a kid under her roof. She took her place to the south and grabbed my hand too.

Holding hands in a dark alley with my grown relatives while my dog took a leak on the sidewalk, I could actually hear my credibility as a reporter crack.

"All right, that's enough." I dropped their hands and removed my hood. "What's this about?"

"I thought reporters were good listeners," said Birdie.

Geez, if she was trying to drive me insane, she was working it well.

"Give me a hint," I said.

Lolly flapped her arms and said, "Bat, bat, bat, bat."

"Right, the bat. Okay, what about it? It was dead in the woods? It flew from behind a shutter? What?" I asked.

Fiona and Lolly shook their heads and Birdie turned to face me. "We were preparing for the ceremony, and it flew through the hearth. Then it circled the kitchen three times before Fiona opened the back door to release it."

I was nodding to show her I was listening and to keep from screaming.

Fiona said, "A bat in February is a bad sign, Stacy. It means betrayal."

"But a bat that circles the house exactly three times is worse," said Birdie. She narrowed her eyes.

"Why? What does that mean?" I asked.

"Death has paid a visit."

Fiona once told me that Birdie made no mistakes. This time, however, I suspected her circuit breaker had blown a fuse.

Who in my family would betray another? And if death had paid a visit, then the joke was on him, because we all escaped that fire unscathed.

I voiced this to Birdie, who put her forehead to mine and whispered, "Not everything is as black and white as the newspaper your words are printed on, my darling granddaughter. Sometimes you have to read between the lines. The message will be clear when the time is right." She popped me on the rear.

A short while later, we finished the spell, and Lolly was packing up. I don't know where she put everything because she wouldn't let me look. Maybe she had a tool belt beneath her cape.

Fiona walked over to me, kissed me on the cheek, and said, "Don't worry. If anyone can overcome, it's you." She tied her hood and followed Birdie.

I resisted the urge to ask, *Overcome what?*

Then I remembered it was cold, I wasn't about to wear this cloak around town, and I had no ride.

"Wait, can you drive me and Thor home?"

Lolly smiled at me, waved, and said, "It's Cinnamon."

I scanned the street. "Where?" I asked just as my phone started belting out a Stevie Nicks tune.

I flipped it open.

"Stacy?" It was Cinnamon.

How did she do that?

"Hang on," I told her. I lifted my head to tell Birdie and the aunts that Cin could pick me up, but they were gone.

I sighed. "Hey, cousin."

"You have to come and get me. Mama is driving me batty, and Mario is on his fourth grappa."

I thought that was an interesting word choice. "Mario's there?"

Mario is Angelica's brother from the old country who visits now and then to the delight of no one. He bathes in Old Spice, sells junk from a shoebox, and has a problem holding his neck up whenever he talks to a woman. Any woman.

"Yes, and he's getting sleazier by the minute. Get me out of here. We're still at the bakery. Mama won't fight me if you're here."

"Cin, I need clean clothes, a coat, and a shower. I was just about to ask you to come get me."

"Tony went by your place and picked up a few things already. I've got all that, and he fed Moonlight."

Moonlight is my cat, who has learned to love Thor. The three of us live in a small cottage behind the Geraghty Girls' house. Aunt Fiona decorated it, so it looks more like a honeymoon suite at a Poconos resort than a Thomas Kinkade painting.

"Okay. I'll meet you at the back door."

"Thanks," she said and hung up.

I looked at Thor.

"Come on, we have to go get Cinnamon."

Thor made a disgusted noise and sat down.

"Thor, up. We have to go." I tugged at his collar, which was futile. The dog is solid as a truck. Sometimes he can be incredibly stubborn, usually when I least want him to be. This might have gone smoother if I had a leash but it was still behind the bar.

"Thor, let's go. *Now*," I said as sternly as I could.

He let out a wail like a tornado warning and put on the brakes. That was his hunger call. "Thor, I am not going in there just to get your four cans of Meaty Dog. Stop acting so spoiled. I'll get you a doughnut at the bakery."

Thor tossed his head back and bayed.

"Fine, a dozen."

He plopped down and turned his head away from me.

I squatted behind Thor and pushed to no avail. It was either leave him there or take a trip to the basement of the Opal and get his dinner.

Not sure I made the right choice.

I tiptoed through the back door of the Black Opal, stepping over the caution tape that Birdie had ripped down.

Sage still permeated the air as I scanned the room. Paintings clung to loose hooks; tables wobbled on their sides. The damage didn't seem too bad, save for the foamy mess from the firefighters putting out the blaze.

I gingerly approached the stairs that led to the basement, where Thor's food was stashed, careful to avoid the front windows.

The beam that separated the back room from the front of the place had crumbled to the floor. Cin always hated those beams. She was saving up to tear them down. She wanted to give the bar a facelift.

Doubt this was what she had in mind.

I peered down the cement stairwell, but I couldn't see much, so I fired up my cell phone for some light.

At the bottom, the stone wall on the left seemed untouched by the fire. The metal shelves were still standing, stacked with napkins, glassware, liquor, and Thor's Meaty Dog food.

I took another step forward and aimed the light to the right wall.

That side of the room was half stone and half red brick, now black and swollen. Loose wires dripped from an opening in the ceiling near a broken window. Bottles of booze had exploded, and glass blanketed the floor.

I crept to the shelves and scooped up several cans of dog food. When I turned back around, something near the corner, behind the stairwell, glimmered.

I set the cans down and crouched in for a closer look. Wedged between layers of sticky dirt and brick was a bit of gold. I decided to use the bottle opener in my back pocket to uncover the source of the sparkle. It was a nifty little tool equipped with a corkscrew, a pocketknife, and a nail file.

The file latched onto just enough chain to extract a long gold necklace. Dangling from the chain was a cross shaped like nails, onyx topping each head. Onyx is great for severing a bad relationship.

Unfortunately, I know that from experience.

"You shouldn't be poking around down here."

I screamed and dropped the bottle opener, nearly wetting myself.

First he mows me down; then he scares the piss out of me. Was this guy trying to give me a heart attack?

"Don't ever do that again," I said to Derek.

"Sorry. I heard you come down the steps, but I thought it was your boyfriend, so I hid. Didn't think it'd be too cool if he caught me."

I didn't even ask how he knew who my boyfriend was. That is the casualty of life in a small town. People scoop into your business, then hand out cones to anyone who asks for a lick.

"What are you doing here?" I asked him.

"Taking some shots." He lifted up one of his umpteen cameras. "They'll look hot next to your article."

I ignored the bad pun.

Wait, my article?

"I told you to tell Parker to get someone else."

"I did. But I thought that's why you're here."

"Oh. No, just picking up dog food." I pointed to the cans.

"They don't have grocery stores around here?"

I blew a strand of hair from my face. "It's a long story."

"What's with the cape?"

"That's a longer story."

"Well, you can tell me on the way out. Ready to hit it?"

Something was pulling me to that corner. Something strong. I stilled myself, then hinged forward for a closer view. My cape was strangling me at that angle, so I unclipped the top hook.

"Derek, do you have a flashlight?"

Derek grunted. "What do I look like, Handy Andy?"

"No, you look like a one-hour photo lab." I squatted down to get another look, but it was too dark.

"Just point your camera over there and snap a shot, will you? Maybe the illumination will highlight the area and I could get a better look."

"Or maybe you'll just get a clear picture? I hear they last longer."

Okay, that was stupid of me, but it had been a long-ass day.

"Just do it."

Derek aimed the camera, twisted a few knobs, and punched a button. The flash revealed nothing more than the charred brick wall, with a few bricks missing.

"We done here?"

I sighed. "I guess." I bent to pick up the bar tool and the necklace, the cross hot in my hand.

"Shh." Derek put his finger to his lips.

I heard it too. Footsteps.

"Go," I said.

Derek took the stairs two at a time.

I shoved the opener and the necklace in my jeans pocket, gathered the cans, and sprinted up after him.

It might have gone well too, if that damn cape hadn't clung to a nail and yanked me back.

The dog food went flying, and my hand caught just enough railing to help me land on a case of wine. I tried to jimmy free, but my ass was stuck. And wet.

"Who's down there?"

Not sure how he did it, but Leo managed to shine a beam of light right at my face.

I delivered my sexiest smile. Which was the only part of my body not covered in muck.

He shook his head and put a finger to his mouth.

That was the second man who had shushed me in the space of five minutes.

"All clear, Mayor. Must be a mouse."

A mouse? There are mice down here? Son of a bitch! I hate rodents. But…oh, he probably just meant me. Duh. A little bit of that Northwestern degree chips away each day I live in this town. Man, I needed a drink. Which was ironic since I was sitting on a box of them.

"Leo, I thought I told you to cordon off the building. It's wide open back there," the mayor said.

Mayor Ritsos is Leo's uncle. He brought Leo in from Chicago to appoint as chief a few years after Cin's father died. Uncle Deck was the chief of police in Amethyst for years, which may have something to do with my cousin's anger-management problem.

The mayor is not my biggest fan. It is not clear why. But if I had to guess, I would say he feels Leo's involvement with a woman whose family dances naked under the full moon on midsummer's eve might hurt both their careers.

Who could blame him?

"What do you mean?" asked Leo. "I had caution tape across there."

Oops.

"Well, it's not there now," the mayor said.

"I'll take care of it," Leo said.

"See that you do. I don't want anyone wandering in here and getting hurt. I want this place locked up until I get a report on what caused the fire. Tommy, what do you think?"

Tommy Delaney is the fire chief. He was a few years ahead of me in high school.

"Can't say yet. I suspect an electrical short. There's a busted fixture down there, and some burned-out wires."

Electrical. Huck was right.

"Well," the mayor said, drawing out the word, "find out for sure."

"Yes, sir."

"All right, let's go."

The footsteps tapered off.

"Just let me secure this entrance. I'll catch up," Leo said.

He ducked down into the basement, shined the light, and said in a low voice, "Do you stay awake at night inventing ways to get me fired?"

"Sorry," I whispered.

"Get that burn looked at," he said.

"Already did." I tugged at the cape, indicating my family had taken care of things.

Leo nodded. "See you later." Before he turned away, he smiled. Uneasily.

Like he'd won the lottery but lost the winning ticket.

Chapter 4

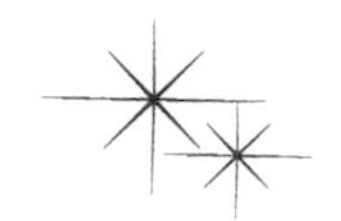

I extracted my fanny from the box and sneaked out the back door. Thor was waiting near the Dumpster and trotted over to me when he spotted the cans of dog food.

"Hope you're happy," I grumbled.

Thor thumped his tail as I used the bar tool to open the cans of food. His water dish was still outside, so I dumped the food in there, and he gobbled it up in about three seconds. Then he belched and wiped his face on my cape. The slobber contrasted nicely with the wine stains.

By the time I got to Angelica's house, Cinnamon was pissed. "Where the hell have you been?" The scent of vanilla and almonds indicated that Angelica was still baking.

"I don't want to talk about it," I told my cousin. "I want to change and go get a drink."

"Your clothes are in here." Cinnamon handed me a brown paper bag. "Bye, Mama!" she called.

"Wait, I want to change," I said as Cinnamon dragged me out the door.

"Change at the bar. We'll go to Down and Dirty. Tony is keeping my mother occupied so I can escape for a little while. She's trying to convince me that we should lend Mario our guest room for a few weeks."

Halfway to the bar, Cinnamon lit a cigarette.

"You're smoking again?" I asked.

"I've had a rough day."

Thor trotted along in front of us, and I said, "Monique will not like this. How are we going to convince her to let Thor in the bar?"

"Easy. I'll promise not to kill her the next time she hits on my husband."

That might work. Monique Fontaine has been a splinter in Cinnamon's behind since we were kids. Her real name is Monica, but she likes French perfume, French toast, and French men. Not to mention Spanish men, Italian men, and African American men, but you get the picture.

Monique has had the hots for Tony for years, so when he married Cinnamon, it really steamed her up. She takes every opportunity to try to seduce him when Cin isn't looking. Of course, he's so in love with his wife that he tells her every time. Which only fuels Cinnamon's anger. Monique finally realized that her facial features were exactly where she wanted them, so she needed a new way to antagonize my cousin. Hence, the bar Down and Dirty. It's located directly across the street from the Black Opal.

Cin said, "I'll have to check it out sooner or later. Might as well be tonight."

My mouth dropped open when we stepped inside.

The walls were papered in burned-out red velvet, gilded gold frames anchoring them, with various burlesque paintings in each. Several cubbyholes lined the left side of the room, harboring love seats with sheer gold curtains hanging above that could be drawn for privacy. Tiny tables supported by miniature Eiffel Towers filled the center of the room, each with little lamps in the shape of a woman's leg, complete with fishnet stockings.

"Unbelievable," I said.

"I've died and gone to cabaret hell," said Cin.

"You think this is what the inside of Monique's head looks like?"

A young woman dressed like a Las Vegas showgirl approached us. "You want to get down and dirty?"

"Excuse me?" I asked.

"It's a shot. Down and Dirty. Like the name of the bar. They're only a buck." She snapped her gum and held out a tray.

"I'm already down," Cin said.

"I'm already dirty," I told her.

The girl skipped away.

Thor parted the crowd as Beyoncé belted from the speakers.

We circled the half-moon bar, and I scanned the place for a bathroom.

"I see two seats in the back," Cinnamon said. She patted Thor to steer him in that direction.

"Son of a bitch," Cin said when we got closer.

"What?"

"Scully's here."

She was over to Scully in two seconds flat. He was sitting in front of a beer tap shaped like a boob.

I squeezed in behind her and held my guard.

"How could you?" Cin demanded, smacking his back.

Scully's face crumpled like a paper bag.

"You weren't open. I wanted a beer," he said.

"He's got you there, Cin," I said.

She darted her eyes at me. Then she looked down. "Is that my goddamn stool?"

Scully glanced around as if the stool had suddenly formed beneath his butt. He sipped his beer and said, "It's my stool."

"That stool is from the Opal," Cin said.

It did seem out of place as the only wooden bar stool in a stream of black lacquered ones.

"See for yourself." Scully thumbed behind him.

Cin and I looked back. Etched in the wood was SCULLY.

Cin slapped his back again. "But why would you come here? You know I hate her."

Scully shrugged and pointed in front of him.

Above the bottles of wine and scotch was a flashing neon sign that read, *Every Thursday—Free Viagra for Senior Citizens.*

Hmm. I thought the crowd was a little gray.

Cin leaned in and said, "You better just pay the bar tab you owe me if you want to use any of it."

Scully's face lost all color. He knew she meant it.

We settled in a corner table, and I was just about to change and wash up when Monique waltzed over to us.

"What the hell are you two doing here? And why is that beast in my bar?"

"Nice to see you too," I said.

Thor growled. Or maybe that was Cin.

"Jesus, Stacy. Why do you always look like donkey dung?" Monique asked.

Monique was wearing black spiked heels, fishnets, a strapless one-piece with gold tassels, and a top hat over her bleached hair. She was also carrying a whip and had enough makeup on to enter the witness protection program.

"Do you talk to all your patrons like that, or is it just when the circus is in town?" I asked.

Her eyes narrowed. "I'll let that slide because I know you've both had a rough day. But, hey, your loss is my gain, right, Cin?" She smiled and jabbed Cin with her whip.

Cin looked down at her arm. I held my breath.

She must have been tired, because instead of jamming the whip down Monique's throat, she stood up and, in a very even tone, said, "If you think you've seen me mad before, imagine what I could do to you when I've just lost everything."

Monique's face froze.

"Now, unless you want me to take that thing and make a s'more out of you, I suggest you turn around and leave me the hell alone."

Monique swallowed and straightened her back. "You can stay. But don't make a habit of it." She disappeared into the crowd.

We ordered drinks and appetizers from the waitress, and I went to change and wash up.

The food was on the table when I returned wearing spandex pants and a sequined tube top that screamed *I grew up in the '90s*. I couldn't believe I even owned these clothes, let alone that Tony had dug them up. I ignored Cin's subtle chuckle and helped myself to a nacho. I told her what I had overheard the fire chief say.

"Really? That's strange because I just had my yearly inspection. They didn't find a thing wrong."

"Maybe they missed it," I said.

"I guess," Cin said, sipping her beer. "The insurance guy is meeting me tomorrow. You want to go for coffee first and then come by the bar? I could use the support. Tony has a long day at the shop tomorrow, and we can't afford not to take the work."

Tony runs an auto body shop on the other side of town.

"Sure."

The lights were still on at the B and B when I got home, but I had had enough spell casting for one evening. I slipped into the cottage, discarded my clothes, and fell into bed.

I can't breathe. It's dark. Cold. I can't lift my head. He's too strong.

The alarm clock jolted me from the dream. Thor had a paw slung across my neck, and I pushed him off and padded to the shower.

I blew my hair dry, slapped on some makeup, and climbed into a pair of jeans. I finished the outfit with a black turtleneck, my amethyst necklace, and leather boots. Moonlight and Thor were in the kitchen waiting for breakfast, so I popped open a can of food for each of them, let Thor out quickly, and headed to Muddy Waters Coffee Shop.

Like everything else on Main Street, Muddy Waters was in walking distance, so I left the Jeep in the drive and hoofed it. My phone blinked three new messages. One was from Leo, telling me to call him back. One was from my boss, Shea Parker, telling me to get my ass to work, and one was unknown. No message.

Cinnamon was already sitting at a table when I got there. The coffeehouse was set in an old 1800s bank, with fluffy couches and earth-toned walls. I draped my jacket over a chair across from Cin and placed an order with Iris at the counter.

"You see that man over there?" Iris asked as she handed me a latte. Her reading glasses dangled from her neck.

I started to twist my head, but she whispered, "Don't look."

I swayed forward and asked, "Then how can I see him?"

Iris ignored me. "He's been asking a lot of questions."

"Like what?"

"About the town. About the tourism. About you."

"Me? What about me?"

"Just little things, like how long you've lived here, how old you are, who your family is, what you do for a living."

"Iris, you're creeping me out."

"I just thought you should know, honey. Never saw him in here before. He must have seen your picture in the paper. Now he's sweet on you." Iris made a kissy face.

"Don't do that," I said.

"Probably just a tourist."

I took my coffee and scooted around the rope in front of the counter. The man in question was hunched over a mug near the window, reading the paper. He was wearing a baggy black suit, felt hat, and gloves. A wool coat was slung across his lap. I couldn't see his face, just sunglasses and a mustache.

I flipped through my mental Rolodex to see if he seemed familiar. Bells were chiming in my ears telling me I knew this person, but for the life of me, I couldn't figure out from where.

I made a note to pick up some pepper spray. Or maybe Thor.

Cin was going over her paperwork at the table.

"You think my premiums will go up?" she asked, only half joking.

"I don't know. But, hey, you were going to remodel anyway," I pointed out.

"Yep. And I took out a big fat loan to cover it." She gave a disgusted look.

"Ouch. Who was going to do the work?"

"I was leaning toward Eddie McAllister for the outdoor patio and stone fireplace."

"Slow Eddie? He's still in town?"

Cin nodded. "He's a great mason, and the city always approves him. I was waiting for other bids to filter in, and Kirk was helping me sort through them."

Kirk is Eddie's brother. He's also the city inspector, and in a town with 80 percent of its buildings on the historic register, every job is subject to approval.

I sipped my coffee and glanced at Mr. Baggy Pants. I got the feeling he was eyeing me, but he quickly buried his face in the paper. "Why didn't you just hire Chance?"

"Because although your high school sweetheart is a great carpenter, he's not an expert in masonry work. He was on the list for building out the new bar, though. Plus, I was going to remodel and expand the bathrooms and refinish the floors."

I flitted my eyes to the man again. Cin caught me and followed my gaze.

"What's that about?"

"Nothing," I said. "What time are we supposed to meet the insurance agent?"

Cin looked at her watch. "Half an hour."

"I'm just going to run and get Thor. I'll be there ASAP," I said, picking up my coat and coffee.

"You spoil that damn dog," she said.

"So did you," I said as I pushed through the door.

As I led Thor down the steps that trailed to Main Street, I could see my cousin waving her hands and yelling at a short bald man with wire-rimmed glasses. I checked the clock on my phone. I was on time. They must have arrived early.

Also in front of the Opal stood Tommy Delaney, Leo, and a man I didn't recognize dressed in some kind of uniformed coat. The McAllister brothers were there too.

The short bald man was doing his best to ignore Cinnamon, taking notes and talking to Eddie and Kirk.

"So you were hired to do the work?" Baldy asked Eddie.

Eddie was wearing scuffed-up work boots and a five o'clock shadow.

"You betcha. That was me," he said.

I inched up to the curb and motioned for Thor to sit.

Baldy tilted his head to peer over his glasses at Kirk. "And you approved it?"

"Yes, I did." Kirk was taller, older, and sharper than Eddie.

"How long have you been doing masonry work?"

"Twenty years," Eddie said, beaming.

Baldy took a few more notes and said, "Thank you, gentlemen. I think I have everything I need from you."

Kirk nodded and guided Eddie away.

"What's going on?" I asked my cousin.

"You won't believe this," she said. I could feel heat seeping from her, her temper in overdrive.

"Miss…?" said Baldy.

"Stacy Justice," I said and stuck my hand out.

"My apologies. I don't do that," he said.

I lowered my hand and raised an eyebrow to Cin, who made a strangling gesture with her fingers.

"I am Benjamin Smalls, and what is happening here is standard company policy whenever a business is involved in a fire. This is the fire investigator for the claims office, Enrique Ortega."

I nodded at Enrique, and he smiled back.

"We already have a fire chief, Mr. Smalls," I said.

Smalls looked at Tommy like he missed the winning kick in the Super Bowl. "Yes, well, sometimes in a town the size of Amethyst, not everyone is…how shall I put it? Up to snuff?"

"I'd like to snuff you," Cin mumbled next to me.

"Pardon?" asked Smalls.

Cinnamon bit her lip.

"Say, you were there when the fire began, is that correct, Miss Justice?" Smalls continued.

"I was setting up behind the bar, yes."

"Would you mind relaying your version of events?"

I told him exactly how everything had unfolded.

"Interesting." He scribbled more notes. "So your dog was there, and you insisted on retrieving him, while your cousin didn't want you to bother," said Smalls.

I stepped back, a bit stunned. "That isn't what I said. She was afraid I would get hurt so—"

Cinnamon pinched me, and I clamped my jaw shut.

"And you were never in the basement?" Smalls asked.

"No," I said.

"And you were the only two people in the building?"

This guy was getting on my nerves, so I decided to return the favor.

"Probably not."

Cin gave me a *Say what?* look.

"Come again?" Smalls removed his glasses and stared me down.

"These are old buildings, Mr. Smalls," I said, sweeping my arm over Main Street. "People have been coming and going in and out of these walls for nearly two centuries." I lowered my voice and conjured up Birdie's witchy tone. "We are never alone when the dead walk among us."

Smalls dropped his spectacles, and I caught them before they hit the ground. I leaned in and slipped them in his breast pocket.

"Thank you," he said, his voice squeaky. He shook off a chill and cleared his throat.

"So then no living people besides the two of you?" Smalls asked, his voice trimmed with sarcasm.

Cin and I shook our heads.

"All right, then. That's all the questions I have. Thank you for your cooperation," he said, and he and Enrique jumped into a van parked on the street.

Cinnamon stood, anchored to the sidewalk, appearing helpless. I jogged over to the van.

"Wait a minute." I knocked on the window, and Enrique rolled it down. "What about the claim? What is she supposed to do now?"

"Now?" Smalls laughed and nudged Enrique, who didn't move. "Tell her to hire an attorney."

"An attorney? Why?"

"Because, Miss Justice, arson is a very serious offense."

"Tommy, what the hell is going on? I thought I heard you say the cause of the fire was electrical," I asked the fire chief. We were in Leo's office at the police station.

Leo shot me a look, and I instantly realized my mistake. I had heard that when I was in the basement, packed in a case of wine. The basement I wasn't supposed to be in at the time.

"I never told you that, Stacy," Tommy said.

Tommy was leaning up against the white brick wall, fluorescent bulbs bouncing light off his prominent forehead. Thor snored under Leo's desk.

"Oh, right...what I meant was I thought I overheard someone else say that you said that."

Geez, I am a terrible liar.

Tommy glanced from me to Cin to Leo. He sighed and pulled up a metal folding chair and removed his Chicago Bears hat.

"That's what it looked like at first," he said. "But then the deeper we got into it, it seemed that wasn't the case. Just didn't add up. And Enrique sure kept digging."

Of course. What insurance company actually wants to dish out money for a claim?

"What didn't add up?" I asked.

"The broken window in the basement, for one."

"I thought the fire caused that?"

"No, someone broke that window. From the inside. Before the fire. I could tell from the glass pattern."

I looked at Cin, who was growing pale. "Cinnamon, did you notice the broken window?"

"No. It's always freezing in that damn basement. I went to grab some napkins and straws, and when I turned around, I saw flames by the far wall," she said.

"Near the window," Leo added.

"Near the light," I said.

"Right," said Tommy. "That's why wiring was my first assumption."

"Okay, so the window was busted, what does that prove?" I asked.

"Have you ever heard of the fire triangle?" Tommy said.

I'd heard of the Bermuda Triangle, and I had a feeling I was about to get sucked into it.

"No," I said.

Tommy took a pencil, a pen, and a sheet of paper off Leo's desk to construct a visual for me.

"A fire needs three things to sustain it," he explained. He grabbed the pencil and angled it. "Oxygen"—he formed a V with the pen—"a fuel source"—he punctured the paper across them—"and heat. Breaking a window in the basement would fan the fire and concentrate it in that area."

"But it didn't burn in just that area. It moved up. Does that mean windows were broken upstairs?"

"We didn't find any. But when you walked in a minute later, Stacy, the gush of wind from opening the door sure helped it along."

That unnerved me. I rarely helped Cin open up the bar. She was usually there alone, and I would swing by if she needed a hand, but we both intended to make the Imbolc celebration last night, before I forgot all about it. Had I not been there, what would have been the outcome?

"So what was the fuel source?" I asked.

Tommy glanced at Cin.

Cin leaned back in the swivel chair and said, "Tell her. Then you'll know why it could not have been me." She twirled.

Tommy put his foot on her chair and stopped her. "Cinnamon, I have known you all my life. For God's sake, I used to buy you beer when you were seventeen. I didn't say you did it, but it will look that way, so you need all the facts," Tommy said.

"Cin, no one in this room thinks for a second you would set your own bar on fire," I said.

"That's right." Leo put a hand on her shoulder.

"Mr. Small Dick thinks I did," she said.

"Well, that's the trouble with being short, bald, and having an unfortunate name like Smalls. Gives a guy a Napoleon complex," I told my cousin.

"I like to call it short-man syndrome," Cin said and grinned.

I turned my attention back to Tommy. "Let's have it. What was the fuel source?"

"We can't be certain at this point until the tests are complete, but we found broken bottles of grain alcohol, so that's where we're leaning."

"You mean like Everclear? The stuff people use to do a flaming shot? Cinnamon would never keep that in her bar," I said.

"Thank you," Cin said and crossed her arms, a smug look on her face.

"Enlighten me, ladies," Leo said. He sat down and put his hands behind his head, trying to look relaxed and confident, but his eyes held a hint of apprehension. He was worried.

"You want to tell the story or shall I?" I asked my cousin.

"Be my guest," Cin said and twirled again.

I took a breath and launched into the story. "It was the town's bicentennial, a few years back. Cinnamon found this recipe for a firecracker shot and thought she would give them away that night. Well, the line was too long, and Scully didn't want to wait, so he swiped a few from the rail when she wasn't looking, lit them all, and started downing them."

"And before he knew it..." She stifled a laugh, and that prompted me to giggle.

Leo raised an eyebrow at Tommy.

"I didn't know a thing about this," the fire chief said, hands up.

I snorted.

Cinnamon pointed at me. "He said he was pissing fire all night!"

"Cin, tell them about Monique," I said.

Cin threw her head back and cackled. "That was the best part." She clapped. "Monique was standing in front of Scully, trying to pick up some guy, and Scully burped on that last shot before he finished it. Her hair lit up like a Christmas tree! It was awesome."

We were both in hysterics now.

"And I did the honors of pouring a pitcher of ice water over her head to put it out," I said. "She never used Aqua Net again."

"And I never ordered Everclear again," Cinnamon said, wiping a tear away.

Leo shook his head and rose. He wasn't laughing.

"Didn't you like our story?" I asked.

"It's a great story. There's just one problem."

"What?"

"I checked with your distributor, and he sent this fax. Cinnamon, it looks like your signature on the invoice," Leo pushed the paper toward us.

I examined the order form. It did look like her signature. Approving delivery of one case of Everclear.

Cin fingered the paper and chewed her lower lip. She stood up.

"Why would I order a single case of anything? That doesn't make any sense." She directed this at me.

"It gets worse," Tommy said.

I waited for the next bomb to drop.

"We found the case of bottles in a corner. There were eight missing." He sighed.

I looked from Leo to Tommy. There was more. I could feel it. "What else?"

"Stacy, the booze was poured all the way up the stairs. There even seemed to be traces on the ceiling and the beams," Tommy said. "And"—he sighed—"the sprinkler system was shut off at the control valve."

My heart thumped at that news. If the fire was contained to just the basement, the possibility of a prank would exist. But for the trail to intentionally lead up the stairs, and with the sprinklers turned off, then whoever set it intended to burn the whole place down.

Or worse. Everyone in town knew Cinnamon would be there at that hour.

My grandmother's voice rang in my head. *Death has paid a visit.*

"What?" Leo asked.

I didn't realize I said it out loud. I shook my head and exchanged an uneasy glance with my cousin. Her face was stone.

"Are you saying someone tried to kill us?" I asked Leo.

"Maybe." He paused. "Or maybe just Cinnamon," he said.

Chapter 5

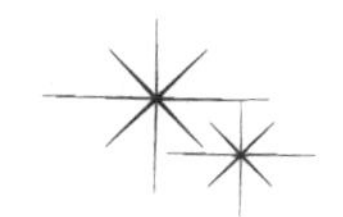

A few minutes later, I parked Thor in my office and barged through my boss's door. He was on the phone, his giraffe legs stretched to the side of his desk. He held up a finger to me, and I watched his Adam's apple bob up and down as he spoke.

In a million years, I never thought I would be working for the *Amethyst Globe.* My father started the paper years ago. Shea Parker handled the business end of things, while Dad was all news. It won quite a few awards back then for our region of the world, and Parker has been hounding me to work for him since I was in high school. But I wanted bigger stories, better scoops. I wanted to work in a city where I made a difference.

Now, it seems, I am.

I put my hands on Shea's desk. "Parker, it's important."

He closed his eyes and nodded, holding up that finger again, still talking.

"Yep, not too much cheese this time, all right, Joey? My star reporter here likes to eat healthy." He made a gun with his finger and shot at me.

I reached over the desk, grabbed the phone from his ear, and slammed it on the receiver.

"Hey, that was Giorgio's! Your favorite," he whined.

"Take me off of everything but the Opal fire."

"Everything?"

"Everything."

"Can't do it."

"You better."

"I need you to cover the ice lizard race."

I don't know why, but I had to ask. "What the hell is that?"

"They take these lizards, you see, and they line them up on the riverbank and then—"

I held up a hand. "I get it. Give it to Iris."

"I can't do that. It's an important piece."

"Ice lizards—that's important?"

"Don't knock it. They raised thousands of dollars last year."

Again, I bit. "For what?"

Parker pursed his lips. "I think it was for a new city sign. They got tired of painting fresh numbers over the old ones when a baby was born, then repainting when someone died. Unless it was for—"

"Shea!" I was this close to shaking the plugs from his head.

Parker stood. "What makes you think you can waltz in here at, uh"—he looked at his watch, which never kept good time—"lunchtime and bark orders at me?"

"Because if it wasn't for me, this paper would still be covering pie-eating contests and your only advertisers would be church bake sales. Now, put me on that story."

"I can't, Stacy."

"Why the hell not? I was there!"

I could feel a vein throb in my neck.

"So was I," said a voice behind me.

Which I now recognized as Derek, sneaking up on me yet again.

I faced him and plastered a hand on my hip. "What do you wear on your feet—ballet slippers?"

To Parker, I said, "You gave the biggest story this year to a kid photographer?"

"I'm not a kid," piped Derek.

I took a long look at Derek. His teeth were bright against his chocolate skin, his hair had a zigzag etched into it, and he was wearing baggy jeans, a Snoop Dogg T-shirt, and a pencil in his ear.

Except for the pencil, he looked like a reality show contestant.

"Right, you're the epitome of professionalism."

"Hey, you were wearing a cape last night," Derek said.

Okay, he had me there. "But I wasn't working."

Derek protested a few more times, but I ignored him.

I poked Parker in the chest. "It's my story. Make it happen," I said and left.

Gladys Sharp's desk was just down the narrow hallway. She was the research assistant for the paper. Gladys used to work at the grocery store, but when I signed on to be a reporter, she jumped at the opportunity to work at the *Globe.* The Geraghty Girls are to Gladys what Elvis was to rock-and-roll fans, so I guess she thought working with me might get her a backstage pass, so to speak. Since she is the hardest-working woman on the planet, I thought she'd be a good fit.

The research room was surrounded by floor-to-ceiling bookshelves with a few computer desks on the outskirts and a conference table in the middle.

"Hi, Gladys," I said. Gladys was surfing the web when I approached. She turned and smiled, her hair puffed out around her cheeks. Blue reading glasses clung to her nose.

"Hi, Stacy," she said. Her dentures clicked as she spoke in her thick Polish accent. On the screen was a web page titled The Kitchen Witch Cooks Without a Stitch.

I pointed to the screen. "That could be dangerous."

Gladys smiled. "Yes, but she has good recipes."

I was all for that, because Gladys couldn't navigate an oven if Emeril Lagasse drew her a map. Which wouldn't make a difference to me if she weren't constantly trying to force home-cooked meals down my throat.

I pulled up a chair and grabbed a pen and pad of paper. "Listen, Gladys, I have some work for you."

Gladys looked relieved. I got the impression she didn't really want to learn how to cook naked.

"I need you to find some records on the building where the Black Opal is located."

Gladys clapped a hand to her throat. "Oh, Stacy, I'm so sorry. You and cousin Cinnamon are fine?"

"Never better," I said.

"You are trumpet."

"Excuse me?"

"You know, like soldier. March on." She made a fist and punched the air.

"Oh. I'm a trooper. Thanks."

I wrote down the information I needed and gave her a list of references she could search. I thanked Gladys and pocketed the pen and paper.

When I got up to leave, Derek was standing in the doorway.

"I'm going to hang a bell around your neck, I swear to God," I said.

"I'm pissed at you," he said, arms crossed.

"You can't be pissed at me. You're not family, and we're not dating."

"What's that got to do with it?"

I shrugged. "Those are the only people who ever get pissed at me. Everyone else finds me adorable." I stepped around Derek and started back to my office to grab my recorder and a bag.

"Mr. Parker took me off the fire story," he said, jogging after me.

"I know."

"Well, that's not right, man. I earned it."

He was on my heels.

"You blew into town five minutes ago. You haven't earned anything, Derek."

"Yeah, but you didn't want it."

"That was yesterday. Today I want it."

"So do I."

"You are a photographer."

"I'm a photojournalist."

"You'll take the next one."

"That could be a while."

"Not in this town, trust me."

We reached my office, and I turned to face him. "Why are you following me?"

"Why are you such a bitch?"

He stepped back as he said it. All I did was glare at him and shake my head.

This was my family we were talking about; it wasn't just a story to me. Cin nearly died in that fire. I nearly died in that fire. I would be damned if I was going to hand it over to a punk with an ego bigger than his camera. This investigation could be dangerous, and I had no idea where it would lead. Derek knew nothing about this town or the people in it. They don't trust outsiders. I couldn't risk him screwing up while my cousin's life was at stake. Because, surely, whoever would go that far once would strike again.

Hand it over to Derek? No freaking way.

I was just about to put my hand on the doorknob when it occurred to me. "You never called him, did you?"

Derek adjusted one of his cameras. He knew I was referring to last night, when I told him to let Parker know I didn't want the piece.

I tapped my foot, waiting for his answer. He didn't supply one, and I didn't have time to slap it out of him. It felt good to slam the door with him standing on the other side of it.

"You're forgetting one thing," I heard him say.

I sighed and peeked through a slat of the blinds.

Derek grinned and pointed to his camera.

Right. The photograph. Dammit.

He was wearing the only recorded evidence around his neck. The physical evidence, if it existed, would be tied up for a while.

Ever since Parker had placed a lunch order, I had a taste for pepperoni, so I called Giorgio's and picked up pizza and salad for a bite with Birdie and the aunts. They needed to hear what Tommy found and—God, help me—I needed to find out if there was anything in their bag of tricks that would help me discover the truth.

Thor and I followed the black iron fence that traced the front yard, and I swung open the heavy gate. The Queen Anne house looked just as it did when I was a kid. Mom and I lived there after Dad died, and when she left, this was home until I went to college.

The front porch circled the frame, complete with wicker rockers waiting for passengers. Gingerbread dripped from every eave, painted in shades of teal, red, and purple, while the body was a buttery yellow, like a Victorian mistress who knew how to accessorize. I climbed the stairs and cranked the antique bell.

A moment later, Aunt Lolly squeaked the door open and blinked big false lashes at me. Her dress was an off-the-shoulder, ruffled number with a pink bodice. A big bow was wrapped in her kinky copper hair, and the blank look on her face told me the boat was in the harbor, but the captain was below deck, sipping a cocktail.

"I'm sorry, we don't take pets," she said.

Thor whined.

"Aunt Lolly, it's me—"

"Please call again," she said and slammed the door.

Damn, damn, damn. I might have beaten her to the finish line if my hands weren't bogged down by a pepperoni pie.

When Aunt Lolly had too much going on, something as simple as one more phone number was enough to crash the hard drive in her mind. To compensate, her internal help desk deleted a file. Like the face of her grandniece.

I leaned on the house buzzer, hoping someone more lucid would show up.

"I'll get it," called a voice from inside.

The door opened again, and my grandfather stood in the frame, his warm eyes happy to see me. I wondered why he was there. Especially since he didn't live there and everyone liked it that way. It was much more peaceful without Birdie whipping platters at his head.

"Hey, sweetheart!" Gramps hugged my neck and said, "Here, let me take that for you." He took the pizza and white paper bag with the salad in it and ambled toward the kitchen. Thor trotted after him.

It was a thirteen-room house with ornate woodwork and delicate furniture. The three guest rooms were located up the curved staircase, and there was a parlor, a library, and a sitting area with a piano for guests to enjoy on the main floor. A locked door led to a long hallway and the private quarters.

"So, you stopped in for lunch on a Friday, eh? You're a brave one," Gramps said when we landed in the kitchen at the back of the house. He placed the food on the old apothecary table that served as a center island. Copper and cast-iron pots and pans dangled just above it.

After I moved out, the Geraghty Girls decided to turn their family home into a bed-and-breakfast, so Friday is the busiest day of the week. Between check-ins, the wine-and-cheese hour, meet and greet with the guests, and menu planning, the day is usually fully booked for all three of them. But I needed their help.

"Well, Gramps, I came to talk with them about Cinnamon and, er..." I wasn't quite sure how to say it since he didn't buy into the Old Ways, but I didn't have to.

He picked up the clue and put up a hand. "Say no more, dear."

Fiona whisked into the kitchen then, carting a tub of laundry. She wore a navy silk pants set, her auburn locks twisted into a chignon.

"Hello, dear. What's this for?" Fiona set the laundry on a chair near the back door and opened the pizza box.

"I brought lunch. I thought maybe the three of you could spare some time to chat. I need a little favor."

Fiona glanced at the rooster clock on the wall. It was twelve thirty. "We have an early check-in this afternoon, but I finished the room already, and I think Lolly prepped the appetizers." Lolly is the chef, and she is a good one too, as long as all her wires are connected.

"What's the favor?" Fiona asked. She pulled plates from the walnut hutch.

"I learned a few things about the fire, and I wanted to go over it with you. I was hoping you could help"—I fumbled for the right words—"sort things out," I said finally, reaching for the silverware.

"All right, sugar. You know we'll always make time for you." She patted my shoulder as she set the plates on the island. "Oh, I almost forgot. Oscar, Birdie's bag is near the front door. She asked me to tell you to load it into the car."

Gramps had just grabbed a slice of pizza and was deciding if he should risk eating first or fulfill my grandmother's request. He looked around and determined what she didn't see wouldn't hurt him.

Wait a minute. Why does she need a bag? "Is Birdie going somewhere?" I asked.

Gramps and Fiona exchanged glances. I didn't like the vibe I was getting.

"What is it?" I asked, a little frantic. Was Birdie sick?

Fiona spoke first. "It was something I planned for her, sweetheart." She nodded toward Gramps, who was inhaling his pizza. "And Oscar too."

I didn't like where this was heading.

I narrowed my eyes at Fiona. "What are you talking about? What did you plan?"

She looked away.

I switched my attention to Gramps. "Gramps, what's going on? Please do not tell me you're going somewhere with Birdie."

My grandfather wiped his mouth with a napkin. "Stacy, I know your grandmother can be a little rough."

"And the *Titanic* hit a little patch of ice," I said.

"But we've been talking and getting along pretty well lately," he said slowly.

This was news to me.

"So you're going on vacation together? Are you kidding me? You can't even a share a meal."

"It's not exactly a vacation," Gramps said and looked to Fiona for support.

"What do you mean? Where are you going?" I asked.

Fiona chimed in. "It's a marriage encounter, sweetie."

My jaw fell open just as Birdie brushed by me.

"Close your mouth, dear," she said, placing her beaded purse and gloves on the counter. She was wearing a flowing skirt with tiny gold medallions tied to it and a crushed-velvet shawl.

"A marriage encounter?" I repeated. My eyebrows rose through the roof.

"Yes," Birdie said, her gaze steady.

I rubbed my temples and took a deep breath. "You do realize you've been divorced for thirty years."

"Has it been that long?" Gramps asked and pulled Birdie to him. He kissed her cheek, and I nearly gagged.

"Birdie, you toss death threats at the man like he's a dartboard," I said.

She put her hand over her mouth and chuckled. If I didn't know better, I'd swear she was flirting. It was unsettling.

"Gramps, you thought she tried to poison you once!"

Gramps wagged his finger. "I never said that. Your grandmother has always been a spitfire." He looked at Birdie, his eyes soft. "Heck, that's why I married her."

Birdie smiled.

"But the woman isn't dangerous."

That's a matter of opinion.

"But you can't live together; you've both said that umpteen times," I pointed out.

Birdie broke from Gramps's embrace and grabbed a plate. "Who said anything about living together?"

"Well, I assume a marriage-encounter weekend implies—"

Birdie cut me off with a wave of her arm. "Enough. It's none of your business. Now, what can we do for you, Anastasia?"

"I'll leave you girls to it." Gramps kissed Birdie, kissed me, and grabbed another slice of the pie before he left the kitchen.

I watched him go and turned back to Birdie, who was helping herself to some salad. I decided it really was none of my business as long as they kept me out of it.

Birdie's head was in the fridge collecting the iced tea, so I smuggled some pepperoni under the table for Thor.

"What have I told you about feeding that dog from the table?" She came back around and set the tea down while Fiona hunted for glasses.

"Sorry," I mumbled. Nearly thirty years old and I still couldn't get away with anything. I got up to let Thor out the back door for a bathroom break.

Lolly came into the kitchen then, a tumbler of whiskey in her hand.

"Hello, Stacy. Oh, did you bring us Giorgio's?" She sniffed the air, her face bright. Perfect. All her bearings were oiled.

The details of the fire and how it didn't appear to be an accident shot out of my mouth in rapid succession.

Birdie, Lolly, and Fiona listened intently, Birdie's green eyes darkening with each word I said. She didn't like what she was hearing. If anyone was going to screw with her grandchildren, it would be her, dammit.

"So I was hoping you could cast some wave of protection around Cinnamon. I think she's in real danger," I said. "And if there's anything you can think of that might help me find the truth faster, I'd be willing to listen. You all have lived here for…?"

Not one of them has ever revealed their age to me. All I know is Birdie is the youngest, Lolly the oldest, and Fiona is sandwiched between them. And thanks to a long-ago courthouse mishap, there are no records of any of them ever being born.

Didn't seem like I would get that answer today, either. They stared blankly at me.

"Well, for a long time, anyway, so after I do some digging, I might need your help on the who's who of Amethyst."

Lolly and Fiona locked eyes.

Birdie stood up and said, "Wait here." Then she disappeared into the cellar.

Thor scratched at the back door, and I went to let him inside. He found a sun spot in the corner and curled up.

When I turned back, the three of them were in a huddle.

"She needs to find her own way," Birdie was saying.

"But Cinnamon..." said Lolly.

"And Thor," Fiona added.

Birdie whispered something I couldn't pick up, and they looked at me.

"Darling," Birdie said, "it's time you did your own bidding."

I didn't like the sound of that.

Fiona floated to the table, carrying a black box with a gold hinge, and set it in the center. I recognized it as the container where their magic tools are stored. She flipped open the latch and pulled out a purple sachet. "Elderberry, hyssop, and rue. Hang it from the threshold of the cottage for protection."

I held out my hand, and she plopped it in.

Lolly stepped forward and dug into the box. She pulled out a gemstone with a coral hue. Agate, I recognized. "Under your pillow. To help you understand your dreams." She set it in my open palm.

Birdie came forward then, a large book in her hands.

I met my grandmother's eyes. "Is that…?"

"The Blessed Book," she confirmed my suspicion.

The Blessed Book began as an oral history of the women in my family. When my great-grandmother came to the New World, she recorded what she knew and what she had learned within these pages. Since then, Birdie, her two sisters, and my mother had added to its knowledge base. I had never actually seen the book before. Never even believed it existed. But here it was.

"Every truth you seek is bound within these pages," Birdie said, cupping the book. She stretched her arms out, and I touched the worn leather cover. "It belongs to you now."

I snapped my hand back.

Oh no. What was I supposed to do with this? They talked in circles, riddles, and rhymes most of the time. I doubted I could decipher whatever was in there. Plus, I knew little about pagans, witches, and especially magic. What could I possibly add to this book? Not to mention the thing was thicker than all the Harry Potter novels combined. It would take forever to sift through.

"Um, this is not exactly what I meant. See, I was hoping you three could do your witchy thing, and I could do my reporter thing, and maybe we could figure this out together." I smiled at Birdie, begging for a positive response.

Birdie set the book on the table and tilted her head high. "Anastasia," she said.

I gulped. "What?"

"You have already accepted your familiars—the cat, the dog. You believe they were sent to you for guidance, protection, do you not?"

I looked at Thor, who was licking his carry-on bags. Not exactly the portrait of protection. Plus, I'd only said that once to appease her. I lied. "Yeah, sure. But Birdie, I need your help on this one. This is serious."

Birdie clasped my shoulders. "The magic is in here." She pointed to my heart. "The knowledge is in there." She pointed at the book. "Now, I have to go. I'll call you later."

"Wait, you're really leaving? Now?"

She was slipping on her gloves, her purse hooked on her wrist. "Of course. And I expect you to look after your aunts."

Now I was getting angry. How dare she take off when I needed her? I was there when she needed me. I came back here for her, to help with the business, the house. Her leaving now was…was…just like my mother.

I shouted at her for the first time in my life. "I have never asked you for anything!"

Lolly jumped and Fiona busied herself by putting away the dishes.

Birdie turned to me, just as the doorbell rang, and smiled. "I know. That is why you have earned this now. Your gifts are your own. Learn them well. My gift"—she threw a look at the book—"is in there." She wafted from the room.

A second later, Fiona said, "That must be Mr. Smalls at the door."

Smalls? As in Benjamin Smalls? "You have got to be kidding me," I said.

Chapter 6

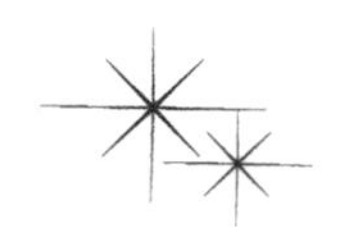

"Darling, would you mind seeing him in?" Fiona asked me.

I was still staring after the empty space Birdie had recently occupied.

"Actually, Fiona I don't think that's wise."

"Please, Stacy. Lolly needs to prepare the other rooms, and I want to finish the food tray."

I sighed. The guy already hated me; it wasn't like it could get any worse. "All right. C'mon, Thor."

I trudged through the long hallway, Thor at my heel, and swung open the front door.

The insurance agent looked at me, backed up, and checked the address on the building.

A gracious hostess would have put aside the pettiness and explained that he was indeed at the right house. But the lioness in me wanted to watch the jerk who was not only denying my cousin her claim but accusing her of arson squirm.

Smalls fumbled for a piece of paper and took his glasses off to read it.

"Mr. Smalls, are you looking for the Geraghty Girls' Guesthouse?"

"Yes, Miss Justice, I am."

"Well, you've found it." I stepped aside to let him in. That's when he saw Thor, sitting still as a statue, his shoulders puffed out.

Smalls jumped. I got the feeling he wasn't enjoying our quirky little town.

"Does he live here?"

Thor regarded Smalls the same way he did the toy terrier down the street—with speculative interest and a knowledge that the creature was beneath his station.

"No, he just visits now and then." I leaned in and said softly, "Helps us weed through the riffraff. You understand. Can't have just anyone sleeping in the family home."

Smalls set his bag down, looking none too happy about it. "Well, I guess I'll be checking in, then."

"Follow me," I said. "This is my grandmother's inn, along with her two sisters. It's been in the family for decades and…" I was walking and talking for a minute before I noticed he wasn't behind me.

I looked back, and Smalls was still standing in front of the door, looking down. I trailed his stare to the bag. He remained still.

"You can leave it there for now. Grab it when you go to your room." I pointed up the stairs.

"Oh, so there's no bellman?"

Was that a joke? A bellman? Who did this guy think he was, Prince Charles?

"Sure, but it's his day off. If you like, we can strap the bag to Thor, and he can haul it up the stairs for you."

Thor groaned and rolled on his back. I smiled.

The insurance agent did not. "There's no call for sarcasm," he said, buffing his perfectly groomed hands.

I had yet to find an occasion that didn't call for sarcasm, but I wasn't kidding and told him so.

It was hard to say if he believed me, but he stepped around Thor and followed me to the registry desk anyway. I got him checked in, gave him a key and a quick tour. Then I called Aunt Fiona.

"So nice to meet you, Mr. Smalls," Fiona gushed, extending her hand. I didn't have time to see if he would shake it because then she said, "My sister has just set out some delectable snacks in the parlor for your enjoyment."

I heard the word *parlor* and ran back fast. Thor was in the middle of accosting a silver platter full of crab-stuffed mushrooms.

"Thor," I hissed, "bad boy." I pulled him from the food and chastised him some more. He dropped his head and slumped to the piano, looking guilty yet unrepentant, while I went about the business of damage control.

It appeared Thor had stolen six mushrooms before he was busted. I scanned the room for a fresh platter but didn't see one.

"Now, won't you follow me to the refreshments?" I heard Fiona say.

The buffet was piled high with napkins, so I swiped one and checked the presentation of the appetizers. The plate didn't look too bad. Just some slobber and maybe a hint of hair. Certainly wouldn't kill anyone.

I sopped up the goo and rearranged the mushrooms, then stuffed the napkin in my pocket just before Smalls and Fiona entered the room.

Oh, please. You would have done the same.

Fiona motioned for the insurance agent to help himself to the snacks. He hovered over them for a minute, planning his attack. Then he plucked a tiny tray from the sideboard and filled it with apples, cheddar cheese, and three mushrooms, one of which had a short tan hair waving from it.

Fiona flashed her eyes at me, then at the dog, who was still licking his lips. Smalls poked the mushroom into his mouth.

I kept mine shut.

"So, Mr. Smalls," Fiona began, "what brings you to our humble town?"

Here we go. I couldn't wait to see how this would play out. My experience in entertaining guests at the inn has, to put it gently, not gone smoothly in the past. So far, though, no guest has accused a family member of a felony.

Until now.

I leaned back against the piano and crossed my arms. Thor laid his head on my feet.

"Actually, I'm investigating an arson," Smalls said, unfolding a napkin.

"Oh my," said Fiona.

I straightened up. "Excuse me, but that's an alleged arson. We are still innocent in this country until proven guilty."

"Miss Justice, I appreciate your passion for the judicial system and your pride for your cousin, but I am confident there is sufficient evidence to support her involvement in the incident."

Incident was emphasized. As if I didn't know what the little weasel was talking about. The more time I spent around this guy, the more I wanted to give him a wedgie. I wondered if there was a spell for that so I wouldn't have to touch him.

Fiona piped up. "Cinnamon? No, sir, you must be mistaken. She is a good girl. She may get a bit hot under the collar now and again, but that runs in the family."

I cleared my throat and sent Fiona a *You're not helping* look. She went about straightening the doilies on the sofa.

"Well, I have all the proof I need right there in that bag," Smalls said and pointed to the leather satchel he'd left in the foyer.

Only it wasn't there.

"Where's my bag?" Smalls looked around the room. He set his tray down and searched behind the curio cabinet, beneath the piano, and near the buffet.

"Are you certain you left it in here?" Fiona asked.

"Yes, I did, it was right there." Smalls was growing agitated, eyes still circling the room. "She said I could pick it up later." Smalls lifted his head toward me. "You"—he pointed to me—"you took it!"

"What?" I asked.

"Where is it? Where is my bag?"

Thor lifted his head and perked his ears.

"I don't know, maybe the bellman carried it upstairs," I said.

I admit I liked screwing with the guy. Which turned out to be a big mistake.

"Is it possible you brought it to your suite?" Fiona asked.

"No, I haven't been to my room yet."

"Well, let's have a look, just in case."

We all climbed the stairs, and Fiona produced a key when we got to the third room on the right.

She opened the door, and Smalls stuck his head inside. Apparently, there was no sign of the bag.

Sweat beads popped up all over Smalls's forehead, and his face was tomato red just before he grabbed me by the shoulders. Through gritted teeth, he hissed, "Give me back my property."

I didn't know where this man was raised that he thought he could put his hands on me and get away with it, but Thor was raised by Cinnamon, who never let anyone get away with anything. Least of all, men who didn't know better than to insult, assault, or just plain piss off a woman.

The Great Dane lunged forward and clamped a jaw on the insurance agent's ham hock of a wrist, forcing him to release me.

Fiona, normally a champ under pressure, froze in shock.

Not a drop of blood was spilled, but Smalls screamed like a girl in a schoolyard. I wanted to bite him myself.

Thor jumped up and planted his paws on either side of the wall, pinning the insurance agent there. The dog towered a good two feet over him and let out a warning that came close to the sound a black bear makes when its territory is threatened.

Frankly, had we not been inside the walls of my family's B and B, I might have let Thor enjoy this little moment. But responsibility took precedence, and I said firmly, "Thor, release!"

He hesitated, so I tapped him by the collar, telling him I meant business. Thor jumped down, the force of which sent Smalls on a short tumble over the carpeted stairs. He stopped rolling when he met the first landing.

It all happened in slow motion, but the reality of it hit me like a tidal wave. My dog had just wrapped his teeth around the insurance agent handling Cinnamon's claim. That couldn't be good.

"Fiona, take Thor down the back stairway," I said.

I skidded down to Mr. Smalls, who was curled up like a ball of yarn.

"Are you okay? Mr. Smalls, are you hurt?"

"Leave me alone," he said and batted me away with his right arm. Unfortunately, I was crouched on my heels at the time, which is a very unbalanced position to put yourself in on a flight of stairs. I tumbled back too and smacked the railing.

Smalls stood up. He was a little wobbly and his suit coat was torn, but other than that, he seemed fine.

"Mr. Smalls, I am so sorry," I said. I got up and took a step.

He blocked me with his hand. "Stay away."

"Please, let me help you. We'll mend that suit coat."

"Help me? Are you crazy?"

Why do people keep asking me that? "Look, this is a huge misunderstanding. I did not take your bag."

I didn't. Really.

Smalls tried to get up. He winced. "I'm pressing charges. You and that dog assaulted me!"

"That's absurd. It was an accident. Besides, you put your hands on me first."

Geez, now I was the one who sounded like a little girl in a schoolyard. But he really shouldn't have done that.

Smalls ignored me and pulled out a cell phone.

"Hello, police?"

Terrific.

Chapter 7

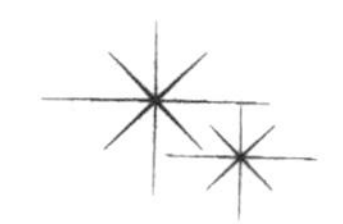

The last time I was in a holding cell I was visiting Birdie. She got arrested for doing a Lady Godiva impersonation down the middle of Main Street during the Fourth of July parade.

Even that day was better than this one.

"Gus!" I called.

Gus moseyed around the corner, drinking a Yoo-hoo.

"Hey, Stacy, what did ya need?"

A clean record? A normal family? An ass doughnut?

"Where is Leo? You said he'd be here by now."

"He was on his way, but he got called out to the Shelby farm because someone smeared Nair on all their goats. Poor things are freezing their walnuts off."

Geez, where do I live?

Thor trotted to Gus and accepted a pat on the head through the iron. I got up and stepped over to the gate.

"Gus, can you please let him out? I think he might have to go."

"Sorry, no can do. He's a prisoner for the time being."

"That's ridiculous. He did nothing wrong. He was looking out for me, that's all."

"Take it up with the judge." Gus grinned and slurped his drink.

My idiot limit had reached maximum capacity, so I stuck an arm through the bars, grabbed him by the belt, found his tighty-whities, and said, "Let. Him. Out." Someone was getting a wedgie today, so help me.

Gus was taken off guard and spit his chocolate drink all over me. "Cripes, Stacy, I was just kidding. Course I'll take him." He backed up and adjusted his uniform, not to mention his unmentionables. He tossed me a hurt look, like a puppy dropped at the pound.

"Sorry, Gus. Can I have a napkin, please, and my phone call?"

"Oh, I made that call for you," Gus said, unlocking the gate. Thor darted through. "Your ride should be along any minute."

"What? Wait a second, who did you call? Gus!"

But he was already gone.

Please, let it be Cinnamon.

My cousin knew the ropes in this department. And by this department, I mean every jail cell in a three-hundred-mile radius. She rebelled against her cop father for years by landing herself in the slammer, which was ironic, since he often slapped the cuffs on himself. Hmm. I never thought of that before. Maybe the violent outbursts, dangerous pranks, and artistic vandalism were her way of seeing Uncle Deck more often.

I, in contrast, never even had a speeding ticket.

The drink was beginning to harden on my face, and since I didn't expect that napkin anytime soon, I untucked my turtleneck and wiped it away.

She came at me while my shirt was stretched over my head. "Can you not keep yourself out of harm's way for five minutes?"

Definitely not Cinnamon.

I pulled my turtleneck down and faced Birdie.

"It wasn't my fault."

"It never is, dear."

"Birdie, I'm serious. That asshole should be in here. Not me."

"Then why didn't you press charges?"

That was a good question. For which my only answer was, "I didn't want to make things worse."

Birdie pointedly eyed every inch of the cell I was standing in. The message was: *And yet, here you are.*

"Please, can we talk about this later?" I said.

Birdie paid the fine as I gathered my things and clipped a leash on Thor. I told her I would wait outside and stepped onto the sidewalk, searching the street for her white Cadillac. I spotted it in the narrow parking lot. That's when I felt a twinge in my chest. Not nausea, not the chills. Just...a tug.

"We go," Birdie said, behind me.

I shifted to face her and spotted the mustached man, lingering near the courthouse.

"One minute," I said to Birdie. I put my things in the car.

When I looked back, he was gone.

As we pulled up to the house, Gramps was waiting in his Buick, tapping his fingers on the steering wheel, probably crooning with Sinatra.

"Are you still going?" I asked Birdie.

"Remember that wonderful talking gadget you gave me for Christmas?"

"You mean a cell phone?"

"Yes, well, we aren't allowed one of those." She rolled her eyes and made a grand gesture with her hand. "Bonding, you know. Getting in touch with our feelings. As if I have any new feelings left to experience in this mature body."

"Birdie, the talking gadget?"

"Right. You see, mine has a little typewriter built in. So we can communicate if the need arises."

I smiled. "Good enough."

We all exited the car, and Birdie got into the front seat of the Buick. She flipped the mirror down and dabbed on some lipstick.

Gramps said something to her and got out of the car.

"There's my star," he said.

I smiled.

"Listen, sweetie, I forgot to tell you that I called Stan Plough and told him that if you girls needed anything, he could tack it on to my bill. I have him on retainer, for my investment properties and such."

By *such*, I assumed he meant the crazy women in his life. He handed me a card.

"Thanks, Gramps. Why haven't you left yet?"

He angled around the front of the car, opened the driver's side door, and shook his head. "Wouldn't you know it? Your grandmother was sorting through the luggage and noticed one of the bags wasn't ours." Gramps shrugged. "See you Monday, dear."

He slammed the door and put the car in reverse. I stood there for a split second processing that little tidbit of information.

I narrowed my eyes at Birdie through the windshield. She smiled at me in return.

Smalls's bag. It had to be. Why she would pull a prank like that, I had no clue.

By the time I changed and fed Thor, it was late afternoon. I would have to submit something by the end of the day to make tomorrow's paper. In a small town, papers don't always publish daily. Some run weekly. The *Amethyst Globe* has four editions: Tuesday, Friday, Saturday, and Sunday. The Tuesday and Friday editions are news, local culture, gossip, sports, want ads, job listings, and anything else you'd find in most city papers. The weekend editions are designed to appeal to tourists, so in addition to the regular features, there are listings for events and entertainment, plus local lore and history. Not exactly cutting edge.

I didn't have enough to go on from my point of view of the fire, nor did I want to highlight anything regarding arson, since that had not been confirmed. In fact, the way the wheels rolled around here, it could take weeks to confirm.

In the meantime, I needed a story today. So I thought I'd interview some of the people who were first on the scene.

I reached for my cell phone and dialed Leo.

"Please tell me you haven't broken another law," he said.

"Funny. It wasn't my fault."

"It never is."

"The moon is in Scorpio or something."

"No, it isn't."

"How would you know?"

"Your grandmother bought me an astrology calendar for Christmas. I check it every day."

"You do?"

"I have to. She quizzes me."

"I'll talk to her about that."

"I wish you would."

"Listen, who were those guys trying to help at the fire last night?"

"You mean the firemen?"

"Ha-ha, smarty pants. No, the three musketeers who headed up the citizens' academy crowd."

"Oh, the Citizens on Patrol. That's Jed, Jeb, and Ned."

"You're screwing with me, right?"

"No, but since you mentioned it, will I ever see you outside of my station again?"

"That depends. Are those really their names?"

"Yes. Two are related. I'm not sure which."

"Where can I find them?"

Leo paused. "Three o'clock on a Friday? Gotta be the Elks Lodge."

"Okay. Pick me up from the paper at six. Aunt Angelica is making dinner for us."

I decided to walk to the Elks Lodge. It was freezing out, but I bundled up and the fresh air felt good against my skin.

The door to the lodge was locked. To the left, a note taped above the bell read, *Ring Bell for entrance. Members Only*.

I was not a member, but I buzzed it anyway. Maybe I could get a free day pass like they hand out at the gym.

A scratchy voice came through the speaker. "Yeah?"

"Hi, I'm looking for Jeb, Jed, and Ned?"

"So?"

"So are they in there?"

"Maybe."

I really was itching to slap someone today, and I wondered if this might be my victim.

"Well, suppose they were in there, do you think they have time for a chat?"

"'Bout what?"

Okay, new tactic. "About the fact that it is freezing cold and I'm wearing my tightest sweater without a coat or a bra."

Magically, the door yawned opened.

The room was dark and musty with a curved bar in the center, cushioned with a leather pad around the edge. A few men sprinkled the bar. One was playing video poker, and three more bent over a shuffleboard.

I walked up to the wraparound bar and caught disappointment on the bartender's face. I almost apologized for my less-than-generous rack before Mr. Huckleberry slid a shot over to me.

"Everyone opens with a whiskey," he said.

The bartender was balancing a glass on his stomach, sliding a towel in and out of it. He drank me in before he said, "Members only, girly."

"Hey, show some respect," Mr. Huckleberry said, puffing on his cigar. Smoking was still permitted in private clubs in Illinois. "That's Oscar's granddaughter."

The bartender looked surprised. "'Scuse, me. I didn't know." He waddled away.

"Well?" Mr. Huckleberry glanced at the shot. "It's Jameson."

I toasted him and sunk the liquid into my belly.

"Looking for three morons?" he asked.

I smiled. "Heard they might be here."

Mr. Huckleberry pointed to the shuffleboard.

"Thanks, Mr. Huckleberry."

"Call me Huck, sweetheart."

I strolled over to the CoPs, as they will forever be known.

"Hi, guys. I'm Stacy Justice. I work for the *Globe,* and I was hoping I could ask you a few questions about the fire last night."

"Hey, Stacy. Sure we know who you are. Heck, everyone knows you, Mrs. Chief," said the shortest of the three.

"Not quite."

"I'm Ned, and them two are Jed and Jeb." Identical twins. Not sure which two were brothers? Funny, Leo.

"Hey, we got a fourth now," said Jed. Or maybe it was Jeb.

"No time, sorry. I just need you to answer a few questions."

Ned crossed his arms. "Maybe we don't have time for questions, then."

What is it with the men today? "If you don't help me, this will go on your permanent record," I said.

Jeb or Jed looked a little scared, but Ned called my bluff. "Shoot, there ain't no such law."

I could have argued further, but I figured the interview would go faster if I just played the stupid game. Apparently

Jeb and Jed are always partners, so I teamed up with Ned, who was a terrible player, thanks to a lazy eye.

Two hours and two beers later, I decided I had wasted enough time trying to get the three blind mice to focus on the subject at hand. Every damn question was met with a story about their high school days, all of which were mind-numbingly boring, I might add. I switched off the recorder and put my notepad away.

"Thanks, guys, you've been no help at all," I said.

"Don't mention it," said a drunken Ned.

Huck was still there, and Kirk and Eddie McAllister had joined him. All of them were hunched over a glass of something, a few stools apart.

I patted Huck on the arm and said, "Thanks for the Jameson."

Huck swung around and said, "Stacy, you're wasting your time. I'm telling you, shoddy work, old wiring. It was an accident."

"Accident," slurred Eddie.

I looked over to the brothers.

Kirk smacked Eddie on the back. "Stop it, Eddie. You've had too much to drink."

"I do good work!" Eddie said.

Kirk put his hand on the back of Eddie's head and pulled his brother close to whisper something in his ear.

I leaned over to Huck. "What's that about?"

"Eddie's a little slow. He gets upset if people criticize him."

"But he never even started the work. And no one criticized him. Why would he take it personally?"

Huck shrugged and stubbed out his cigar. "Well, he worked on the place a few times over the years. Hired him myself. But like I said, he's slow."

The older brother guided his sibling off the stool and pointed him toward the door. When they walked by, he said to me, "He just gets upset sometimes. I shouldn't let him drink at all."

He tapped my shoulder, and instantly my head swirled and I faltered. The bar was close enough to steady my stance as I watched the pair leave. Then a picture of Kirk McAllister flashed in my head. His face streaked with water, he was bent over muddy earth, shoveling dirt onto a fresh grave.

I shivered. What was that? A memory? Something that had happened long ago? Or something that was about to take place?

The picture still in my mind, I pushed open the door to the newspaper offices.

"About time," Parker said, looking at his watch. He flicked the face, then lifted his wrist to his ear, frowning.

"Sorry, Boss. I was in the field conducting interviews."

I had to walk past him to turn down the hall to my office.

"You smell like beer," he said. He sniffed my hair. "And some kind of spicy cigar."

"Yeah, well, what can I say? The field is stinky." I tossed Parker a grin and told him I'd have the story on his desk in an hour.

I twisted the key to my office, dropped my bag on the chair near the door, and screamed bloody hell.

"Take it easy, Miss J," Derek said, a smug look on his face.

I clutched at my chest, making sure my heart was still beating, and glared at Derek. He had the nerve to put his feet on my desk and lean back in my chair.

The pent-up anger was too much. I walked over to him and flung his ankles over his head. He crashed to the floor, and papers swam through the room. I reached for the ritual sword I kept propped beneath my desk. Birdie had given it to me when I started this job. It was adorned with the three muses, each holding a tiny crystal ball.

I bent the sword toward Derek's neck.

"Why do you insist on screwing with me?" I demanded.

Derek's line-free face gathered just enough wrinkle to let me know that he was about to piss himself.

"Hey, I just wanted to give you the pictures, I swear."

"How did you get in?"

"The door was unlocked."

I added more pressure.

"Okay, okay. I picked the lock."

I picked up one of the papers and scanned the text. It seemed to be from an abstract on a piece of property.

"Gladys got that information you wanted—you know, from the building," Derek said, trying to smile. "Can I get up now?"

"Where are the photos?"

"Really, this isn't funny anymore."

Parker walked in then, eating a bear claw, and said, "Woops, I'll come back."

"Wait, get her off me!" Derek squeaked.

Parker paused. He looked at me and raised one eyebrow.

"Creative differences." I shrugged.

He sighed and slid a chair over to my desk.

"Why can't you two play nice?" he asked.

"Because he is a weasel," I said.

"And she's a nut job," Derek said.

Parker considered this and polished off the bear claw. "Stacy, I know you're very protective of your work. But have you considered the fact that collaborating with Derek could make it that much better? He is talented, trust me. I didn't hire him for his looks." He glanced down. "And, Derek, you can't string two words together. Stick with what you know."

Derek blinked.

I really could use a decent photographer. But I could do without the douchebaggery.

"I have terms," I said.

"Go on," Parker mediated.

"No more sneaking up on me, breaking into my office, or following me."

Parker glanced at Derek.

Derek nodded.

"Done," Parker said.

"He does what I say, when I say it, and he respects that I am his superior."

Derek slid his eyes sideways.

"Seems reasonable," Parker nudged.

Derek rolled his eyes and nodded.

"One more thing," I said as Parker stood.

"What?"

"Thor takes his nap in Derek's office."

Derek shrugged, and I got up.

"Hey, no prob. I like dogs," he said, straightening his shirt.

Parker and I exchanged a knowing glance.

Chapter 8

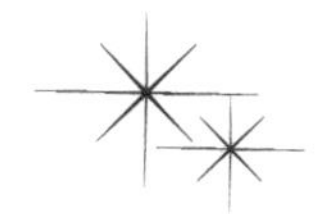

An hour later, I e-mailed the story to Parker, packed up the research, and stepped into the night. The sky was black, stamped with a crescent moon and a kaleidoscope of stars. Leo was waiting for me inside his Mustang.

He jumped out and grabbed my bag, packed with Derek's photos and the abstract, and tossed it on the back-seat. Derek had chosen a picture of the Opal spitting out bright-orange flames, a fireman battling them, to run with the story. Everything else, he passed off to me.

I squeezed the door handle, but Leo stopped me and spun me into his chest. He gazed down at me, the crisp scent of his aftershave inviting me to lean into him. So I did.

He cupped my chin, his hands still warm from the car, and hungrily sunk his lips into mine. I slipped my arms beneath his leather jacket and melted into him for what seemed like forever. When he finally pulled away, he opened the door and tucked me into the car without a word.

If we never had to speak to each, our relationship would be perfect.

"Did you find anything out?" we asked at the same time.

I laughed.

"You first," he said. He shifted the gears expertly and pointed the car toward Angelica's bakery.

"Well, not exactly. Your CoPs were wasted, so they were no help at all, but I had an interesting encounter with the McAllister brothers."

Leo glanced at me. "And?"

I told him about the image of Kirk at the grave site.

At the mention of my vision, Leo cringed.

"Hey, I don't know if it means anything." I try not to get defensive whenever this subject comes up, because I myself don't understand it, nor do I necessarily buy into it. But the image was vivid, strong enough to knock me off balance.

"Maybe it was a memory from the past. A friend or a neighbor's funeral?" Leo offered as he cut the engine behind the bakery.

My voice had an edge when I spoke. "Why do I bother telling you these things? You never believe me."

"Whoa. In my defense, *you* don't believe you."

"That's not the point."

That was exactly the point, but he should believe *in* me, at least. Even if I don't. I shook my head.

"Forget it," I said and exited the car.

Leo got out too and shut his door. "I'm just saying it might not mean anything."

I didn't respond. Instead, I reached into the backseat and pulled out my workbag. There was really no point in discussing it. I had a job to do and so did he.

"What are you doing?" he asked.

"I have to go over some things with Cinnamon. Derek—" I cut myself short. Leo couldn't know that Derek snapped those photos in the basement. If he did, he might confiscate them for evidence.

He narrowed his eyes at me over the roof of the car. "Derek what?" he said slowly.

I fumbled for a lie. "He was looking through the abstract of the Opal—that's the entire history of ownership—and he thought it might be helpful, so he gave it to me." I chewed my lip.

It wasn't technically a lie.

"Let me see it," Leo said, always the cop, suspicious to the core.

"I can't."

"Why not?"

"Reporters' code of ethics. Can't reveal my source."

"It's not a source, it's public information."

I rolled my eyes. "Fine, Chief, if you don't believe me..."

Praying to the goddess that the photos were buried beneath the document, I pulled out the thick envelope.

I slid it over to him via the roof of the car. Leo caught it, unhooked the tie, and thumbed through the pages. After a minute or two, he walked around the car and handed the envelope back to me, his face softer.

"I'm sorry," he said and reached for my hand.

I snapped it away. "No, you're not," I said and stuffed the abstract into my bag.

"What is that supposed to mean?"

I met his stare. "You are who you are. You can't turn off being a cop."

"And you"—he tapped the bag—"can't turn off being a reporter. This is supposed to be our night, and you'll be working. Again." He folded his arms in protest.

"This is different, and you know it. I have to—"

"Hey!"

We both looked up. Aunt Angelica was standing on the upper deck of the building. "You gonna smooch all night, or you gonna eat, hah?" She waved a meaty arm. "Come on, *mangia*!"

We both forced a smile and trudged up the stairs. Angelica hugged me, then Leo, and ushered us inside.

The crisp scent of lemon mingled with roasted garlic as I stepped into the small kitchen. My stomach growled in anticipation.

Cinnamon, Tony, and Mario were spread around the dining room table in the next room. My cousin and her husband both looked exhausted. Leo shook Tony's hand, and they began chatting about basketball. I crouched to hug Cinnamon, but Mario interrupted.

"There she is. How you doing, *mi bellissimo*?" He snatched me away from Cin and pulled me into a hug, which put him at perfect boob-sniffing height since I was taller than him.

I pulled away, choking on that awful cologne he marinated in.

"Hi, Mario," I said.

He pulled a cigar from his shirt pocket and said, "How come you not married, yet, hah?" This was directed at my rack.

"Well, I'm still practicing, I guess." I willed his eyes to travel up.

Mario slapped his knee and chuckled. I looked to Cin for assistance.

She got up and put an arm around Mario. "Why don't you go on the porch and smoke that, Uncle Mario?"

"But it's cold," he said to Cin's cleavage. "Your mama won't mind."

"Mario!" Angelica barked from the doorway.

"*Un momento,* Angelica. I was just talking to Stacy, hah?" Mario liked to end most sentences with a question.

"Now, Mario," Angelica growled.

Mario looked at me and shrugged. "Women, hah? She thinks because she older she still can boss me." Mario searched for a match, pulled out a packet from Down and Dirty, and glanced back at Angelica. She had a good fifty pounds on him, and he decided it might be easier to abide by her wishes.

I watched him leave as Cinnamon poured me a glass of wine.

"How long is he staying?" I asked when she handed me the Chianti.

"Probably until I've plucked every strand of hair out of my head." She moved to the floral sofa and I joined her. "Now he wants to be my lawyer. For a fee, of course." Besides boob watching, drinking, and cologne shopping, Mario's favorite pastime is scamming people out of their money. Cin continued, "He thinks it's a shame that the insurance agent would refuse a payout." She sipped her wine and puffed out her chest, mimicking her uncle. "'In Italy,'" she began in a deep voice, "'buildings burn all the time. You have problem, you burn building. Nobody mind.'" Cin looked at me. "Can you believe that? Like I really did it. What a jackass."

Ugh. I'd have to keep an eye on Mario. "We need to go over a few things, Cin. Tonight, okay?"

She nodded.

Dinner was delicious and uneventful. Leo and I stole glances across the table every so often, but there was a distinct nip in the air. In between idle conversation, bites of steak, and false smiles, his jaw was set, indicating he was still angry.

My anger faded after the second portion of pasta and the first Chianti, but I didn't have the energy to smooth things over with him. Maybe after dinner.

Leo's phone buzzed, interrupting my thoughts. He clicked a button, paused for a minute at the display, and shook his head.

"Damn," he mumbled. "I have to go."

"What's up?" asked Tony.

"The Shelby farm."

"The goats again?" Tony asked.

Leo stood up and sighed. "Yep."

"What is it this time?" Cin asked.

"Someone strung battery-operated Christmas tree lights around them and opened the gate. Damn things are wandering all over the road, flashing and blinking."

Leo looked at me and said, "I'll call you later." Then he thanked Angelica and slipped out of the dining room.

My cousin and I cleared the table, despite Angelica's protests. When I went back into the dining room to retrieve my bag, Mario had his greasy hands in it.

"Mario! What are you doing?" I snatched the bag from him, but he had the abstract sprawled on the table already.

"What I do?" he asked. His pants were unbuckled and a caper clung to his chin.

I gathered the papers, mopped at the sauce stains, and said, "You don't go through a woman's things. Shame on you."

Mario raised his eyebrows. "*Mi scusi.*" His voice was mocking, as if I were the nosy pig in this scenario.

I shook my head at Cinnamon, who had no trouble reprimanding bad behavior, even dishing out punishments, but this was her uncle. She was raised to respect her elders, but I could tell she was considering a showdown.

I heard the sound of running water, and Tony emerged from the bathroom a minute later.

We all turned toward him, and he said, "What did I miss?"

"Tony, take Uncle Mario out for a drink," Cin said.

"But I got no money," Mario whined.

"It's okay," Tony said, eyes locked on his bride. "It'll be on me." He didn't seem too thrilled about it, and I didn't blame him one bit.

"No," I said. "You stay here. Cin and I will go to the cottage."

He didn't bother to hide his relief. I imagined letting Mario loose to prowl was worse than containing him in the apartment.

I kissed my aunt good-bye, and Cin and I traipsed out the door. Her Trans Am was parked in the back lot, and we piled in.

I unlocked the door to my cottage, and Cin walked in first. Most people don't lock their doors around town, but it's a habit I picked up living in the city that I can't break.

I had been in the house for about three months, but I still wasn't used to Fiona's taste. The place was a tidy one-bedroom with a Jacuzzi in the living room. The carpet was leopard print, the focal point a giant shoe chair, and the drapes looked like they were ripped off from Caesar's Palace. See what I mean? Not quite my style.

I fed Moonlight and Thor in the pink kitchen and spread the photos and the paperwork over the counter. Cin sat across from me, and I passed her a water bottle.

"What are we looking at?" she asked.

I reached for a magnifying glass, and we examined the first photograph. "Derek snuck into the basement and snapped a few shots. Something felt strange about the corner behind the stairs, but I couldn't figure out what it was."

"Do, do, do, do..." Cinnamon sang.

"Knock it off."

The first few shots were of the fire itself. The blaze was so bright it practically leaped off the page and heated the room. The next few shots were of the town: Main Street, buildings, people milling about, gawking, CoPs getting in the way, and the kid.

The kid! He was right there in one of the snapshots. Only it was just the back of his head. I touched it, and there it was again—the feeling of a spider crawling up my back.

"Cin, that's the kid I saw." I pointed.

"All I see is the back of someone's head."

I held the magnifying glass to the image.

Cin squinted. "Oh, that's Chip Lewis. He helps out once in a while. I hired him a couple months ago to wash floors, move stock, that kind of thing." She lifted her eyes to me. "But he wasn't there that day. He had some school function. Chip only shows up when he feels like it."

I frowned.

"Stacy, I know what you're thinking, and there is no way that boy started the fire. He's a punk, but he isn't evil."

"Why is he a punk?"

"Oh, I don't know. He's got a mouth on him, and I think he's lifted a few beers. I can't prove it, though."

"Then why is working for you?"

"Well, he isn't now," she looked at me pointedly. "But I was in a bind when Bay left, and I needed someone who only wanted to work a few hours a week. I didn't know he had his head up his ass." Bay is Cin's brother. He left to play in a band in California after the New Year.

We scoured the other photos. There was debris all over the charred floor—broken glass, stray nails, and an old tin sign. I got up to stretch, and Cin shrieked.

"I knew it!" she said.

"What?"

"Look." She tilted the magnifying glass to the last photo and shined it on a pack of matches. I peered in. The label read, *Down and Dirty.*

"That bitch!" Cin hopped off her stool and Thor barked.

I lifted the picture and something else caught my eye.

"Cin, calm down. Monique was at her place that night," I said.

"Oh, please. How easy would it be for her to sneak out?"

I didn't say that I thought Monique would be conspicuous if she were a slot machine in a casino. What I said was, "I'll check it out." But my money was on the cigar stub lying inches away from the matches.

We glossed over the photos for a few more minutes, and Cin turned to the abstract.

"So what's this?"

"This"—I pointed to the thick packet of paper—"is the abstract for the building. It lists all the owners from the time of construction."

"I've seen this before. What does that have to do with anything?"

I shrugged. "It might be helpful, and it might not. I thought it was at least worth a look. Maybe someone who had it once wants it back? A fire would cause a lot of damage, but in a brick structure like that, it could be repaired."

"But why burn it at all? Why not just make an offer?"

"Because it's a lot cheaper to purchase a damaged piece of property."

Cinnamon looked doubtful. I kicked off my boots and hoisted myself onto the counter.

"They probably thought you wouldn't sell it. But maybe with all the trouble of repairs—"

Cin cut me off. "Stacy, you do know I don't own the building."

No, I did not. "What do you mean you don't own it? It's your bar."

Cin laughed. "You honestly think I could afford a half-million-dollar piece of property?"

Good point. "Well, I just thought, after your dad…"

Cin was shaking her head. "Honey, I just bought the Black Opal. The business. Not the building."

I threaded that through my mind. "But the repairs…"

Cin shook her head. "All cosmetic. That's why I was going to pay for them."

It hadn't even occurred to me that she didn't own the building. She rented. Which meant she had a landlord.

"Cin?"

"Holy hell," she said. Was she thinking what I was thinking? "What is that?"

My gaze trailed her arm. She was pointing at the desk in my bedroom. Or more accurately, she was pointing at the Blessed Book lying on top of the desk.

"Is that what I think it is?" she asked.

I rolled my eyes.

"So you are a believer!"

Cinnamon jogged into the room and began flipping through the pages. "This thing is huge. I thought they were full of it, carrying on about this damn book." She did a sweeping bow toward me. "And now, it belongs to you, the Seeker of Justice."

I smirked and hopped off the counter.

"You are hilarious. It wasn't like that. I went to them for help and...Wait a second, you're changing the subject, Cin."

"That's because I know your next question, and you won't like the answer, and then I'll have to tell you you're wrong again, and frankly, I'm beat."

"Who is it Cin? Who owns the building?"

Cinnamon paused. "Huck."

That was all she said before a rock slammed through my kitchen window.

Chapter 9

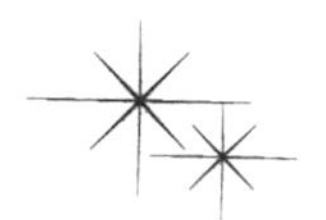

I hit the floor, and Thor exploded into a rage. He ran to the window, bellowing fiercely. I crawled into the bedroom to meet my cousin.

"Are you okay?" she asked.

I nodded and looked back. The rock lay on the counter where I had just been sitting.

We waited a few minutes, listened for a car engine, footsteps, any sign of further harassment.

When it seemed safe, we peeled ourselves off the carpet and crept toward the counter. Thor was still barking, but he stopped to sniff us, making sure we were both unharmed.

I touched the rock. It was big and flat and cold. My stomach roiled as I felt the stone between my palms. What was it Birdie used to say about feeling nauseous? A sign of harmful intent? Yes, that was it. A gut feeling that someone meant to inflict physical harm. I could feel it then, right through the rock. Whoever launched it through the window meant business. This was no prank.

Then I felt the note taped to the bottom.

I flipped the rock over and peeled back the masking tape. The note was folded in quarters. When I opened it up, I saw my byline. Beneath that were individual letters cut from the paper:

LEAVE IT ALONE OR MORE WILL DIE

Cin squeezed my hand and nodded to Birdie's bible. "We're gonna need a bigger book," she said.

That won a smile, and my heartbeat slowed to a fast trot.

"I'm calling Leo," Cin said.

The impact of the shattered glass had fanned the photos across the carpet, and I bent to collect them. Shuffling through the prints, I noticed one was stuck to the back of the last photo we had examined. I held it up. This was the photo I had asked Derek to shoot. The wall, the missing bricks. Missing bricks. Something was bothering me about that. I found the magnifying glass and held it to the photo.

"Cin, hang up," I coughed.

Suddenly, my throat tightened, and my breath came in spurts. It felt as if I had just been punched in the neck.

"Why?" Her phone was cradled in her hand.

"Look at this," I said.

Cin hurried toward me and peered at the photo while I massaged my neck.

In the space of one of the missing bricks, the flash had caught something…shiny.

"What is that?" Cin asked. She lifted the photo and the magnifying glass.

"I don't know. But something is behind that wall." I sucked in more air and exhaled long and hard. Whatever had constricted my breath was passing.

Cin looked at me, then did a double take. "Holy cow! Stacy, you've got a bruise on your neck. Did you crash into something when you dove?"

"I don't think so." I padded into the bathroom for a look. There was a slash of deep purple across my throat.

As I stared into the mirror, fingering the bruise, a reflection not my own shot back. I screamed and scrambled out as fast as I could.

"What? What is it?" Cin asked.

"I…I…" All I could do was point.

Cin rushed into the bathroom. "I don't see anything. What happened?"

My whole body shook. "In the mirror. There was… someone in the mirror."

Cin looked at me like I had completely lost my mind.

"Cinnamon, call Chance," I said.

"Your old sweetheart? Why?" she asked.

Before I could tell her about the girl in the mirror, before I had time to study the book, before I could say we had to get to the Black Opal right now, tonight—and Leo couldn't know about any of it—my front door flew open.

A wave of cold air rushed in, Fiona and Lolly trailing it. "What is it? What's happened?" Fiona asked.

Cinnamon and I exchanged glances. This would be bad. If some wack job was trying to get rid of us, the last thing I wanted was for my aunts to get caught in the web. Not only because they were my family and I didn't want them hurt, but because they were unpredictable and had the uncanny ability to turn a sticky situation into a super-glue situation with honey all over it.

Cinnamon must have been thinking the same thing, because she curled around to the front of the living room so the aunts would face her and I slid the rock behind a phone book.

"Hi, aunties!" Cin said.

"What's happened?" Fiona asked.

"What do you mean?" Cin asked, all wide-eyed and innocent.

She overplayed her hand, because as soon as she said it, Lolly and Fiona locked arms in a standoff between Cinnamon and me. They glared at us, narrowing their eyes. Lolly was in focus, so I guessed the wine held over from the cocktail hour was still swimming through her brain waves.

"Don't play coy, Cinnamon, I know something is amiss in this cottage," Fiona said, and Lolly nodded.

The walls were thick in their old house, practically soundproof, so chances were they didn't hear the glass shatter. But they knew something was very broken in our little town. Fiona swung her head to the doorway.

"Where is the sachet I gave you?" she asked.

Oops. I forgot to hang the protective potpourri. I shrugged. "I just didn't have time, I guess."

She craned her neck to view the kitchen, but Cinnamon rushed over and gave them a hug.

"I'm sorry I missed the Imbolc. Thank you for the spell."

Fiona never could resist a hug, and she squeezed my cousin close.

I inched around, aiming to cover up the glass and hide the rock, but my cell phone rang and broke the silence.

"Say hi to Birdie," Lolly said.

My phone was in the bedroom. If I moved, they were sure to snoop. "I'll let it go to voice mail," I said.

"Where is that draft coming from, dear?" Fiona asked.

"We just let Thor in from outside," Cin said.

At the mention of "outside," Thor jumped up and trotted to the back door, where the jagged shards lay.

"Thor, no!" I ran to check his paws, but he must have missed it. I unlatched the back door, let the dog out, and turned to face my aunts.

They had such an utter look of disappointment you would have thought I just had a baby out of wedlock.

"Let's have it," Fiona said.

I bowed my head as Cin tried to explain. I brushed past Fiona to get my phone, and she gasped at the sight of the bruise on my neck. When she touched it, I flinched.

"It's okay. It's just a bruise."

But Fiona seemed skeptical. She held my wrist, willing me to face her. Her forehead wrinkled into a question, like she had seen that mark before. She dropped my hand, kissed the bruise, and shuffled toward the kitchen.

I picked up my phone and pressed the message option. I had two texts. While Cin and the aunts tried to talk over each other, I read the messages:

FROM: Birdie 8:49 p.m. Hey Sunshine, Gramps here! Not supposed to call, but Grandma has her ways. This is fun!

Journal writing, cozy room, talking. Dinner great. Tomorrow we share feelings in group.

FROM: Birdie 8:57 p.m. If I believed in hell, this would be it. No clocks, no calendars. How will I know when the moon enters Gemini? Sleeping in a closet, eating shoe leather. Oscar won't shut up. Wait 'til I tell my feelings. Anastasia, danger descending. Read the book. Protection.

I tucked the phone in my pocket and went into the kitchen, where Fiona and Cin were duct-taping the hole shut while Lolly was sprinkling salt all around the house. The glass was in the garbage, and the rock was still on the counter. I looked at the note without touching it, because I didn't want to feel sick.

"I called Chance," Cin said to me. "He said he'd help out with whatever we need. He is free tonight, so he said he would stop by."

Fiona dropped the tape and looked at her. "Whatever for?"

Cin tilted her head back and shrugged. "Ask Stacy."

Chance and I were high school sweethearts, and when I first got back to town, it looked like we might revive our romance. He was my first love, and I have to admit that seeing him again—tanned and muscular from working construction, with bright blue eyes and Brad Pitt's hair—I was tempted. But I'm not one to read a book backward.

"Actually, I need him to do something at the Opal." I was still staring at the rock.

What did that note mean? More will die? Where did the *more* fit in? As far as I knew, no one had died.

"Uh-oh," Lolly mumbled.

I lifted my head. Her eyeballs were bouncing around in their sockets. It looked like she popped a fuse.

"Lolly, you okay?" I asked.

Fiona said, "She's fine, dear. We'll just be off now. Looks like you girls have everything under control here." Fiona was ushering Lolly to the door, and I saw a spider dance across the carpet. That was a sign I knew all too well. An uninvited guest.

"Stop!" I yelled.

My aunts halted and slowly circled to face me.

"What did you do?" I asked, hands on hips.

"Whatever do you mean?" Fiona asked in her sultry *You'll believe me because I'm gorgeous and charming* voice. But that doesn't work on me.

I tapped my foot, and Lolly suddenly became fascinated by her split ends.

Fiona sighed. "Well, dear, we felt something was wrong here, so we called your friend Leo."

"Wait a minute. You called Leo?"

"Eek," Cin whispered behind me.

The only thing Chance and Leo have in common is me, and neither of them is thrilled about that. But what I was going to ask Chance to do, Leo couldn't know about.

He would think it too dangerous, or he'd want to follow the rule book, or he might try to convince me that it was illegal.

Which it might be.

"Cin, call Chance back. Tell him to meet us at the Opal ASAP. And you two"—I pointed to my aunts—"stall Leo and—"

The doorbell cut me off.

Son of a bitch.

Chapter 10

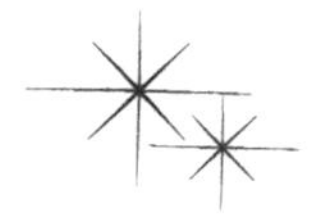

Through clenched teeth, I barked a few orders so everyone knew what to do before I opened the door. I wasn't sure if Chance or Leo had arrived first, but I had a plan in place for either scenario. If it was Chance, Cin was to head to the bar with him in his truck and wait for me. I would wait for Leo, tell him there was no emergency, but ask him if he would like to stay for a beer. I would make up with him, and Cin was to phone and say she needed something or other and ask if I could I bring it to her.

If Leo was standing behind the door, Fiona was to fake some kind of emergency at the inn. He would follow the aunts there, and they would stall him in their own way for at least an hour (which I was sure to hear about later). That way, I could still leave, and he wouldn't know where I was headed.

With everyone manning her station, I straightened my hair, tugged my top down, threw on a smile, and twisted the handle.

Chance and Leo both stood on my front porch.

Unfortunately, I didn't see this one coming, and I had no Plan C.

I slammed the door shut and turned to my family.

"Okay, new plan," I said.

"Uh, I can hear you," Leo said.

"Me too," said Chance.

What the hell good is magic if it can't foresee these kinds of scenarios? And what the hell is a family full of witches for if they can't predict disaster?

I swung the door back open and beamed. I heard movement behind me, probably all three of them planning an escape.

"Sorry. Wind gust. Must have yanked the door from my hand. So what are you doing here?" I asked.

Chance and Leo spoke at the same time.

"Cinnamon called me," Chance said.

"Fiona called me," Leo said.

"Oh." I smiled stupidly, blocking the entryway.

"Stacy?" Leo said.

"Yes?"

"Are you going to let us in?"

I laughed. "Of course, I'm so sorry." I stood back and watched my ex-boyfriend and my new boyfriend walk into my house.

Fiona went to work, gushing forth with hugs and welcomes.

Get the book, I managed to mouth to Cinnamon.

She shook her head.

I gave her a livid look. *Get the book!*

Again, she declined.

"How about some tea, boys?" Fiona said.

I didn't know what Cin's problem was, but the Blessed Book was still in my bedroom, so I went in and scooped it up so that I could put it in Cin's car before we left. I figured at this point I could use all the help I could get. Funny, it seemed even heavier.

"Dear, come out here and have some tea," Fiona called.

"I'm just going to put this in Cin's car. Be right back," I said. Chance leaped up to open the door, and Leo rushed to unburden my arms. Cinnamon dropped her head in her hands.

"I'll get that for you," Leo said and reached for the book.

"It's okay," I said and pulled back.

"Stacy, that looks heavy. I'll take it," Leo said. I knew this little performance was for Chance's benefit, so I retreated as Leo pulled forward. We both lost our grip.

The realization hit me before the binding hit the floor.

The rock slipped out between the pages. It was a large rock, but rather flat, so for some stupid reason, either my cousin or an aunt had decided to tuck it between the pages of the giant book.

Cinnamon's face told me she was the genius behind the ruse.

"You couldn't have tossed it in a drawer?"

She shrugged. "A drawer they might check." She eyed the book. "I knew they wouldn't look in there."

The teakettle whistled, and Fiona announced, "Soup's on."

Chance and Leo stared at me, then at each other.

Leo picked up the rock, and Chance leaned in to read the note that Cin must have taped back onto it.

"What the hell is going on?" Leo asked.

Chance's face hardened. "I'd like to know that myself."

"Oh, boys? Won't you sit in the living room and have some tea, and we can all discuss this?"

"Fiona, please, not now," Leo said.

Chance looked at him like they were two men standing in front of a grizzly, and he could run faster. He had been around the Geraghty Girls long enough to know that you do as they requested, or you might wind up with a frog infestation in your shower.

Leo felt the heat of Fiona's stare and met her eyes.

"I said, sit." It was not a suggestion.

See, when Birdie isn't around, Fiona is first in command.

Leo and Chance shared my sofa while Fiona poured the tea. She handed each of them a dainty floral cup and saucer, complete with ladyfingers. I would have burst out laughing if I didn't think one of them would have strangled me.

There was no avoiding the subject, so I launched into an explanation. Leo looked at the rock, then at me. Chance shook his head.

Leo sipped his tea under Fiona's watchful stare, choosing his words carefully before he spoke. "This is serious. You could have been hurt."

"I agree with Dirty Harry over here," Chance said. "Whoever did this means business, so whatever you're involved in, stop it."

"Bob the Builder is right." Leo glared at Chance. "We need to file a report."

"A report?" Chance said. "What good is that? You need to find this asshole, Joe Friday."

Leo gulped his tea and said, "Listen, Tim the Tool Man—"

"Enough!" I shouted. Geesh, where were we, in high school? "Neither of you gets to tell me what to do. I make my own decisions. That's the beauty of being an adult."

Leo was about to say something else, but stopped. I thought he was stopping because he knew he crossed a line, but when he set the tea down, his head swayed a bit; then his dark eyes drooped and his body slumped. He crashed into Chance's lap.

Chance looked up.

"Oh my God," I said, rushing over to Leo. "Is he okay?"

Chance put his finger to Leo's neck. "He's fine, but my nuts took a hit."

I spun around. "Fiona, what was in that tea?"

The cup was still in Chance's hand, and I heard a clink as he carefully set it back on the coffee table.

Fiona shrugged. "Chamomile, valerian, a touch of this, a pinch of that. He's sleeping, dear, that's all." She looked at Chance. "Yours was licorice root, dear."

Chance whistled his relief.

I looked at Leo, also relieved. Now that I knew he was just sleeping, I figured we might as well get on with the task.

"How long will he be out?" I asked.

Chance helped me arrange Leo on the couch as I explained what I was hoping he could do at the Opal. I removed Leo's shoes, tucked a pillow under his head, and covered him with a blanket. Then Cin, Chance, and I all piled into his truck.

"I still don't like this," Chance grumbled as he backed out of the driveway.

Fiona and Lolly waved.

"Well, I don't, either, but we don't have a lot of choices. Whatever is behind that wall might have something to do with the fire. If I told Leo about it, we would need permits, approvals, and inspectors just to get the ball rolling. Then it might take weeks before they would even get in there to take a look. Besides, what would I tell them? My grandma says I have special powers and I should follow every hunch?"

Chance smiled and shot me a sideways glance. "Well, what are you going to tell Captain America when he wakes up?"

"Okay, that isn't even a cop reference. That's just a cheap shot, and I've had enough study hall antics for one night," I said.

"If you two are done bickering, can we get on with it, please?" Cin said.

We had just pulled up to Angelica's bakery, where Chance would park the truck. We'd walk from there.

He grabbed his toolbox and we hoofed it the block to the Black Opal in silence.

Chance let out a low whistle when we got to the basement. It still reeked of stale booze and charred wood. "Wow, Cin. Tough break." He squeezed her shoulder, and she sighed.

"Okay, which wall is it?" Chance said.

"Over here, behind the stairwell." It wasn't until I got down there that I recalled the necklace. I made a mental note to show it to Cinnamon later. I pointed to where Derek shot the photos of the wall with the three bricks missing.

Only, now, there were no bricks missing.

I thought I was losing my mind before Cinnamon said, "What the hell?"

"Cin, you saw that photo, right? There were three bricks missing from that wall," I said.

Cinnamon nodded.

Chance turned from us and examined the wall. He brushed his hand lightly over the soot until he found a spot where the black ash flicked away with ease. "It's been patched. This one is newer," Chance said, tapping the brick.

Patched? Who would do that? And more importantly, why? I had to find out what was behind that brick.

"Well, can you still try to chisel away at the wall?" I had hoped we could wedge a crowbar between the empty spaces, pop out a few more bricks, to see inside.

Chance ran a hand through his hair and flicked on a flashlight. "It could take a while. I might have to drill."

I checked the time on my phone. It was nearly ten p.m. on Friday. The town was busy already, but it was sure to get louder, with the sounds of packed clubs and restaurants and music spilling out onto the streets.

I ducked down to show Chance where I thought I had seen something sparkle in the photograph and ran my hands along the wall. As I did so, I felt heat, and a wrenching cough choked me.

The flashlight shone on my face, and Cinnamon said in a hushed tone, "Oh, Stacy, that bruise is getting worse."

Chance took a step forward. "Jesus, Stace, maybe we should get you looked at."

I had to admit I was feeling pretty funky. As if a nerve in my throat was pinched. I stood up—about to agree that maybe this wasn't the greatest idea—when, next to me, a nail flew from the mortar, taking a crumbling chunk of the wall with it.

We all stared at the mound of rubble.

"No. We need to do this," I said.

An hour later, Chance had punched a twelve-inch hole in the wall. Cinnamon stepped forward and flashed the light into the black space. We all inched forward. As I looked in, I saw the face of the girl in the mirror, just for an instant.

Cinnamon and Chance saw something completely different.

Leo was still groggy and none too happy about taking a catnap. In fact, he woke up with my cat draped across his head, completely disoriented. I couldn't offer much in the way of an explanation, so I avoided the subject entirely by telling him what we had found. That made him lose all interest in the possibility that someone slipped him a mickey.

Now the four of us were standing in front of the wall, staring at the face of a girl. She couldn't have been more than eighteen years old.

Leo's hand slowly washed over his own face. "You were never here," he said to me.

"Actually, I was," I said.

He looked to Cinnamon for support.

"Yep, I can vouch for her."

Leo turned to Chance. He was getting desperate. "You helped them. What the hell were you thinking?"

"Hey, man, if I didn't, they would have tried it themselves, and who knows what sort of a mess they would have made. They could have gotten hurt."

Leo knew Chance made sense, but I was offended by the sexist comment. Even if it was on the near side of the truth.

"I cannot let this go, Leo. I have to report on it. Besides, we all know this is the reason the Opal was set on fire."

"Stacy, that hasn't been confirmed yet. Let Tommy do his job first, and then we'll know for sure," Leo said.

"What about the person who filled in the missing bricks?"

"You can't be sure that there really were bricks missing."

"I know what I saw. I have—" I stopped short before I said proof. He would kill me if he had known I withheld that information.

"Stacy, it was dark down here. You can't be certain." Leo grabbed my hands and searched my eyes for a hint of reason. "All I am asking is that you hold off until we get the body out. I'll call the coroner tonight, get a crew out here, and when that's taken care of, I will tell the mayor. Then it can be made public. I just don't want it known that you were here when the body was discovered. Agreed?"

"Agreed," I said.

I looked toward the hole, aching for the poor girl who was entombed there. It had to have been at least half a dozen years, maybe more. Cin had had no brickwork done since she owned the bar.

"She must have been so scared," I whispered, rubbing my neck.

I felt eyes burning the back of my head. I turned to find three puzzled faces.

"She?" Cin asked.

"Yes, she." I shifted back toward the corner. That's when I realized the face behind the wall was like black leather. Mummified. I shivered.

"How do you know it's a woman?" Chance asked.

"Because. I saw her face. Once in the mirror…and… and then here." I waited for one of them to tell me my gears were slipping.

Leo and Chance exchanged glances. For some reason, Cin smiled.

"So you can identify her?" Leo asked. I nodded, and he gave me a weary look. "Don't repeat that to anyone, kitten," he said and pulled me close.

I heard Chance whisper to Cinnamon. "Kitten?"

Cin chuckled. "You gotta admit, the girl has nine lives."

Chapter 11

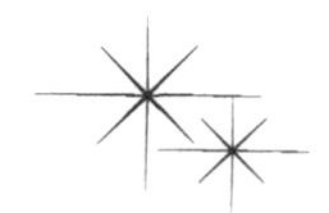

The agate crystal was tucked inside my pillow all night, but it didn't do any good. Lolly had promised it would help me understand my dreams, but all it did was disrupt my sleep. I tossed and turned all night, images of Leo, Cin, and Chance drifting through my mind. The last thing I saw before I woke up was the high school kid, Chip, walking through fire.

I rolled out of bed and glanced at the clock. It was after nine on Saturday, and I wasn't expected at work. Instead, the plan was to get to the coroner's office to find out who the girl in the wall was and how she had died.

First, a bathroom break. When I finished, a shriek escaped my throat as I stepped into the living room to find a man sitting on my couch, reading a magazine.

"Chance! You scared the crap out of me. What are you doing here?"

Chance smiled. "Hey, angel. Just keeping you company."

"How did you get in?"

He stood up, pulled a key from his jeans pocket, and dangled it. "Fiona told me to keep the key she gave me after

I put the new roof on." He walked over to me. "I didn't mean to scare you," he said and cupped my shoulder.

"Leo won't like this," I said.

"Who do you think asked me to come here?"

Great. Now I had a babysitter. That left me speechless. Then he tilted in and swept his lips across mine, his hand still guarding my arm.

"Now, *that* he wouldn't like," he said and pulled away.

It was a soft, friendly kiss, but there was meaning behind it. I knew Chance was toying with me, tempting me. I wasn't sure I was strong enough to resist.

A phone rang, rattling the room. Chance lifted his cell from the coffee table and answered it.

"Yep, she's up…Will do, Chief," he said and hung up. He looked at me. "Why don't you get dressed? I'll buy you a cup of coffee."

I washed up, slipped into cargo pants and a wool sweater, and reached for my amethyst necklace, wondering why the only man in my life who didn't irritate me was my dog, when I remembered the onyx cross necklace from the dirt in the basement of the Opal.

The jeans from the night of the fire were still crammed in the corner of my closet. I rifled through the pockets and pulled out the chain. I stuffed it and the bar tool in my pants pocket, grabbed the book and my bag, and told Chance I was ready. He had fed Moonlight and Thor as I changed.

A dull gray settled over the county, but the air had warmed a bit. Muddy Waters Coffee Shop was bustling with people when we arrived. The scents of hazelnut and roasted coffee beans teased me as I walked in. We scooted to the counter, and Iris called to me. She waved us over to the side bar.

"What's up, Iris? Got some dirt for the column?"

"Please. As long as Monique is running a brothel disguised as a bar, I got lots of material."

Chance raised his eyebrows.

"Free Viagra for the elderly every Thursday," I told him.

Chance nodded. Monique is well known around town for being perpetually in heat. At least now she's spreading the wealth.

"My poor Henry couldn't put his jack in the box for seven hours. The husbands love it. Wives, not so much."

I thanked Iris for planting that image in my head and asked what she called me over for.

"Remember that man that was askin' all the questions? He left you a note." She plucked a white envelope with my name printed on it from her canvas apron. Then she turned to pour us two cups of house blend as I stuffed the envelope into my pocket.

"What is she talking about?" Chance asked.

I told him about the skinny guy with the mustache and sunglasses. As soon as the words left my mouth, I regretted them.

"Did you tell Leo?"

"No. I forgot all about it until now."

"You forgot?"

Iris rang in the order, not bothering to hide the fact that she was cataloging every word. I arced around to the side bar for cream and sugar. "It's nothing. I've had a lot more things to worry about lately." Fires, dead bodies, rocks through my window.

"Stace, he could be the guy who lobbed the rock through the window."

Never thought of that.

"Who?" Leo said behind me.

Holy crap, now I had two watchdogs.

"No, he isn't," I said to Chance. "I didn't get that kind of feeling from him. He's harmless." But familiar, which I did not say.

"Who?" Leo asked.

"How do you know? And since when did you start trusting your instincts?" Chance asked, eyes blazing.

"Who the hell are we talking about?" Leo demanded.

"Tell him," Chance said. They both crossed their arms and stared at me.

I wasn't enjoying this one bit. I felt like a Ping-Pong ball caught between two players who enjoyed the game as long as the little ball didn't bounce off the table.

"All right, what is this? You two are buddies now? And you"—I pointed to Leo—"what are you doing here?"

"I came to pick you up. The coroner said he has time to talk to you."

I took a huge sip of my coffee, ignored the fact that I just burned my tongue, and said, "Listen to me very carefully. I do not appreciate being passed around like last month's *Playboy*. I don't need either one of you to babysit me, and the only man I need in my life right now is the one with balls big enough to handle who I am."

I left them there trying to figure out which one of them was equipped for the job, when behind me I heard Iris say, "I think she means Thor."

I couldn't tell if they were fighting over me or ganging up on me. At times like this, I ache for my parents. My father was tender with my mother. I loved to watch them sharing a moment when they thought I wasn't near. A touch. A look. A smile. Meaning behind all of it. Sure, there were disagreements, but always there was a mutual respect. I couldn't imagine my father bossing my mother around, treating her like a wounded bird. But if he had, I bet she wouldn't have trouble defusing the situation.

I was not gifted with that talent.

For a second, I envisioned my mother walking in stride with me. *How do you command respect from a man?* I would ask. *How do you know someone is* the one*? What is love, really?*

Then I would ask why she had left after Dad died, never to be heard from again.

I crossed Main Street and headed up the hill to White Hope Road, dodging piles of gray slush and salt. The note in my pocket piqued my curiosity, but that would have to wait until I got some information under my belt. I stopped off at the corner store to arm myself with the usual bribe. Even though the coroner and I go way back, it never hurts to present an offering to gain entrance into his kingdom. Mr. Sagnoski was smoking a Pall Mall outside the back of the building when I got there.

"Hi there, Stacy." His teeth were chattering because he wasn't wearing a coat. His fingers are gnarled from years of cutting open the flesh of friends and neighbors. He is a foot shorter than me and wears the same Coke-bottle glasses he wore back when he was my eighth-grade biology teacher, although the lenses had thickened some.

"Mr. Sagnoski, it's freezing out here. Where's your coat?"

"What are you, my mother?" He laughed as if that were the funniest thing in the world and then coughed up some phlegm.

Guess when you spend most of your time with the dead, you have to find ways to amuse yourself.

He flicked the cigarette butt into the street and said, "The usual arrangement?"

I pulled out a giant box of Skittles and a lottery ticket from my coat.

"You don't tell Helen, and I won't tell the chief," he said and held the door open for me.

"I still don't understand why she lets you smoke, but you can't gamble or eat sweets," I said.

He shrugged. "She believes a man is entitled to one vice."

The toxic scent of embalming fluid wrestled with the stiff aroma of Pine-Sol for the honor to empty my stomach.

I swayed a bit, and Mr. Sagnoski steadied me with one arm.

"Whoa, kid. You sure you're up for this? You couldn't even dissect a frog in my class. And this ain't no frog." He laughed again, followed by a gurgling sound.

She was everywhere. All around me, the presence of the girl in the mirror. The dead girl we rescued from the wall.

What was she trying to tell me?

"I'm fine. Let's see what you've got." I smiled weakly at my old teacher and followed him through a narrow corridor and down a few steps into a stale room.

The body was covered with a powder-blue sheet on a stainless-steel table. There was a humming, possibly from the furnace, as Mr. Sagnoski walked up to the table and hopped on a stool, lifting the sheet. He flipped on a light that dangled over the table, painting every corner of the cold room with odd shadows. Various clothing remnants sat on a counter, waiting to be inventoried and bagged. I paused to examine the garments.

"So, at first, I thought maybe it was a head injury that caused the death," Mr. Sagnoski was saying.

Among the clothing remains were a poodle skirt, faded and torn; a cashmere cardigan, which could have once been pink; a scarf; and tired, worn saddle shoes. Had she been there since the fifties? Funny, the hairstyle from the image in the mirror didn't fit that era.

"But now, that didn't jive, so then I thought maybe she was buried alive, okay?" The horror of that theory made me want to run from the room. Then I saw a pin. *Is that a* K? *Yes, K.*

"But if you look real close, here, you can barely see"—A sharp scream echoed in my head. I looked at Mr. Sagnoski. He hadn't heard it. Did I imagine it? I palmed my temples—"there are some imprints where pressure was applied."

Then I too felt pressure around my throat.

"So my report will indicate the victim was —"

I couldn't breathe all of a sudden. It was as if I were being…"Strangled," I said, my hand around my neck.

Mr. Sagnoski chuckled. "That's right. Guess you were paying attention, Stacy."

"Guess I was." I met his stare. The pressure around my neck faded. I nodded toward the clothes. "Are those hers?"

"Yep." Mr. Sagnoski stepped off his stool and waddled over to me. "In a manner of speaking."

"What do you mean?"

"Look at the label there."

I squinted at the label he pointed to on the poodle skirt: CLEVER COSTUMES.

I looked down at the coroner. "It's a Halloween costume?"

Mr. Sagnoski shrugged. "Could be."

"I've never heard of Clever Costumes. Is it around here?"

He peeled off latex gloves and tossed them in a metal container as he spoke. "They were located in Culver City. Only costume place in the county. Closed in 'eighty-nine."

'Eighty-nine. I glanced at the body, picturing the blackened, thin form as the girl she once was. Young, fun-loving, full of hope. She could have been anyone. She could have been me. "Don't suppose she had ID?" I asked.

"Course not, what fun would that be?" He winked.

"Age?"

"Hard to tell."

I sighed.

"You can get a copy of the report when I'm through, Stacy," Mr. Sagnoski said, dismissing me.

I was about to shake his hand and thought better of it. I thanked him and told him I would be in touch.

As I stepped off the curb, heading to the newspaper office, my cell chimed in a text message. I glanced at the phone and got the distinct sensation of déjà vu:

FROM: Birdie 10:02 a.m. Gramps again. What a hoot. Hike after brkfst, in tune with nature. Kissed Birdie in the woods. C u soon.

FROM: Birdie 10:04 a.m. They asked me what I wanted to get out of this experience and I said me.

I clicked the phone shut, knowing in my heart this would not end well, but it wasn't up to me to keep my grandparents' love lives in order. I couldn't even keep tabs on my own.

As if on cue, Leo pulled up to the curb just as I crossed Main Street, and I stuffed my phone into my pocket.

"Need a ride?" His warm breath cut the air in a whirl of smoke.

"I'm good." I kept walking.

He cruised next to me anyway, and my pace quickened.

"Who was the note from?"

"I don't now. A source, probably," I told him, still looking ahead.

"Is it chilly out here, or is it just you?"

The ground was covered with prime packing snow, which I liberated and lobbed at Leo's face. He ducked, and the snowball splattered across the inside of the passenger window of his cruiser.

"What the hell is wrong with you?" he asked.

"I could give you a list, but it would take too long." I dusted my gloves off.

The newspaper office was a few blocks away, but if I cut to the stairs, I could shake him.

"I could have you arrested for that." He wiped his window.

It was still early, so there weren't a lot of cars on Main Street. This allowed for a clean exit and a straight shot up the stairs toward the newspaper office. The city workers kept the streets and walkways well salted and my boots had good traction, so I wasn't too worried about slipping as I ran up the stairs. I should, however, had lifted my head, or at least slowed down, as I rounded the corner after the last step.

"Jeez, girl! Why you always runnin'?"

That voice was beginning to imbed itself into my brain, so I knew it was Derek I had slammed into, even if I couldn't see him.

"Agghhhh!" I yelled from the hot sting of some gooey substance blanketing my eyes. I put my hands in front of my face and felt for a snowdrift. "Help! It's burning."

"Well, of course it burns. You just ran into a chili dog."

Feeling my way toward the embankment, wet, cold relief was inches away, and I washed myself off as best I could.

"Who the hell eats chili dogs for breakfast?" The snow lifted the heat from my face. I felt a little better. I just hoped there were no burns. God, this guy was a nightmare. I looked at him, and he shrugged.

"I like chili dogs."

"Is it all off?" I asked.

Then he smiled.

"What, you think maiming a person is funny?" I shouted.

"No." His eyes cut to the snow bank behind me. "But I do think that's funny."

My gaze traced his view, and I gasped, not finding it one damn bit funny. Yellow snow. I hinged forward and spat saliva from my mouth, brushing my tongue with my scarf.

"That's it. You're coming with me," I said.

"But I'm still hungry," he whined as I dragged him up the street toward the office.

Derek stood outside in the cold, on the lookout for Leo, as I sneaked through the back basement of the building. I figured I could cash in on about ten minutes of guilt before he gave up and left, so I gingerly approached my office in the dark. When I reached the oak door, I was surprised to see the lights on inside. I shoved the key in the lock, but it was already unlocked.

The distinct odor of Aqua Velva charged at me and I gagged.

"Hello?" I said to the person turned around in my comfy high-back leather chair. The chair pirouetted, and I was face-to-face with the mayor, a situation I have earnestly tried to avoid the few months I'd been back in town. My heart skipped, anticipating an awkward conversation.

He didn't speak at first, just flashed a brilliant smile, which made me shift uncomfortably. The mayor was a generation older than Leo, but he still resembled him quite a bit. He wasn't as tall, maybe a bit heavier, but he had the same smoldering eyes, same olive skin, and enough silver around the temples to make him look authoritative.

"Hello, Miss Justice." He sounded like the guy who narrates movie trailers.

"Mr. Mayor," I said, "how nice to see you." I removed my gloves and approached him, hand extended.

The mayor stood and circled to the front of the desk. He clasped my hand and then paused, squinting at me.

"Is that chili in your hair?"

"Old family recipe. Brings out the shine."

His brow bent for a second. Then he said, "I suppose you're wondering why I'm here."

"Okay."

"I need a little favor."

The room was suddenly very warm, so I took off my coat and draped it over the filing cabinet.

"Shoot."

"I understand that it is your job to report the news in this town," he said, "and as a journalist, I have great respect for you."

As a witch's granddaughter, I was guessing, not so much.

I leaned against the windowsill, wondering where he was headed with this.

He strolled around the office, eyeing the awards, stories, and photos that lined the walls.

His back was to me when he spoke again. "But this is a tourist town, and frankly, occupancy rates have been down, which means less revenue. Less revenue means cutting spending, maybe even jobs." He stopped and looked at me. "I don't want to see that happen to my town. Our location is central to the Midwest. Visitors can bypass us and head to Milwaukee, St. Louis, Chicago, but they don't. They come here. And do you know why?" He turned to face me.

"Chili dogs?"

He shook his head, as if that were a serious guess. "They come here because they feel safe in our friendly little community."

I thought about Cinnamon threatening her customers with bodily harm, Monique handing out free Viagra with a whip strapped to her thigh, and Lolly operating at half-mast most of the time.

I didn't even feel safe in this town.

Nevertheless, I nodded in agreement.

"So, I'm not so sure that a story about a body discovered inside the wall of one of our quaint establishments would be good for business. Do you follow me?"

"I know you're not asking me to compromise my ethics, Mr. Mayor."

He laughed. "Nothing like that. But if you could wait until the weekday edition, I'd sure appreciate it."

I hesitated, then said, "I guess I can do that."

The mayor nodded and grabbed his coat, crossing to the door. When he reached the handle, he looked back. "Might be a good idea to leave out some of the specifics. If the killer is still in the area, we would want some leverage."

"I'll talk to Leo about what he thinks is important in that regard."

"You do that." He nodded and smiled before he left.

Derek walked in a few minutes later. "No sign of the chief. I'm headed out."

I asked him to snap some photos for the copy before he went in search of a fresh pork product.

It took half an hour to pump out a rough draft on the murdered girl. I omitted the details of the case—the costume, the suspected strangulation. I saved the file to a flash drive, e-mailed a copy to Derek so he could match a photo to it, and tucked the drive into my bag. Then I left a message for Gladys to search the archives for any missing girls from the mid-1980s to 1990. Something about the hair in my vision told me that girl was an old-school Bon Jovi fan.

The soap in the bathroom was like waxed paper, but I used it to wash up anyway. I parted the blinds near the front door of the office and spotted a police cruiser at the curb, so I waited, then sneaked out the back door ten minutes later.

"Stacy Justice, you're under arrest" were the words that greeted me.

Chapter 12

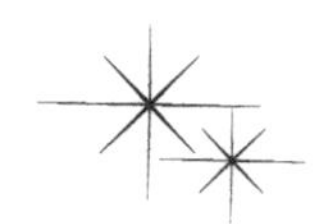

"I am not amused!" I yelled through the bars at Leo.

"You assaulted a police officer. That's a felony," he said and locked the cage. Then he was gone.

I sighed and sat heavily on the bench, pouting and cursing Leo under my breath. He confiscated my bag, so I couldn't even get any work done or read the Blessed Book. Who was going to bail me out if he didn't drop this? Birdie wasn't around. I didn't know what Cin was up to, but I was sure she had her hands full. Chance? Yeah right, then I'd have two jailors to contend with. That's when I remembered the note that was shoved in my pocket.

I took it out and unfolded it.

The text was printed in all caps.

DOWN AND DIRTY, 1 P.M. COME ALONE.
I HAVE INFORMATION FOR YOU.

There was a clock across the hall and it read 12:53. *Crap.*

I read the note again, running my hands over the penciled letters, willing a vision to come to me, anything that would indicate who it was from. I closed my eyes. Nothing. So much for these "gifts" Birdie is always ranting about.

"Leo, you have to let me out!" I screamed.

"Is that it?"

I popped my eyes open and crumpled the note. "What?"

"Is that the message Chance was talking about?"

"I don't know what you mean." I crossed my legs and tried to look demure.

Leo held up my black leather satchel. "It's not in here, so my guess is that's the big secret you're holding."

"The big secret is you're an ass." I made my way to the bars. "Let. Me. Out."

"Not until you tell me what that note business was all about."

"You're abusing your powers, Chief," I said through gritted teeth.

"I can wait all day."

"Well, you just might have to," I said and stuffed the paper in my mouth, chewed, and swallowed.

A vein throbbed in Leo's forehead, and he said, "You are just as stubborn as your grandmother."

I narrowed my eyes and said, "And just as powerful."

Not even close, but I was betting he wouldn't call my bluff.

For a split second, his eyes flashed uncertainty. Then his lips molded into a grin, and he said, "You could have just flushed it, you know."

Before I had time to process that, yes, there was a commode behind me, his radio beeped. "Hey, Chief. We have a situation here."

Leo put the radio to his mouth, his eyes still on me. "What is it, Gus?"

"Yeah, um, you need to get to the firehouse."

"Why?"

"Well, you remember Mr. Peterson was building a plane in his backyard? Yeah, well, he thought he'd test out the engine, so he drove it down here, and now he can't get it back up the hill."

Leo paused and blew out some air. "Why didn't he just fly it?"

"No wings."

Leo tapped the bars. "So call some of the CoPs and push it back up the hill."

"Already did, but Jed and Jeb knocked back a few and they're arguing about which one gets to steer." Gus paused. There was shouting in the background. "Hey, break it up!"

Rustling came through the radio, followed by more yelling and then a buzzing sound.

"Gus! Gus!" Leo demanded.

There was another pause.

"Hey, Leo," said Tommy Delaney after several seconds.

"What the hell is happening, Tommy?" Leo asked.

"You better get down here. Deputy Dog just Tasered himself."

"Christ. I'll be right there."

Leo was contemplating if the streets would be safer with me locked up, and I shot him the deadliest look I could muster.

"No," was all I said.

The door was heavy, but he slid it open with ease and pulled me to him for a lingering kiss, which my mind objected to but my body didn't.

When we parted, I searched his eyes for an emotion.

"Do I smell chili?" he asked.

By the time Cin picked me up it was close to two p.m.

"Drop me off at the corner, wait a few, then come inside," I told her.

Cin shot me a gaze over her sunglasses. "Who do you think you are, Nancy Drew?"

"I just want to get to the bottom of this creepy little guy slinking around town."

"What's with all the cloak-and-dagger stuff? And who meets at a bar at one in the afternoon?"

"I know. Weird, right?"

I hopped out and sprinted up the block, then pushed through the double doors of Down and Dirty, hoping my liaison was still inside.

Monique had done a little decorating since the other night. Velvet heart pillows were tossed in booths, plastic ruby lips hung from the ceiling, and every table had those tacky valentine candies in crystal bowls.

I scanned the bar. It was dark and glittery, with no sign of the mustached man. I walked through and checked the bathrooms just to be sure, then hopped on a stool next to Scully.

Monique wove her way through a beaded curtain and sashayed up to the bar, wearing a red-and-white satin cupid costume with huge heart-shaped, feathered wings floating behind her.

She aimed her bow and arrow at me and said, "You better be here to drink, because I'm not in the mood for any bullshit."

"Hello to you too, Monique. Still spreading the love, I see."

She blinked purple false lashes at me.

Scully tried to order a beer, and Monique interrupted him, "Don't you have a home?" Then, to me, she said, "Can't your cousin set up a beer tent or something on the sidewalk? This guy's a pain in the ass."

Cinnamon walked in then and said, "Not as easy as it looks, is it?"

"Oh, for fuck's sake. What do you want?" Monique barked.

A bemused smile spread across my cousin's face as she sized up Monique's attire. "Aren't you supposed to return the costume when you graduate from clown college?" Cinnamon asked.

"You see, this is why I want to douse you with gasoline every time I see you," Monique fired back.

Really poor choice of words. Before Cinnamon tried to implant a bar stool in her head, I said to Monique, "Monique, has anyone been in here asking about me?"

Monique opened the cooler and pulled out a Pabst Blue Ribbon, clipped the top open with her crimson talon, and slid the beer to Scully. Then she turned to me and said, "Actually, yeah. Short guy, mustache, talks funny."

That was him.

"What did he say?" I asked.

Monique shrugged. "Just wanted to know if you'd been in here. He waited about a half hour, then took off."

"Damn," I said.

"What, are you into trolls now, Stacy? Because I could take Leo off your hands."

I just bet she would. Monique would take the entire defensive line of the Chicago Bears if she could. Including the Gatorade boy.

I felt Cin stand on point next to me and I grazed her hand, signaling that I didn't need assistance.

"Monique, I realize that it's a short list of men in this town you haven't tied up, held down, or sent to the free clinic, but why don't you just leave Leo alone. At least until he can update his vaccinations."

Monique smoothed out her feathers and said, "Very cute. So, you drinking or what?"

Cin ordered us a round, and Monique dug in the cooler for more beer.

Before I had a sip, my cell phone rang.

"What's up, Gladys?" I answered.

"Hello, Stacy. How are you?" Work or no work, Gladys thought it was rude to just get to the point.

"Good, thanks. You?"

"I'm fine. Picked up a nice chicken for dinner."

"Did you get my message?"

"Maybe you come by for dinner, eh?"

"Maybe. Gladys, did you find anything out?"

"Sorry, Stacy. Nothing on the computer files about a missing girl."

"Nothing?"

"Ya."

I ran my hands through my hair as I thought about that and a red bean fell out. "What about the hard copies? There have to be hard copies archived in the library, at least."

"No. Gone."

"What do you mean, gone?" Why was I repeating myself?

"Ya. Gone. No hard copies."

"You're kidding."

Gladys didn't know how to respond to that, so she didn't. Instead, she said, "So, you come for chicken?"

"I'm not sure, Gladys. I'll let you know, okay?"

"Sure, sure," she said.

I thanked her and we disconnected.

Cin was sipping her beer, staring at me. I grabbed her arm and dragged her into one of the private booths and drew the curtain.

"Why does a historic town not have any newspaper records?"

My cousin shrugged. "They were in the library for years, but the last fire chief thought they could be a hazard."

"Why?"

"Because space is limited, so the librarians started stacking papers up the chimney. Then they forgot all about them until the high school put on *A Christmas Carol* and—"

I held up my hand to cut Cin off. "Got it."

"What's this about?"

The story poured from me quickly. The girl's clothes, the K pin, the fact that someone must have reported her missing. I was sure there might have been an investigation, and the paper would have covered it. The problem was I didn't know if this girl was from Amethyst. If she was from another town, I wasn't sure I'd find anything in the local paper.

But I had to start somewhere.

"Are you sure about the time frame?" Cin asked.

I squeezed my eyes shut, conjuring up the image of the dead girl I saw in the mirror. It was still vivid, the hairstyle, the makeup.

"Pretty sure."

"I think I can help," Cin said, smiling wickedly.

Scully was still perched on his bar stool when we returned, and there was a young couple in the corner. The woman didn't look too pleased as feathers smacked her in the face while Monique's boobs entertained her date.

"Scully," Cin said, squeezing next to her ex–best customer, "I need a favor."

"So!" Scully said, still drinking his beer and not looking at her.

"Dammit, Scully, you are dangerously close to pissing me off. Do not forget I am the only bartender in town who will run you a tab."

Scully frowned, his face a tree trunk. "What do ya want?" he asked.

"I need you to let me and Stacy rummage through your newspaper collection."

Scully put his beer down. For the first time ever, I think. "No," he said slowly, his watery eyes gaining focus.

"Yes. It's really important, Scully," Cin urged.

"Why should I?" he asked, squaring off with her.

"Because I asked nicely, you toothless old crocodile!"

That wasn't the approach I would have taken, but my cousin had her methods.

"Bah!" Scully said and turned back to the ale.

Cin's fist flexed, and I was afraid she might coldcock him. Instead, she bit her lip, and I waited.

"Okay. How about this?" She hesitated and looked at me. "If you do"—she scratched her chin—"I will"—Cin glanced around, then bent toward Scully and whispered—"erase your tab."

And that was when I discovered Scully had legs.

When we got to Scully's apartment over the bookstore on Main Street, the bubble of hope I held burst.

The entire tiny apartment was floor-to-ceiling newspapers. No television, no kitchen table, no couch. Newspapers.

I raised one eyebrow at Cinnamon.

"It's a hobby," she said.

"It will take all of my childbearing years to go through these," I told her.

Cin shook her head, stepping over a short stack of newspapers with a coaster on top. "They're sectioned by decade."

I wrinkled my brow. "How many decades are we talking about?"

Cin called out to Scully, who had wandered into another room. Or maybe he was just lost in the maze, I couldn't be sure. "Scully, how long you been collecting?"

"Oh, 'bout sixty years, I guess," he called.

"Want to order a sandwich?" Cin asked me.

Two avocado turkey wraps and four hours later, we found it.

"There!" I said to Cinnamon. Scully had fallen asleep on a futon that passed for his bed and was snoring. He woke with a start when I yelled.

Cin had just pulled a stack of newspapers from a built-in bookshelf near the radiator, and on the top, in a black-and-white photo, was Kathy's face.

I stared at the picture, so enthralled with the beautiful, haunting eyes of this young wisp of a girl that I nearly forgot to read the caption.

She was wearing a taffeta dress and short black heels, a K pin over her heart. The same pin that now lay on the coroner's work space. Next to her, his arm casually draped over her bare shoulder, was a tall football player wearing a bejeweled crown.

The caption read, *In a 42–14 sweep, the Amethyst Eagles beat the Briertown Bucks. Shown here is Matthew Huckleberry, homecoming king, and his date, Kathy Sims, of Culver City.*

Culver City. Clever Costumes. Bingo.

Cin was reading over my shoulder, and I heard a small gasp leave her lips. My eyes were glued to the page, and I read the caption again.

"What are you thinking, Stacy?" she asked softly.

Matt Huckleberry was Huck's son from his second marriage. The paper indicated he was a senior in 1989, and although I didn't really know him, since he was much older than me, he was a celebrity of sorts, having carried the team to the state championship for four consecutive years.

I looked over my shoulder at Cinnamon. "We have a name."

Cin groaned. "Huckleberry."

I traced the photo with my fingers. "No, cuz, I mean Sims." I picked up the newspaper, studying the girl's face. "Kathy Sims."

Chapter 13

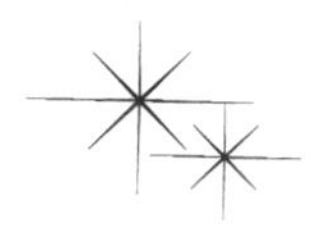

It was that time of year when the sky darkens so early you can't tell if it's dinnertime or bedtime, but I was sure it was getting late and Thor was probably turning blue. Cinnamon agreed to drive me home, but she had to pick up Mario first, at Angelica's request.

An only child myself, I suppose the bonds of sibling love are loosely tied.

Cin led the way up the steps, and I followed her. Aunt Angelica would never let me hear the end of it if I didn't at least pop in and say hello, so I did, against my better judgment.

She was tinkering in her workshop, a rich marinara piping out the essential oils of basil and parsley. Pavarotti floated from the CD player.

"Hi, Aunt Angelica," I said, leaning in to kiss her cheek. She hugged me with one arm, concentrating on the sauce.

"Stacy, my little cannoli, you stay for supper?"

"Sorry, just tagging along for a ride," I said.

"Well, I fix a plate for you to take." She reached for a ceramic bowl with pasta in it just as Mario walked into the kitchen.

"*Che curve*," he said. This was directed at me, although I had no idea what he'd said.

Angelica heard it too and smacked her brother upside the head with a wooden spoon, so I assumed it wasn't exactly an appropriate comment.

Cinnamon's annoyance quota for the day had been met, which she made clear by announcing, "Uncle Mario, we go—*now*."

"*Un momento*, Cinnamon," Mario said, winking. He bent over the kitchen table, which I noticed was swathed in a black velvet cloth, and began extracting gold watches from his pocket, lining them alongside one another on top of the cloth. Then he pulled out a few gold nugget rings and placed them next to the watches. He stopped and looked at me, holding out a pinky ring. "Stacy, for your boyfriend, hah?"

Although Leo could pass for a key member of the Greek Mafia, I wasn't about to encourage that look.

"No, thanks, Mario," I said.

"Eh, too bad," he told my cleavage.

A few minutes later, we pulled up to the inn, and I thanked Cin and sprinted around the side to the door of my cottage, hoping Thor hadn't destroyed the couch. The lock had hardly clicked over when the dog rushed out, claiming the nearest tree as his own.

Moonlight was sprawled across my desk. He stretched, yawned, and meowed at the same time, then hopped on my shoulder and rode me to the kitchen.

I was preparing dinner for the three of us, making a mental note to call Gladys and request a rain check, when the text alarm sounded on my phone. I put Moonlight's dish on the counter, opened the door to call Thor, and placed his food on the floor. The pasta circled in the microwave as I sat down with a glass of milk to read the message:

FROM: Birdie 7:12 p.m. Home tomorrow. Danger lurks. Feathers, a bow, a warning. Careful. Keep reading the book.

I thought about the rock crashing through my back-door window. Then I thought about Monique in her stupid cupid costume with the bow and arrow and heart-shaped feathers. Then I deleted the message. Next, I gave Gladys a ring and asked if we could have dinner another time.

The sauce was thick, rich with layers of garlic and oregano that danced perfectly together. I wondered what Kathy's last meal was. Her thoughts before she took her last breath. And what role, if any, Mr. Huckleberry had played in her life.

My stomach full of Angelica's food, I showered, slipped into flannel pj's, then spent about an hour surfing the Internet for Kathy Sims's parents' last-known address. It seemed they still lived in Culver City after all this time, if I had the right family. Hopefully they'd be up for company in the morning.

The information printed and my fur kids soundly sleeping, I settled on the couch and cracked open the elusive book of my family theology, apprehensive and eager at the same time to discover its secrets.

The pages were thick, the binding in surprisingly good shape. The first fifty or so were penned in a sharp, decisive script that I knew belonged to my great-grandmother Maegan Geraghty. There was a hand-sketched map of Ireland, labeled with landmarks, rivers, and cities. A tree outlined my familial ancestors, whose history reached back to the Druids. The Celtic tribe they founded settled near County Kildare, Ireland.

Maegan wove tales around wise women, like Birdie, who healed the sick through medicine grown and cultivated with their own hands. There were recipes for tonics, potions, and poultices, with specific details for applying each one.

She spoke of mediators, like Fiona, who calmed tempers and settled disputes. The triads were spelled out there too, Celtic laws of three regarding everything from land ownership to family quarrels. *Truth*, *honor*, *respect*, and *diplomacy* were the words that repeated over and over.

There were also stories about women of the hearth, like Lolly, who stoked the fires and cooked the meals. Enchantments were splashed across the margins of every page, from protecting the home to safe travel to mending a broken heart, showcased in step-by-step detail.

Maegan also wrote of high priestesses singing the dying to sleep, of elderly prophets and courageous warriors. There was an intricate drawing of the Wheel of the Year, explaining the eight Sabbats of the pagan religion, and discussions on the Roman invasion, the Burning Times, and the Salem witch trials.

I was mesmerized by the melody of her words, the rhythm of her ink strokes. Her stories entranced and inspired me, both in the language she used to relay them and the moral woven into each one. The tales filled me with an admiration for the men and women who have gone before me and a pride in the Geraghty name that I'd never quite felt before. Now, I felt a little ashamed of that.

Hours passed before I finally looked at the clock. When I couldn't keep my eyes open any longer, I closed the book, stretched, yawned, and shuffled to the bathroom. It was getting late, and tomorrow would be a long day. Birdie was coming home, which meant I might be obligated to console Gramps. I usually ate breakfast at the inn on Sundays, if I wasn't helping out, which meant I could run into Smalls. Plus, there was the visit to the Simses, a good thirty-minute drive with church traffic. I brushed my teeth, gulped some water, and flipped off the light.

When I returned to the living room, the book was upside down on the floor, open. I glanced at Thor, sprawled across the carpet, one brown eye following me.

"Were you on the couch?" I asked.

He sneezed in response.

I wagged a finger at him and knelt to pick up the book. My hands had just grazed the binding when something gripped my shoulder and I froze.

Nails, long ones, lightly fingering my sleep shirt.

Had I not just relieved myself, another shower would have been in order.

I glanced at Thor again. He was still watching me. Surely, if someone were touching me, he'd growl, bark, or attack, right?

Thor lifted his huge head, perked his ears, and cocked his snout, sniffing the air. He stared at something just over my head.

I still couldn't move.

And then warmth hugged me, like being wrapped in an afghan delivered straight from the dryer. I closed my eyes and swallowed hard.

Just your imagination, Stacy. Deep breaths, happy thoughts.

That's when the voice came, soft and fluid, like a birdsong.

As the surviving matriarch, it is my duty to pass knowledge to my children and to my children's children. Throughout the ages, our histories have been sung around bonfires, whispered near hollyhocks, gasped from deathbeds. But with a New World comes new traditions. And so my purpose for putting ink to paper is twofold. The first—to keep the spirit of our ancestors alive. The second—and most important—so the next seer in the Geraghty clan will know she will not walk the path alone. There are few of us. Your challenge is great, my child. Let your dreams guide you, your strength carry you, and the truth light the way.

I sat back on my heels after the voice faded, wondering if that was a hallucination or if Angelica had spiked the pasta sauce.

The book still within reach, I feathered the binding with my thumb, yearning to flip it over but afraid there'd be a message like, *Yes, Stacy, there is a seer.*

I turned it over anyway, and the text was there in black and white. Every word I just heard in my mind, there on the page. I didn't remember reading it, but I must have before I closed it.

That was the only reasonable explanation.

I ignored the part of me that knew very well there was no such thing as reasonable when it came to the Geraghty Girls. But more importantly, was Maegan referring to me? Did Birdie think I was a seer? Because if that was the case, then I sucked at it. Besides, she told me I was the Seeker of Justice. So how can one be both?

Unless...Was she referring to my mother? Was she the seer? Was it too much to bear?

Or was it someone else entirely?

A loud thump rattled my thoughts as Thor surfed the countertop. I yelled at him to get down and he did. Then he came over to me, sat, and pawed at the air, whining loudly.

"What?" I asked.

He rested on his haunches and I caught both paws in my arms for a second as he reared up. Then he jumped down, grunted, and trotted back to the counter, now pacing.

"What? There's no food on the counter," I told him.

He threw me a disgusted look, curled his teeth around something near the toaster, and tossed it at my feet.

I recognized the purple protection sachet that Fiona made for me and scratched Thor behind the ears. "Good boy!" I couldn't believe I'd forgotten to hang that thing after she scolded me once already.

I carried the book to my bedroom, flipping through pages of spells, ritual recipes, and crystal enchantments, marking the last page I read before setting it on the dresser, then went back and scooped up the herbal pouch, untying the ribbon as I approached the threshold. I hung it from the entryway light. That done, I hit the lights and crawled into bed.

He's here. I've been waiting so long for this. Tonight, I tell him. It's dark. Cold. He leans in and whispers, "Kathy," as my supple face shrinks into a leathery shell and life slips from my body.

I woke up gasping for air and accidentally launched Moonlight off the bed. Bright sunlight penetrated the shade, casting a colorful prism on the far wall of my room.

Just a dream. That's all. A vivid, disgusting dream.

I threw the covers off the bed and climbed into a robe and slippers. Eyes at half-mast, my first stop was the kitchen because that's where the coffee was. Thor darted for the front door, so after the pot was set to brew, I opened it for him. He galloped out but then forgot he had to pee as his nose coaxed him to my wicker rocker. There, a chicken sat with my name on it. Literally.

I shook my head. "Gladys."

The note was taped to a red cellophane bag tied with a bow. My hands trembled from the cold as I read it: *Made especially for you, Stacy.*

For some reason, Gladys thinks I can't cook. Maybe it's because Cinnamon can operate a drive-through window better than her own stove, and that reflects on me, but the truth is I love to cook and I am pretty good at it. It's just not that fun cooking for one, and I've eaten enough cold dinners waiting for Leo to finish working that it isn't worth the effort.

My stomach rumbled as I tucked the chicken into the fridge, searching for nourishment. I decided on a yogurt. *Mmm. Blueberry. My favorite.* I shut the refrigerator door, flipped the top off the yogurt, and was just about to dip in when I stopped.

Something about that chicken was odd—aside from the fact that it was left on my front porch, I mean.

I peeked in the fridge. Without my jolt of coffee, my mind was jogging to catch up with my eyes.

There was string tied around the legs of the bird. Sure, that was normal. People tie the legs together before they roast a chicken.

Wow, was I paranoid.

I shut the fridge and leaned against it.

A familiar feeling crept into my stomach, and this time, I recognized it.

Uh-oh. Harmful intent. My eyes jumped to attention.

Moonlight snaked through my legs as I opened the fridge for the third time.

String on the legs. Normal.

Wire sticking out of its ass? Not so much.

I slammed the fridge shut, grabbed my cat by the scruff, and dove out the front door just before the explosion.

Chapter 14

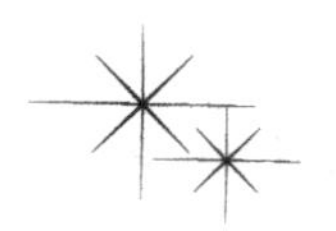

"Well, I never heard of such a thing," Fiona said as she poured me coffee. "Who leaves an exploding chicken on someone's front porch?"

"Who picks it up and brings it inside?" Leo said.

"Look, I told you, I was half-asleep. I thought it was from Gladys."

"Why would Gladys cook you a bird that blows up, dear?" Fiona asked.

"She didn't, Auntie. But last night I declined her dinner invitation, so I thought she made one anyway and brought it by this morning," I said and sipped the coffee.

Leo raised his eyebrows at me.

"Well, sure, *now* it sounds stupid," I said.

I was sitting in the dining room in the center of the Geraghty Girls' Guesthouse. The claw-foot table sat twelve and always wore antique Irish lace. The sideboard leaned against the far wall, its etched mirror illuminating a silver tea set.

The room was lovely, a stark contrast to my appearance this morning. My hair was in knots, my face was imprinted with bedsheet wrinkles, and my shoulders were bare because

Lolly had dressed me in a strapless lace cocktail dress, claiming that pj's were not proper breakfast attire.

Leo sat across from me, Lolly was in the kitchen, and Fiona was setting the table. No sign of Birdie yet, thank the goddess. I was not looking forward to explaining why my refrigerator—or rather, her refrigerator—was standing near the curb awaiting execution.

"I'm home."

Crap.

"We're in here, Birdie, in the dining room," Fiona sang.

"Well, I'm out of here." I stood as Lolly came into the room with biscuit dough.

"Breakfast is ready," she announced and dumped the glob onto the table. She then began sectioning it with her hands.

Leo made a face.

Fiona chuckled and guided Lolly, who was wearing a World War II Navy uniform, to a chair. I felt bad for a second, since I was sure it was the task of finding me something suitable to wear at this hour that crashed her database. But then I remembered my grandmother was present, and I figured it was every woman for herself. I sprinted to the kitchen and broke one of the four-inch heels in the process. I was almost at the back door when she called, "Anastasia!"

I considered hiding out in the fruit cellar.

"Come out here," she said. It wasn't a suggestion.

I sighed. What was the point in putting it off?

I limped back into the dining room.

It was difficult to interpret the look on Birdie's face. Not worried. Not angry. Not sad. More like *I cannot believe this girl shares my blood.*

She didn't speak, just looked at me like I had bird droppings on my head. Which I very well could have at that point.

Thor was under the table, and he belly-crawled closer to Leo. I took that as a bad sign.

"Hey, Birdie. How'd the marriage encounter go?" I asked, attempting a smile.

"Yes, dear. Where is Oscar?" Fiona asked. She stepped forward and took Birdie's bag.

Birdie was still looking at me when she said, "I dropped him at home, where he belongs."

Damn, she must know what happened. How could she, though? Okay, the marriage thing had to transfer some of the heat from me to Fiona. I could have told her that wasn't going to work.

Lolly started singing "Anchors Away" just as Mr. Smalls entered the dining room.

He removed his hat and asked Fiona, "Will there be breakfast this morning?"

"Of course, we have a seat all ready for you, Mr. Smalls." Fiona motioned to a high-back chair, and Smalls sat, still staring at my aunt. Under her spell, you might say.

"Thank you so much," he said as if he were a starving man and she'd given him her last cupcake.

"Knock, knock?" It was the trace European accent of Gladys.

Oh good, more witnesses.

"Hello, everyone," Gladys said.

Nods and salutations all around.

"Mr. Leo, you want to speak with me?" she asked.

"Please, sit down." Fiona escorted Gladys to a chair, and Gladys drank them all in, Lolly included, with the admiration of a celebrity stalker.

I was slowly tiptoeing toward the kitchen when I bumped into Tommy Delaney.

"Good morning, everyone. Leo, I think we're all done."

"What did you find out, Tommy?" Leo asked.

Fiona pulled up a chair for Tommy, who thanked her and sat down.

Tommy glanced around uneasily. "You sure you want to do this now?"

Leo nodded and sipped his coffee. He smiled at me, and I wagered another step back toward the kitchen. Might have gotten away too if Birdie hadn't clapped her hands and said, "Who's hungry?"

Seven hands shot in the air, including my own.

"Put your hand down, Anastasia," Birdie said and made her way to me. She gripped my shoulder, a bit too hard, and announced, "My granddaughter and I will make breakfast."

I looked to Fiona for support. She raised her palms and took a seat. Grasping for straws, I tried to catch Lolly's eye, but she was relaying a story about fighting the Japanese at Pearl Harbor, and Gladys was transfixed.

I threw up my hands in surrender and limped into the kitchen.

Birdie moved to the center island that once served as an apothecary table. She grabbed a mixing bowl from the shelf below and a whisk from a pewter pitcher. Fiona had already set the eggs out, and she began cracking them.

I reached for a heavy cast-iron skillet and crossed to the old black stove, flipping on the burner and lobbing some butter into the pan. I chopped red and green bell peppers and tossed them with sweet basil before adding them to the skillet.

It wasn't until she ducked into the refrigerator that Birdie spoke. I was grateful she broke the silence.

"Do you ever listen to me?"

Well, almost grateful.

"I read the book," I said over the pop of peppers.

"All of it?" she asked, holding the milk.

I faced her. "Are you serious? That thing is thicker than the Library of Congress."

Birdie rolled her eyes and sloshed some milk into the bowl, whisking the eggs together. I reached for a potato and started to grate it.

"My warning, the message I sent you—didn't you at least give it some thought?"

"Of course I did, and who ratted me out?"

"That's not important. Why didn't you understand it?"

"I thought I did, but I made a mistake." I remembered the image of Monique with those feathered wings and shivered.

Birdie looked up and stopped whisking. "How could you have been mistaken? I made it very clear, Anastasia. Feathers, a bow, danger."

"Well, you left out the *kaboom* part, Birdie. That would have clinched it."

She handed me the eggs, and I poured them in with the peppers and grated potato. I topped it all off with a hearty helping of fontina cheese and a dash of paprika and popped the frittata into the oven. I set the dial to 350 degrees.

Birdie was peeling pears when I turned back around, so I handed her the large saucepan and went to the pie safe for cinnamon sticks.

"Are you telling me you had no warning signs? No feelings at all?" Her voice shot up an octave, and I turned to watch her work, thankful I wasn't that poor pear she was carving.

I stared at my uneven shoes and thought back to earlier this morning. It seemed like a week ago. My stomach had been rumbling, but I was hungry. Seemed like a reasonable enough assumption since I had just woken up and didn't eat much the night before.

"Maybe. I'm not sure, but I hung the protection charm. Right inside the threshold like you taught me," I said. That had to count for something.

"Magic isn't effective without common sense, Anastasia. I told you this was serious. You make mistakes, people get hurt," she said. "This isn't a game."

"And I told you, I am not a witch." I tossed the cinnamon into the pot with the pears and added pear nectar and a splash of blackberry brandy. "Besides, the only one that got hurt was that poor chicken, and I'm pretty sure he was already dead."

The look on Birdie's face told me my humor was wearing thin. "You need to study the spells, the enchantments, relearn the early chapters of your youth you've tried so hard to forget."

"I read as much as I could. I got tired. How was I supposed to know someone would send me an exploding chicken?"

"The rock through the window should have been your first clue."

Right. Of course she would know about that too, even if she had been in a cabin in the woods. That message taped to the rock made sense now. *More will die.* It was referring to Kathy Sims.

"I'm trying," I said.

Birdie planted her hands on the counter and leaned in. "You came to me for help."

"Yes! And you ran away."

We were glaring at each other when Leo walked in. He looked from me to my grandmother, debated if an interruption would be wise, and decided to take his chances. "I think your aunt Lolly's a quart low," he said, thumbing behind him. "She's in there pretending Thor's a plane, and she's trying to land him on an aircraft carrier."

I didn't ask what the aircraft carrier was. I just grabbed the brandy and headed into the dining room.

Turned out Mr. Smalls was the aircraft carrier, and since Fiona was smiling at him, he didn't care one bit. Thor gave me a long-suffering look.

I shuffled to the sideboard for a goblet and set it in front of Lolly. Birdie came in with a fresh pot of coffee. I could tell she was loading up more ammunition.

I filled Lolly's glass with the brandy and patted her shoulder. She gulped the liquor like a thirsty sailor.

"You are old enough to practice on your own. Everything you need is in that book."

The bell chimed on the stove, so I ignored my grandmother as I hobbled back into the kitchen.

"That would only make sense if everything you believe about me is true," I hissed to Birdie, who was on my heels.

"It is," she said firmly.

"Right. Seeker of Justice and all that. But that's not all your mother saw, was it?"

"Of course not," Birdie said.

I stopped and looked at her. "Are we talking about the same thing?"

"Maegan made many predictions. I gather you didn't get that far."

"The last paragraph after the history." I didn't mention the voice I had heard. "She spoke of a"—I glanced toward the doorway, making sure we were alone; everyone seemed to still be invested in breakfast—"a person like her. A seer. Am I?"

I heard Lolly suck in her breath, all the way from the dining room.

Birdie threw her shoulders back, looked me in the eye, and said, "I don't know."

"You don't know? Well, thank you for clearing that up." I waved my arm, swigged the brandy, and immediately coughed. The oven mitts were hanging from the wall, and I stuffed my hands into them to check the dish.

"The point is," Birdie said, "you don't need me anymore." Her voice was steady, determined. Pushing me away just like my mother had. Just when I needed her the most.

I slammed the oven door shut and spun around. "That's just it, Birdie." It wasn't until that moment, when I said it out loud, that I believed it myself. "I do need you. You're all I have left."

Something flickered behind her eyes. A light. A truth. Hope. Then it was gone.

Chapter 15

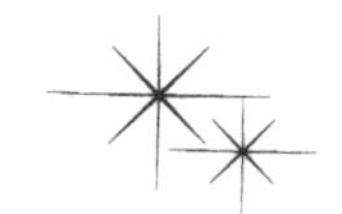

Birdie and I never finished our conversation because Leo insisted that Tommy explain to me the dangers of handmade pipe bombs and how you should never, ever put one in your refrigerator. He also let me know that the bomb was small, activated remotely, with enough kick to burn up my hand, but not enough to kill me. Probably.

Whoever planted it had intended it as a warning.

Which didn't really make me feel better.

I helped feed everyone and slipped out with Thor on the excuse that I desperately needed a shower and a change of clothes, promising to call Leo later that evening.

Right now, though, I was bundled up in my Jeep, Thor in the back with a scarf around his neck and Bruce Springsteen on the radio, begging for Rosie to come out tonight.

According to MapQuest, the Simses lived at the edge of Culver City and the drive should take about twenty minutes. It was after eleven, so I didn't think I would be interrupting breakfast, and if they were churchgoers, they should be home already.

Culver City was a blue-collar town. A sheet metal factory was the main industry. It had its fair share of bars, a corner grocery, and a sprinkling of churches, but it lacked the luster of Amethyst. Although the terrain was right out of a Thomas Kinkade painting, the houses, streets, and buildings could have posed for a Mellencamp album.

I pulled up next to a modest clapboard house with black shutters, two of which were missing slats.

I threw a blanket over Thor and told him to wait, grabbed my notebook, clipped off my spare key, and left the car running with the heat on, but the doors locked. I took a deep breath and punched the doorbell.

A small woman with ribbons of gray hair and huge eyes creaked the front door open.

I knew those eyes.

"Mrs. Sims?" I asked.

"Yes, how can I help you?" Her words trickled from her lips like raindrops.

"Hi. You don't know me, but I—"

"Then why are you here?" She avoided looking right at me like you might a solar eclipse.

"Well, ma'am—"

"Are you selling something?"

"No, ma'am. My name is—"

"Because I don't need anything."

"Of course. I just wondered if I might speak with you a moment?"

"Are you one of those Jehovah's? Because we aren't Jehovah."

This woman should be guarding the president, I swear.

"No. I'm not a Jehovah's Witness. I'm from Amethyst, and I—"

"I have to go now. I'm sorry."

"Wait!" I put my hand on the door, and Mrs. Sims screamed like I had stabbed her.

"What the hell?" boomed from another room, and a barrel of a man with a beard and a mop of curly hair was at the door in a flash. He glared at me and gingerly touched the woman's shoulder. "Alma, honey, go fix some tea," he said.

He watched her leave the room and snarled, "Lady, whatever you're sellin', we don't want it." Then he slammed the door.

I paused for a minute and decided to just go with, "It's about Kathy."

When the door didn't open right away, I assumed he thought I was a nut job and went to get his shotgun. I wondered if maybe I had made a mistake. Perhaps I had the wrong house?

Then, slowly, the door opened, and Mrs. Sims stood there, those wide eyes seeking answers I wasn't sure I had.

When we all had our tea spruced up and I was certain Mr. Sims wasn't going to snap me like a pool cue, I began.

I chose my words carefully. I wanted to be sure I had the right family. "I'm a reporter for the *Amethyst Globe,* and I stumbled across an old newspaper clipping with a picture of a young girl I thought I recognized. Her name was Kathy Sims, and she had accompanied Matthew Huckleberry to a 1989 homecoming game in Amethyst. Is that your daughter?"

Mrs. Sims clapped her hands, and Mr. Sims sat up straighter, but still reserved.

"Yes, yes!" squealed Mrs. Sims. "That's her. That's Kathy. Oh, is she okay? Do you know where she is?"

Oh. My. God.

How could I have been so stupid? It hadn't occurred to me that these people might consider their daughter to still be alive.

I really should have thought this through.

Mrs. Sims held her breath, her teacup clanking against her wedding ring. Mr. Sims scratched his beard, and I saw a sparkle of hope.

They must have wanted to know the truth, one way or another. Not knowing—that would be much worse.

I took a deep breath and said, "Did Kathy have a gold pin, shaped like a *K*?"

"Yes. Yes, she does." Mrs. Sims bobbed her head in agreement, but something on my face extinguished the sparkle in Mr. Sims's eye.

"Do you have a picture of her?" I asked.

The Simses ushered me into the room of their dead daughter, and the scent of Love's Baby Soft smacked me hard. Then a rush of damp death consumed the air.

It was her. She was here.

"I got it," I whispered so Kathy would stop beating me with her scent.

"What's that?" asked Mr. Sims.

"Um, I spot it. The pin." I straightened and walked toward the dresser, pointing to a photograph of Kathy wearing the brooch, Matt's arm around her.

"Was he her boyfriend?" I asked.

Mrs. Sims started twirling her hair between her fingers. "Why do you talk about her like she's gone? She just ran away, is all. We was hard on her, see..."

"Alma," Mr. Sims said gently. He met her gaze and smiled. Then he looked at me and frowned. I wasn't winning any brownie points with Mr. Sims.

"Let's talk in the living room," I suggested.

After so many tears, I explained to them what we had discovered, leaving out the details of where, why, and how, careful to stress that I wasn't sure it was Kathy. They understood they would be contacted should they need to come to Amethyst to examine the belongings for a positive identification. The Simses opened up then. They relayed how they had gotten into a huge fight with their daughter near the end of her senior year in high school. She wanted to go to some "Back in Time" dance, and they wouldn't allow it. She was a rebellious girl, and she sneaked out through the window after dinner with a packed bag—to meet up with her boyfriend, Matt Huckleberry, they assumed.

Back in Time. That explained her costume.

"We never heard from her after that," Mrs. Sims sobbed.

"I'm so sorry," I offered. "And Matt—did he hear from her?"

Mrs. Sims shook her head. "That's the kicker. He never heard one word from her. Said he was asleep in bed all night. Said she never came by. He was such a good boy. We sure liked him." She looked up at me. "I thought maybe she run off to Hollywood, like she was always talkin' about, you know? We checked with the train people, and well..." Her words fell off.

I nodded, aching for her. I knew what it was like to lose someone and not know why or how. Always wondering, questioning what could have been done differently.

One way or another, the Simses were going to get their answer.

"Did you file a missing persons report?"

Mr. Sims scoffed. "Damn cops just kept telling us she run away, is all. Said she was eighteen and since she took a bag and there wasn't no trace of foul play wasn't much they could do. They sniffed around, asked a few questions here and there, but no one seen her. They figured she hitchhiked outta town."

I learned that Matt Huckleberry sent the Simses a Christmas card every year. Matt lived on a farm in an unincorporated section of the county, off the beaten path. It was lunchtime when I finished speaking with the Simses and I had yet to eat, so I swung through a drive-through and ordered Thor a couple of cheeseburgers, and a grilled chicken sandwich, no mayo, for myself. We ate in silence as I jotted a few notes and contemplated what I was going to say to Matt. I was sure he knew of my family, even if he didn't know me. Since his father was close with my uncle, he had to know Cinnamon, at least.

Come to think of it, I wondered why I didn't see more of him around Amethyst. I had assumed he lived nowhere near town, but he was only a few miles away.

A soft snow began to fall as I backed out of the parking lot and pointed the Jeep west. I circled down an empty road, as the Simses had instructed, and found myself winding around a frozen lake with no houses in sight.

The wipers were doing their job when I spotted a hand-painted wooden sign dressed with twinkle lights ten minutes later. The sign read, HUCKLEBERRY'S FRESH-CUT TREES.

I turned down the long driveway. Acres of snow-capped pines and firs drifted by, leading me to a grand Victorian draped in fresh garland. Candle lights in each window and red velvet bows along the porch railing made me think for a second that Bing Crosby was about to tap-dance across the hood of my car.

I got out of the Jeep and clipped a leash on Thor, who immediately whizzed on my tire.

"Dammit, Thor, there's a thousand trees around here," I scolded.

"Ah, but warm rubber doesn't poke like a Scotch pine," said a voice behind me.

I jumped and scooted around, face-to-face with a man who had to share Robert Redford's genes.

He wore a blue scarf that matched his eyes and a thick down jacket that hid all the good parts.

"Hi, there," he said, extending his arm, "Matt Huckleberry."

I shook his hand, expecting a bad feeling, but got nothing through the gloves.

"Hi, uh, I'm..."

Thor ran past me, and I stumbled into Matt as the dog pounced on the porch.

Matt smiled at me and helped me right myself. Then I yelled, "Thor! Come!"

"Oh, he's fine. He's probably cold. Why don't you both come inside? I have some fresh hot chocolate."

"Well, um, I..." *Complete sentences, Stacy, you know this.*

"Come on." Matt put his hand on the small of my back and led me to the front door. I moved forward.

The smart girl inside me was saying, *Don't go inside. What if he killed her?* But the shallow slut was duct-taping her mouth shut.

Blame it on the winter wonderland.

A bell chimed as we entered the foyer and a train sped over my head, whistling. Thor bounded after it and Matt laughed.

As promised, hot chocolate steamed on a buffet with a bowl of miniature marshmallows next to it and oatmeal cookies stacked high on a plate.

There was a crisply scented tree just to my right covered with heart-shaped ornaments and pink tinsel.

It was all too surreal.

"This is our Valentine's display, but we still have seventy-five percent off on our Christmas decorations," Matt said as he poured the cocoa.

This was the guy? Santa's hot little helper?

"Marshmallows?" he offered.

I shook my head.

"So, what can I help you with?" He handed me the warm mug.

"Actually, Matt, I don't know if you recognize me, but my name is Stacy Justice and I wanted to talk to you about—"

"Stacy? Oh my gosh. Look at you all grown up! Of course I know who you are. Wait, are you here about my father?"

"No. I'm here about Kathy Sims."

Matt stepped back and stared at me for a beat. "I haven't heard that name in a long time," he said quietly. He removed his scarf and hung it on a hook.

"Yes, well, I wondered if I could ask you a few questions about her?"

"Why?" His voice raised an octave.

"Well," I stammered, unsure how much I should reveal. I placed the cocoa on the side table.

"Has she contacted you?" he asked.

Yes. She appeared in my bathroom mirror. "No, but I may have stumbled across something that belonged to her, and I wanted to return it, but I was told that she…left the area."

Please don't ask what I found.

Matt stalked forward, eyes glued to me. I took a step back and clutched my amethyst necklace.

"What did you find?" His voice told me he didn't believe me.

I took another step back, reaching behind me for the door handle.

"What. Did. You. Find?" He grabbed my wrist.

"A pin," I blurted.

"You're lying," Matt said, still holding me.

"No, I'm not. Thor!" *Where the hell is that dog? Protector, my ass.*

"Tell me, Stacy, did Kathy come to you?" Hell, it was like Jeffrey Dahmer disguised as Jimmy Stewart.

"What? No."

He grabbed my other wrist, urgency in his tone. "Did she come to you? Did Kathy visit you, Stacy?"

Holy cockgoblin, this guy's going to slice and dice me, and no one will ever know.

"Look, I know what you are, Stacy Justice. I know all about the Geraghty Girls," Matt said.

"Thor," I squeaked.

"Is she dead?" he asked.

I gave a slight nod.

Matt pulled me to him with force, and I held my breath.

"I knew it. I knew it," he said and hugged me. Then he buried his head in my hair and sobbed.

Okay, this guy is officially a whacknut.

"Come into the parlor. We'll talk," he whispered.

"No, thanks, it's late. Thor!" *Cripes, where does a 180-pound dog hide?*

"Come on." Matt pulled at me, still holding my arm, and dragged me farther into the house.

I counted three doors and twelve windows, deciding Thor was on his own, before Matt said, "I loved that girl. She was my best friend."

He sighed and ushered me to a settee as he sank into a chaise lounge, rubbing his temples.

"Friend?"

Matt looked at me and nodded.

"That wasn't the impression I got."

"What do you mean?"

"I thought you two were a couple."

Matt laughed. "Yes, well, when you're captain of the football team in a small Midwest town and your homophobic father runs a dive bar, people make assumptions."

Wait, what?

Matt sensed my confusion. "That's why I haven't talked to the man in years. I'm gay, Stacy."

"Darling!" said a thin man with a goatee, accompanied by my wayward dog. "Look who I found lounging on our bed."

I glared at Thor, who completely ignored me and sat next to our host. Matt ruffled his ears.

The man approached Matt and kissed him, punctuating the fact that I was a complete jackass.

Matt introduced me to Blake, and the conversation went on for another half hour as he explained that Kathy was his date whenever he needed one for appearances, but other than that, they were the closest of friends.

"She was seeing someone seriously those last few months of school, and I got the impression from our last conversation that she wanted to tell me something. She never had the chance," he said, choking back more tears.

"Was she going to tell you who it was, do you think?"

Matt shook his head. "No, something else. She made it clear she didn't want me to know who her secret lover was." He shrugged. "I don't know. Could have been kid stuff. Everything's so dramatic when you're a teenager."

Kid stuff. What do teenagers engage in that they hide from their parents? Drinking? Drugs? Sex? Was she going to sneak off for a weekend getaway? Maybe tell her parents she was visiting a college. Did she really plan to run off to Hollywood like they thought she might? Get married? Join the circus? What was it she wanted to tell Matt?

I thanked Matt and left with a promise that I would help the couple perform a séance. Turns out the Geraghtys are popular among the gay community, and Matt is fascinated by the supernatural.

"Well, that was another dead end. And you were no help at all!" I said to Thor as we backed out of the driveway.

Matt and Blake waved good-bye.

It was early afternoon, and the roads were a bit slick, so I took the turns a little slower than I had on the way there. I reached for my cell phone and called Derek, telling him to review the story and choose some pictures to go with it.

"No problem. Hey, some guy was calling here asking about you."

"Who?"

"Didn't say. Said he'd leave you another note. What's up with that?"

Great. The little troll is back.

Next I called Leo, asking if he had dinner plans.

"I know the answer, but I still have to ask," he said. "Did you visit the Simses' residence?"

Holy crap on a cracker.

"*Is that her?*" I heard the mayor yell in the background.

Well, this could be problematic.

"Tell her she'll be lucky to get a job writing for the back of cereal boxes when I'm through with her!"

"What's that, Leo? You're breaking up." I cut the call.

This was so not good.

I flipped the wipers on high, coasting around the lake, thinking about what a girl might want to tell her gay best friend. Want to, but was afraid to. Or ashamed to. Or uncertain about. Or worried. Or...

And then it hit me.

Was Kathy pregnant?

I called the coroner and asked if there was any way to determine that possibility.

"What? Why?"

"Please, Mr. Sagnoski. If there's anything you could do. It's important."

He sighed. "I'll try, kid, but no promises."

I hung up the phone just as a car smashed into me from behind.

Chapter 16

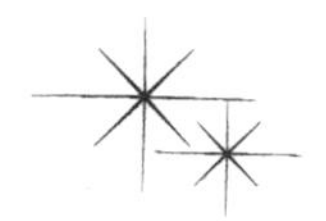

My skull throbbed as I forced my eyes open. Everything was fuzzy. I looked in the backseat, and my neck cracked. Oh no. The back hatch was open, and Thor was gone. I peeked in the mirror, frantic. Another crack and blood oozed down my eyelid.

Where am I? Where is Thor? What happened?

Every bone in my body ached and cracked each time I moved, and a distinct chill settled over me.

I leaned forward to peer out the windshield.

White all around. But it had stopped snowing. The sun washed the sky in waves of pink and purple brushing against the surface of the untapped landscape. It was dusk. I had been out for at least a couple of hours.

I unhooked my seatbelt and heard another crack.

That's when I knew it wasn't my bones.

It was ice. And I was in my Jeep, in the middle of the lake. I sat very still for about a tenth of a second before I threw the door open and dove onto the ice. I landed on my chest and skidded across the glassy surface. I turned back to see the lake swallow my Jeep one fender at a time.

Deep breaths. Deep breaths. Seemed I was far enough away from the dark hole. If I could just run to the shoreline...

CRACK.

Uh-oh.

I flipped on my back and crab-walked as fast as I could toward what I hoped was land, all the while watching chunks of ice breaking in front of me.

Then I felt wet.

And the platform that held me caved.

I plummeted into the water, grasping for an edge of ice, bobbing.

Finally, I gained purchase. I pulled myself up, but the frozen lake shattered in my hands. My arms flailed wildly. Reaching, grabbing, desperate for a solid connection, but the slippery surface gave way, again and again.

The chattering of my teeth drowned out all sounds, but I was sure I screamed, "Help!" at the top of my lungs, my last bit of strength gone with it.

And then I heard, "Woof!"

Treading water, I looked up and saw Thor.

He was paving a path along the embankment, a car's length away, galloping back and forth.

Certain I could make it, I tried to secure some real estate on the lake, but my arm weighed a hundred pounds, and my coat, scarf, and gloves were anchors. I wiggled from my coat and scarf, hot breath slicing the air, and let them sink. The gloves were leather, so I thought they'd offer some protection for at least a few more minutes.

Again, I grabbed the frozen surface—and it held. I rested for a minute, gasping for breath. Then I tried to pull myself up. It was futile. My strength was gone, and my jeans bogged me down.

When I looked up again, Thor was on the ice, crawling toward me.

"Thor! No!"

He slithered forward, and I said a little prayer to Diana, goddess of the hunt and canine protector.

My fingers were stiff, probably blue beneath the leather, and I couldn't stop shaking.

Thor moved forward, and I noticed he was shivering too. Great Dane fur isn't exactly insulation.

"Go back," I croaked.

He didn't listen, and I realized he still had a leash on, plus the scarf.

I briefly wondered how my day could start with a poultry bomb and end up with me as fish bait.

Thor crept closer, and I was warming up to the idea, afraid that even if I could hoist myself up, the ice that kept me afloat would crumble again.

Of course, I had no clue what I would do once I got out of there. It had to be miles back to Matt's place, and my cell phone was swimming inside my Jeep at the bottom of the lake.

Thor was about three feet away, and I told him to stay there. He had a good seventy pounds on me, and I didn't want to risk us both going under.

But his weight was more evenly displaced. So maybe...

"Down," I said to Thor.

He obeyed.

"Come."

He crawled slowly toward me. When he was about a foot from the shelf, I said, "Stay."

The leash was buried beneath him by the time he reached me, but the scarf was tied around his neck. If I could just snag it, maybe he was strong enough to pull me up.

Thor whined softly.

"Okay, buddy. Hang on."

Gingerly, I extended my right arm and propped myself up on the ledge with my left. I was just able to tangle my fingers around the fringe of the scarf.

I looked at him and said, "Back."

Thor inched back.

"Up."

He stood, and I was lifted a few inches, my legs still in the water.

"Back."

Another step.

Another.

My chest emerged from the water, and Thor hesitated, looking to me for further instruction.

"Back."

I still couldn't access the leash, and the scarf began to unravel.

CRACK.

Uh-oh.

Before I slipped into the water, I felt something clamp my arm.

Then I passed out.

Chapter 17

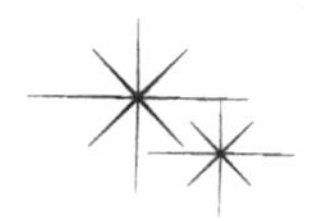

"I cannot believe you put a tracking device in my car!" I said to Leo later.

"Actually," Chance said, raising his hand, "I did."

I glared at him. "You did?"

"Yeah, but he told me to," he said, pointing to Leo.

"Okay, that's it. I don't understand this bond the two of you have formed. You don't even know each other." I waved my arm, and the wool blanket around me fluttered. "What am I? Some prize you're competing for at the state fair?"

Leo and Chance exchanged a look as I caught my reflection in the mirror over the fireplace. We were in the Geraghty house parlor, and my forehead was plastered with a butterfly bandage, my nose was runny, my eyes bloodshot, and I was pretty sure strands of frozen hair had broken off in the squad car.

"You know what I mean," I mumbled.

It turned out Leo had grown concerned when he couldn't reach me for so long and no one else had heard from me. He called Chance to track my car, and when they discovered it appeared to be in the middle of a frozen lake, they rushed to find me. They arrived just as Thor was struggling to pull me from the freezing water.

Fiona floated in with hot coffee and herbal tea. The coffee was for Leo, who sniffed it first.

My great aunt set down the tray and said, “Well, dear, they did save your life.”

“That isn’t the point,” I said.

“Come now, you need to rest.” She shuffled me to the sofa and tucked an extra blanket around me.

My teeth had only just stopped chattering.

“Don’t you think she should be in a hospital?” Leo asked.

“Nonsense!” Birdie said. She drifted through the entryway with Irish whiskey and warm scones that hinted of nutmeg. “There’s nothing they would do for her that we can’t do here. It isn’t like she lost a limb.”

I’m guessing if I had, though, the Geraghty Girls would have been in the fruit cellar fashioning one from hay and twigs.

“Birdie, she could have pneumonia,” Leo insisted.

“I’m fine, Leo,” I said and sneezed.

“You are not fine.” Leo stood over me. “First you think you’re Nancy Drew, then you’re Dora the Explorer. I mean, what’s next?” He threw his hands in the air and looked at Chance.

Chance helped himself to a scone and said, “If you say Bob the Builder, I swear I will punch you.”

Birdie prepared a hot toddy for me and said, “That’s quite enough, boys.”

I looked around the room. “Where’s Thor?”

“Lolly’s bringing him around now, dear,” said Fiona.

It wasn't a minute before Lolly wove into the parlor, in full Geraghty regalia. She smiled at me, curtsied for Chance and Leo, and swung her cape around to meet the fireplace. She fumbled for a minute, bent down, worked her arms every which way, and when she stood, there was a Thor-sized bed with a canopy on it near the hearth. She whistled, and Thor, wearing leggings and a fleece tunic, trotted over to me, licked my hand, and retired to his boudoir.

I heard him slurp something, burp, and plop down.

"Hmm. I thought Fiona was the one with the knack for animals," I remarked.

"*That's* what sticks out as strange in this picture? Are you kidding me?" asked Leo.

Chance avoided his eyes, fearing guilt by association, and I chugged a shot of whiskey.

"Where's Smalls?" I asked, ignoring Leo.

"Oh," Fiona's tone was a cool breeze, "he won't be bothering you anymore, dear."

I sat up. "Why? What did you do?" I looked at the three of them, and they all just stared at me, blank chalkboards.

"Don't give me that," I said. "I want to know what you said. Or did."

"We just had a chat, dear," Fiona said. She poured herself into a chair and crossed her legs.

"Your aunt can be very persuasive, Anastasia," Birdie said.

The implication hinted at some kind of seduction scene. If you could carve out an image from your brain with a melon baller, I would have done it on the spot.

"Not like that!" Lolly slapped my knee.

Now, how did she know what I was thinking?

"Can I see you for a minute?" Leo asked and pulled me into the hall.

The look on his face was a combination of longing and pity. Not exactly what a girl likes to see in the eyes of her suitor.

"Stacy, I am serious. You need to get some real medical attention. I'm worried about you."

"That's very sweet, but I really am Okay, Leo. Trust me." I squeezed his hand.

"Trust you?" He tilted his head and laughed. Then he counted off on his fingers. "You've been investigating a homicide."

"I am investigating a story."

"You put a bomb in your fridge."

"That wasn't my fault."

"You got run into a lake."

"Again, how could I see that coming?"

He leaned in as the little vein on his forehead throbbed. "You informed a family that their runaway daughter is dead."

"She is."

"You don't know that."

"I'm almost positive."

"Even if it is her, that's not your call."

I blew out a long sigh. He was a little bit right, although, truthfully, I hadn't intended to tell them about Kathy. It just slipped out.

"Stacy, look, I care about you." He kissed my forehead. "I don't want to see you get hurt." He kissed my eyelids. "I want to be with you. Alone. On a real date. Remember those?" He lifted my chin and kissed my lips. "But it's always so crazy around here. It's tough to handle."

"Then you aren't equipped to court my granddaughter," Birdie said behind us.

"Birdie!" I was exasperated.

Leo looked at her and shook his head slowly. I saw a little bit of his fire fade in that moment. "Maybe you're right, Birdie. I might not be. But it's worth it to me to find out." Then he looked at me, my face shining back in his eyes. "Please stay out of trouble," he said before he closed the door.

I whirled around at Birdie. "Why? Why would you say that?"

Birdie made a disgusted sound. "He needs to toughen up."

"He's a cop, for Chrissakes."

"That means nothing. And don't curse."

"I like him the way he is."

"Men who love Geraghty Girls have to find a delicate balance between resolve and tolerance. He's a lion in his sun sign, a leader, one who controls. You, of all people, should know that Geraghtys cannot be controlled." She clasped her hands in front of her.

She had a point there, but this was none of her business.

I opened my mouth to tell her to stay out of my love life, to tell her that my decisions are my own and that I certainly do not need her advice when it comes to relationships, but then I glanced into the parlor and something stopped me.

Fiona, Lolly, Birdie. All of them single. And after my father died, so was my mother.

I flashed forward thirty years and saw myself sitting on the settee, alone, reading a book. And I didn't even have any sisters.

"I'm going to die alone in this house," I said like I was reading a headline.

"Don't be so dramatic," Birdie said, examining her nails. "I didn't say he wasn't trainable."

The doorbell chimed before I could ask what that meant.

A very pissed off–looking Cinnamon stood on the porch next to Mario, who didn't seem to notice she was giving him a death stare.

"Hey, cousin. Fiona told me what happened. How you doing?" she asked, rushing to hug me.

"I'm good, thanks, Cin."

"You need to lie low, Stacy. This is getting scary." She searched my face and said, "But you won't. Well, at least call me next time you want to risk your life." Then she looked around, said hello to Birdie, and asked, "Chance is here, isn't he? I thought I saw his truck in the driveway."

"In here, Cin!" Chance called.

I followed Cinnamon into the parlor, and she explained that she needed Chance to pull her car out of a snowdrift.

"Because my idiot uncle told me he knew how to drive." Her eyes shot daggers at Mario.

"I'm right here, Cinnamon," Mario said. "You should respect your elders, hah?"

Cin grumbled something about not being sure they were really related. Then Mario spotted Fiona's legs and forgot all about the respect thing.

I retrieved my hot toddy as the bell rang again, and Mr. Huckleberry entered the parlor.

"Well," Birdie announced, "our dinner guest has arrived."

Lolly clapped her hands, and I spit boozed-up tea through my nose.

Fiona rose and said, "Why don't you all stay? There's plenty for everyone."

Well, this should be interesting.

Upstairs, Lolly was hammering down the gin and tonics as she dug through her closet searching for proper dinner attire for Cinnamon and me.

The two of us were crouched on the floor of Lolly's private dressing room, spying out the upstairs window at Mario and Huck smoking cigars on the side porch.

"Remember that photo, Cin? The one Derek snapped in the basement?" I whispered.

"Yeah, so?"

"The cigar butt. Didn't it have that same color ring? Like the one Huck's puffing on?"

Cin squinted. "Oh yeah. I think so. But that doesn't mean anything. He used to own the place. It could have been there for years. Besides, look, Mario's is the same."

She was right, and we met each other's eyes. Could Mario have set the blaze? But what would have been the motive? Money?

"Mario?" she said. "Man, if I could get that guy out of my life." She went back to watching him, a smile framing her face.

"Girls," Lolly called, "makeup time."

Cinnamon's mood returned to pissed off as we entered the dining room in matching crinoline-stuffed dresses, with pigtails and neon-blue eye shadow.

We looked like the Judds. The early years.

Chance laughed, and Cin kicked him. Hard.

Even Mario flinched.

"Feeling better, dear?" Fiona asked me as she scooted her chair up to the table.

Yes, I always feel better when I'm dressed like the cast from The Beverly Hillbillies. "Fine, thanks," I said.

Huck was piling scalloped potatoes onto his plate. "I heard about your accident, Stacy. What were you doing out in the boonies?" he asked, although I suspected he knew.

"Just sightseeing," I said and helped myself to a buttermilk biscuit. Mr. Huckleberry probably knew I had been close to his son's tree farm. Why didn't he mention it? He certainly would have known Kathy if Matt and she were so close.

Not to mention he did own the building at the time of her disappearance. He would have been aware of any work that had gone into it, whether he ordered it or even if it was rented out at the time. But if he was responsible for Kathy's death, the reason eluded me.

Mario asked Chance to pass the wine, and Fiona piped up. "Look, Stacy, Mario brought this lovely jewelry from Italy." She motioned toward the buffet where Mario had displayed the wares he was packing up the other night.

"Very nice," I said.

"I sell you cheap, hah?" Mario said.

"Stop it, Uncle Mario," Cin said.

"What I say?" he asked.

"Stacy, come, look." Mario yanked my chair from the table and dragged me to the buffet.

"You want bracelet, you want ring, watch? What you like?"

I browsed the display, prepared to buy something just so he'd take his hand off my ass. Then I spotted a necklace I had to have.

Chapter 18

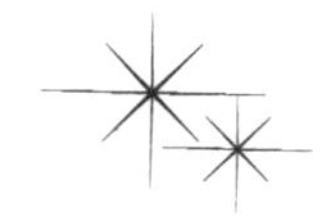

My eyes opened to the image of three cloaked heads staring at me intently and I yelped.

"What the…?" I said.

"Settle down, Anastasia," Birdie said.

They were hovering over me, each holding a candle.

Disoriented, it took me a minute to realize I was in one of the guest rooms of the inn.

"Why…?"

"You fell asleep after dessert, dear. So Chance carried you up to your room," Fiona informed me. "He's such a nice boy."

Right. Dinner. Chance, Huck, Mario. Mario! Oh no, I didn't get an opportunity to tell Cin about the necklace. My chest felt bare, and I patted where my purchase should have hung.

Gone.

"Looking for something?" Birdie asked, and Lolly held it up.

The onyx cross matched the one I had dug from the basement floor.

I rubbed my eyes, suddenly very awake. "Okay, what are you up to?"

"Scrying," said Lolly, grinning.

Oh boy.

"What time is it?" I asked.

"Almost midnight," said Fiona. "The perfect time to talk to the dead."

"No, no, no." I rose up and realized I was wearing a cape too. *How the hell…?*

"Birdie, I'm not quite ready," I said.

"Nonsense, we're here to help." Then she winked.

I had never seen my grandmother wink, and it unnerved me.

"Please don't do that," I said.

The duvet slipped from me as I swung my legs over the bedside. "What exactly are we scrying for?" I asked.

"Answers," Birdie said, and Fiona propped me up.

It seemed Chance had filled them in on Kathy Sims, so they got the idea in their heads that they should aid me in my quest for the truth. I wasn't in a position to argue with them, so I followed them downstairs.

An altar had been set up in the kitchen. On it sat a crystal ball, illuminated by a moonbeam that bounced off a black mirror. There were lit candles and sprigs of coltsfoot and elfwort—good herbs for divination—spread around it.

Lolly reached inside her cape and retrieved a cigar butt. She balanced that and the necklace on the purple scarf that draped the altar.

Even in my freshly awakened state, I could see that something was missing.

"We can't do this. We need an object that Kathy might have touched. Something her energy had transferred to," I said. *Whoa, where did that come from?* I guess the studying was paying off.

"You mean like this?" Fiona asked, producing the original necklace, still caked with dirt.

I didn't even ask how she got it.

"Shield yourself," Birdie instructed.

Scrying is a form of divination. A crystal ball, a black mirror, even a bowl of water can all be used to scry, in hopes of invoking a vision, receiving a message, or opening a gateway to the other side. Before scrying, it's best to form a mental shield for protection. You never know what will come through in a scrying session.

This was not, as they say, a job for amateurs. Which of course, I was, so my heart nervously fluttered.

I closed my eyes, imagining a white light molded to my body. Then I took a deep breath and kneeled, clasping the hands of my great aunts. With Birdie completing the circle, I dove in.

The cigar butt was Huck's, which explained why Birdie invited him to dinner.

I held that first, staring intently into the mirror. Within seconds, the Black Opal, freshly painted and dressed with new tables, a digital jukebox, and an unmarred floor, popped into sight. I could see faceless people sipping cocktails against the antique bar, and I wasn't sure if I was looking at the future or the past. I fought harder, delving into the scene, wading through the sea of customers. There was a door marked OFFICE, and after a moment, Huck—a version of him, anyway—swung it open. Then the vision blew out like a match.

My hands were hot, and I broke the circle, shaking out the tension.

"Well?" Birdie asked.

"I don't know. Nothing concrete. Not with Huck, anyway," I said.

"Continue," Birdie said.

One more deep breath and the shield embraced me again, my concentration sharp. I reached for the cross I bought from Cinnamon's uncle, and a roller coaster of laughter rushed at me. I saw Mario talking to a man dressed in all black. They stood in front of a table, the man talking with his hands and Mario picking up pieces of jewelry. They were on a bridge punctuated with shops, a river flowing beneath it. The melodious chatter of happy tourists drowned the conversation, but I knew from the feel of the scene I was looking at Italy. Then it fizzled.

Fiona handed me a glass of water, and I gulped it down. "Take your time," she said.

"Just the man Mario bought the merchandise from," I said.

I sat on the floor, refocused my eyes, and looked at the last object.

The visions came to me so clearly. Huck, the Black Opal, Mario, Italy—all of them I could see and hear and taste. I hadn't had that kind of connection to magic since I was a kid. It frightened and exhilarated me at the same time. I stood, rolled my neck around, and massaged my temples.

"Two down, one to go," I said.

I returned to my perch and lifted the hood over my head.

When I had first dug it from the dirt, I thought the necklace I found belonged to whoever set fire to the bar. Then I thought perhaps it was Kathy's. Now I wasn't sure if it had anything at all to do with the fire or the murder. But this was my chance to find out.

The chain was cold as I curled my fingers around the links. I slid my hand down the length of it to meet the cross. Four corners of blackness emerged as the dirt rained on the floor, exposing the onyx.

I closed my eyes and called to Kathy through my mind.

At first, there was nothing. Only darkness. I waited and mentally said her name again.

Then the scent of damp earth crept in before a flash of red shocked me into her world.

Trees budded around me and there was no trace of snow on the ground, telling me it was spring. I shivered. That's when I noticed I was wearing the clothes Kathy had been buried in. Only they were bright and crisp. New.

"Just a little further," I heard behind me.

I stiffened, every muscle on high alert. I wasn't alone. And this was three-dimensional. I was there. In the woods with…who?

Don't panic. It's not real, I told myself.

I spun around, clinging to my composure.

The silhouette of a man loomed ahead, the waning moon providing little light.

"Come closer. I can't see you," I said. If I could just get a glimpse of his face…

"Right behind you," he said and waved me on.

The voice. Was it familiar? I couldn't place it.

I ventured forward, my heels snapping twigs with each step.

"Do you see your surprise?" he asked.

At the end of the path lay a checkered blanket, a bottle of wine, and two glasses.

"Wine?" I looked back. He was closer, but I still couldn't define his features. Not too tall, not too short.

"Don't play innocent with me, Kathy. I know all your dirty secrets." He sounded like he enjoyed them too.

I made my way to the blanket and toed it. It felt so real.

Gloved hands cupped my shoulders from behind, and he said steadily, "Perfect, isn't it?"

"Mm-hmm." My head tilted, but he snapped it back into place.

"Just like us." The words were whispered like a confession.

I didn't respond.

"But you had to screw it up!" he hissed.

I tried to dart away, but he lassoed my neck and jerked my head back. I flung my arms and legs, kicking and punching, hitting nothing except thin, moist air—air that wasn't making it into my lungs. My neck muscles strained as the cord tightened, and I felt myself losing consciousness. Before my eyes, a star flashed.

Then a tiny voice whispered, "Carol," before the world blackened.

Chapter 19

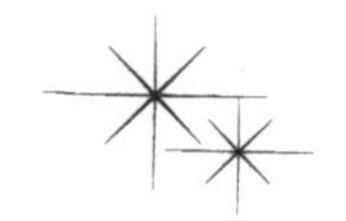

"Tether her!" Birdie yelled, and I could feel the aunts pulling me back from wherever I had been.

"Stacy!" Fiona was speaking, and Lolly was slapping me silly.

"I'm okay. I'm good. Stop!" I said, and they backed off.

How many times can you pass out in a twenty-four-hour period before it starts to affect your brain?

I leaned over the sink and splashed water on my face. When I turned back to them, they stared hard at me, waiting for a report.

"I saw her," I panted, "and him. But I didn't see his face. And what the hell happened? I felt like I was dying. I thought you knew what you were doing here."

"You went in too deep, dear," Fiona said, and Lolly nodded. "It was our fault, really."

"But," Birdie interjected sharply, "you came away with answers, did you not?" She looked pretty proud.

"Some." I relayed the whole scenario from start to finish. Then I asked, "Do you think the man was named Carol?"

The three of them huddled and then stood to face me.

Birdie said, "In the event of a murder, the dead cannot speak the name of the person directly responsible. So they point you to someone else. Someone who may know the killer."

"Great. So I'm back to square one."

The Monday-morning sunlight danced off my white bedspread as I rummaged through my sock drawer. I caught myself whistling as I showered, replaying the scrying session over in my head. It had gone rather well, I told Thor as he inhaled his breakfast. Maybe there was something to this magic business? Maybe, if I practiced hard enough, I might be good at it.

I decided there was no time like the present, so after I made an appearance at work, I would stop by to see the coroner. If he hadn't discovered any new information, like a pregnancy, then perhaps being in the same room with Kathy's body would lead to another clue or maybe a vision.

I grabbed the Blessed Book, tucked both necklaces away, patted Moonlight on the head, and swung open the door.

I had to get creative in the wardrobe department since the lake swallowed my winter wear. It didn't bother me that the only boots in the back of my closet were moon boots from middle school or that I looked like something the Cookie Monster swallowed in Lolly's faux fur. Nope.

What bothered me was that I had no car, no wallet, no driver's license, and I just remembered all that when I stepped outside.

Even my recorder was buried in the lake.

Normally I would just walk, but I had a lot to do today. I slammed the door shut and called Gramps on the prepaid phone Leo had brought me yesterday.

"Well, sure, honey, I'll drive you. But why don't you just ask your grandmother?"

"Need I remind you of my college graduation?"

"Oh yeah," he laughed. "Well, it was the solstice, after all, and Birdie is a purist. You wouldn't have even known she was naked under that cloak if her bobby pins hadn't fired off the metal detector."

I cringed at the memory.

"Why don't you just take her car, sweetheart?"

"Allow me to redirect you to Thanksgiving two thousand two."

"Now, you know your grandmother didn't realize that there was marijuana mixed in with the mugwort she picked on the side of the road."

I thanked Gramps for the ride, and he told me I could borrow one of his vehicles as long as I needed it. Gramps made a bundle in real estate some years back and had a car for every day of the week.

He said he might drop one off later in the day and surprise Birdie with a lunch invitation. I smiled and sent a silent prayer for him. Then Thor and I went to work.

I snagged some coffee, booted up my computer, and edited the story. Then, after making a considerable dent in my inbox, I scanned through the photos that Derek had chosen for the piece, just as he walked in my office door. Thor was under my desk, and he ran out to greet Derek, lifting the desk off the ground and spilling the remainder of my coffee across my lap.

"Hey, big guy," Derek said, knuckling Thor's ears.

I grabbed the roll of paper towels I kept in the bottom drawer and starting mopping up the mess.

"I like the shots," I told Derek. "I just edited the piece, so I'll send it to Parker and you can go with those photos. Why the hell are you looking at me like that?"

Derek was grinning like he got a hot tip on a horse. He closed the door behind him and trotted to my desk.

"You are going to love me," he said.

"I seriously doubt that."

"Too bad." He crossed his arms and looked away.

"What is it?"

"Say I'm the best partner you ever had."

Now he thought we were Woodward and Bernstein.

"We are not partners."

"Say it."

"Derek, I don't have time—"

"Ah, ah." He wagged a finger at me. I hate when people do that. "You'll make time for this."

I crossed my arms and stared at him. Thor's head was bobbing back and forth from me to Derek. He sensed my annoyance, but I guessed he also suspected that the kid wasn't a bad egg.

"Fine. You're the king."

"Even better." He sat on my desk. "I just got a call from the hospital. It was your friend Lyn. She said some kid was admitted to the emergency room last night for second-degree burns."

"So?"

"So the kid was at a party."

He paused for emphasis, and I grunted for the same reason.

"Spill it, Derek."

"Fine, but you're ruining my buildup."

"I'll risk it."

"The kid was doing shots of Everclear and singed off all the hair on his head. He looks like a bowling ball." Derek chuckled.

"And you don't think he could have swiped it from a liquor store?"

Derek shook his head. "I checked. No one carries it in the whole county."

I rolled that around in my head.

"There's more," he said, excited.

I hiked both eyebrows to let him know that if he didn't just come out with it, I might bitch-slap him.

"He listed the Black Opal as his place of employment."

Now we were getting somewhere.

Derek waited for a pat on the back.

"Okay, good work. I'll let you live today." I smiled. "Tell Parker the story's good to go for tomorrow's edition and that we'll be gone all morning." I grabbed a notebook and hurried out of the office.

Derek hung his head out the door. "Where you going?"

"I have to meet with the coroner first."

"What should I do?"

"It's Thor's nap time. Bring him to your office," I called over my shoulder. "Then come by and pick me up."

I dodged snowdrifts and black slush as I made my way down Main Street, heading to the coroner's office. The sun fed me energy, and renewed confidence settled in as I pushed through the door.

"Mr. Sagnoski?" I called.

No response. The hallway was dark, so I flipped on the light.

"Hello? Mr. Sagnoski?"

It was a little after nine. Maybe he was in the autopsy room. Doubtful he could hear me out here.

The hallway lights flickered deeper into the building.

"Mr. Sagnoski?" I called. I popped into the stale room he had escorted me into on my last visit. It was freezing, and I rubbed my hands together. "Hello? It's Stacy Justice. Wondering if you had any news for me?"

The blue sheet was tossed across the table, instruments scattered on top of it. A cold rush of air slashed my face, and I turned to find the window gaped open.

When I rubbed my neck, I realized Kathy wasn't grabbing my attention by force any longer. If divination carried that kind of perk, I was all for it.

A crow flapped in the open window, and I jumped back. I grabbed the table to steady myself, which had the exact opposite effect. The table slid over the linoleum, and I landed on my ass, my notebook skating behind me.

I flipped over to look for it, but instead, I found Mr. Sagnoski lying in a pool of blood, a scalpel planted in his neck.

Chapter 20

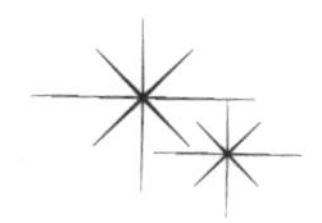

Seconds later, I burst through the door so hard I was sure I broke it.

I ran across the street and called Leo.

That's when the mustached man decided to make another appearance.

He was coming toward me at a brisk pace, and I couldn't shake the feeling that something about him was familiar.

I also couldn't stop shaking.

Inching backward, I hung up when I got Leo's voice mail and called dispatch. The words tumbled out as I told Betty that I needed an officer right away at the coroner's office and please hurry, hurry, hurry. I heard her call it in before I clicked off the phone.

It wasn't long before the Citizens on Patrol showed up. Jed held up his police scanner and said, "Whatcha got, Mrs. Chief?"

"Don't call me that," I snapped.

"Sorrrryyyy. Geez," said Jed.

Ned, Jed, and Jeb surrounded me, and the mustached man stopped, then turned and went the other way.

Wow, these guys aren't useless after all.

Ned swayed a little bit, his lazy eye on the fritz.

"Has he been drinking?" I asked Jed.

"Nah. Still drunk from last night."

Of course.

Jeb lit up a cigarette.

We all stood there a moment, Jeb puffing away, avoiding eye contact.

"So, what's the problem?" asked Jed finally.

"You know, I think maybe we should wait for Leo," I said.

"Why? We can handle it." Jeb hiked up his jeans and sniffled.

"It's not that." Yes, it was. "I just think the chief will want to take a look first. He likes to be in charge, you know?"

"I do, do I?" said Leo, his voice amused.

I turned around. "I didn't hear you pull up," I said.

"I was just getting coffee when you called. Parked in back." He managed to look warm and sun-kissed even when it was twenty degrees outside. My Irish skin was envious.

"What's going on? Betty said you hung up before you gave any details," Leo said.

I looked at the CoPs, then at Leo.

"Hey, guys, give us a sec?" Leo said.

"Sure thing, Chief," said Jed.

"Is he gonna make out with her right here on the street?" Jeb muttered.

"Am I?" Leo asked, his tone smooth as leather.

"I want to show you something," I said.

"Kinky, Stacy," he said.

His playful tone vanished when he saw Mr. Sagnoski, realizing that I was the one who had found him and that Kathy's corpse was missing.

"What in God's name do you feed this mutt?" Derek asked when he picked me up. "He's passing gas like a trucker on a burrito binge."

"It's not that bad," I lied.

"Why is he here?" said Cinnamon. She'd packed up a few things I thought we might need for this powwow and met me at the coroner's office.

"Hey, it's my car," Derek said.

"Yeah, well, I could do without the bitching, thanks," Cin said.

"Stop it, both of you. I need Cin because Chip might talk to her, and Cin, I need Derek because he has a working car and a recorder."

Tony was aligning the front end of Cin's Trans Am after Mario played chicken with the snowdrift.

"Well, why do we need the dog? You can't bring him into the hospital," Derek said.

Oh, but I had a plan.

I filled Cinnamon in on the scrying session, the necklaces, and Mario. I didn't know what, if any, connection there might be, but those necklaces looked an awful lot alike. Gus had filled them both in on the coroner and Kathy's missing body while I was giving my statement to Leo.

At the mention of the scrying session, Derek shot me a sideways glance and said, "What are you talking about, voodoo? Because I got an aunt who's into voodoo, and that's some scary shit."

"Now can I hit him?" Cin asked.

I poked her.

"It's not voodoo, and I don't have time to explain it." Mostly because I didn't know how.

"Hey, invite him to the inn for dinner one night. Birdie can explain everything." Cinnamon smiled wickedly.

"You chicks are nuts, man," Derek muttered.

I couldn't argue with that, and since we had arrived at the hospital, Cin didn't bother.

"This will never work," Cinnamon said as we walked through the doors.

"Trust me," I said to Cinnamon, "Lyn looks up to you. She'll do anything you ask."

"What about the nurses?" Derek asked.

"Once we sail past the front desk, it shouldn't be an issue," I said, feigning confidence.

Lyn's head was dipped into a book when we approached the front desk.

She looked up, and I swear, if she had a tail, it would have wagged. "Hi, Cinnamon. Gee, I tried to call you direct about the kid in two twenty-seven, but I didn't get you, so then I tried Stacy, but her phone wasn't working, and did he steal from your bar? Because I hear that Everclear is—"

Cinnamon halted Lyn. "It's okay, Lyn, really."

Lynn looked relieved, and then she said, "Hey, is that Thor?"

"Yep," I said. "Thor's a certified Canine Good Citizen now. We thought he'd cheer Chip up."

Derek beamed at Lyn.

Lyn's eyebrows danced up and down as she shifted from one foot to the other. "Oh. I see. Gee, I think I'd have to clear this with someone." She shuffled through some paperwork.

"Already done," Derek said, flashing a manila folder as if it contained some top-secret documents.

Thor sat down, perfectly still, showing off his fake CGC tag we pulled together from a key ring Cin had in her purse.

"Oh. Well, okay, then. Come to think of it, I did hear something about implementing a special program for the patients. Studies show that animals reduce stress."

"Thanks!" I said, and we hurried away.

Since Thor refused to ride the elevator, we climbed up the stairwell and shuffled down to 227.

Cinnamon ducked into the room, shutting the door behind her. Derek, Thor, and I waited in the hall.

Fifteen minutes later, Cinnamon stalked out, nostrils flaring.

"That little cockroach. When he gets out of here, I swear, I'm going to put him right back in, because my foot will be planted so far up his ass he'll need a surgical team to remove it."

"So it went well, then?" Derek asked, and I grabbed her hand before she could punch him.

"What happened?" I asked.

"He just smirked at me, the little snot. He wouldn't tell me how he got the booze or what he knows about the fire. But something's up. I can feel it. He had to be the one to forge my signature. Maybe he even called in the order," Cin said.

Of course, if that were true, someone else had put him up to it. He wasn't even born when Kathy was murdered. So who was it? That's what we had to find out.

"Okay. Plan B," I said. "Ready, Thor?"

Thor perked his ears up, and his body followed.

Derek stood guard while my cousin and I attempted to shake some information out of Chip. She told me he had just turned eighteen, so I wasn't concerned about corrupting a minor.

He was slapping his knee at the television when we walked in, oblivious to Thor slithering under the foot of the bed. I grabbed the remote and clicked the screen off.

"Hiya, Chip! How are the eyebrows?" I asked.

"Better yet, how's the balls? Because when I get through with you—"

"Cinnamon," I interrupted. "The kid's hurt. C'mon. Lighten up."

"What is this? Good cop, boob cop?" Chip cackled again. His face was layered in salve, and his shiny head had red scabs all over it.

"Well, yes, that was the plan," I said.

"Look, lady, I already told that one"—he pointed to Cin, whose face boiled with rage—"I had nothing to do with the fire."

I ignored the "lady" comment and forged ahead.

"You were there that day, Chip. I saw you."

"I don't know what you mean." He crossed his arms.

"This look familiar?" Cin said as she produced the jeans pocket Thor had ripped off of him the night of the fire.

Chip scooted farther back on the bed and kicked off the blanket. He studied our reactions, then relaxed and said, "So what? I was in the crowd with everyone else, watching. I should sue your ass for what that dog did."

"You know, Cinnamon, I never thought of that." I twisted my neck toward her.

Cin crossed her arms and said, "Hmm."

"I bet someone could get in a heap of trouble for being so careless."

"Mmm." Cin nodded.

"I mean, say, for instance, you're a minor and you forge someone's signature on a liquor order. Then say that liquor was traced to an arson."

"Interesting," Cin said.

"Hey, I don't know what you're talking about. I don't even work Thursdays." Chip smirked and cocked his head.

"Then how do you explain your handwriting in Cinnamon's name on the liquor order?" I asked, and Cin held it up.

Chip licked his lips. "That's not my handwriting."

"Well, the lab tech at the police station says differently. Helps to be tight with the chief." I narrowed my eyes.

Chip's pink face lost a bit of color as his head trailed from Cin to me.

"Yep," she said. "Good thing you filled out this application when you applied for the job."

"We had the handwriting analyzed, Chip. Guess what we found?"

Of course, none of this was true. Even if Amethyst had a lab, which it doesn't, that would take weeks. But I was banking on the fact that Chip was as dumb as he looked.

Chip snatched the papers and tore them up. Then a switch flipped, and he must have recalled a recent *CSI* episode, because he shook his head and said, "You two are full of it."

I leaned away from the bed and caught Cin's eye. "Guess we can't fool him."

"Guess not," she agreed.

It was a shame that Chip wasn't as dumb as I had hoped. Things might have gone much smoother for him if he were.

In my pocket was a stick of pepperoni I had asked Cin to bring along for Thor as a snack. I grabbed it, waved it low so he could smell it, then said, "Fetch," as I tossed it onto Chip's crotch.

"What the...?" was all Chip could get out before Thor's front paws were on the bed, his mouth secured around the pepperoni Cinnamon brought and Chip's own.

"Thor, hold," I commanded.

"Get him off!" Chip yelled and eyeballed the call button.

"Don't you dare," I said. "Don't move, don't scream, don't even blink, because I only have to utter one simple command and you'll be as smooth as a Ken doll. Do you understand?"

Chip nodded.

"Good. Did you sign that order form?" I asked.

Another nod.

"Why?" Cinnamon asked.

He shrugged.

"You don't know?" Cin threw her hands up. "This isn't helping, Stacy. I say we let Thor eat his snack."

"Wait, there's more, but..." He stopped.

"But what?" I asked.

"What if I accidentally say the command?" He looked at Thor.

"We'll risk it," I said.

The kid was really sweating now. He whispered the rest of the story. "When I got there on Wednesday, you weren't there yet. I was sitting out back waiting for you to show up and this liquor distributor asks me to sign for an order. Said he was in a bind and couldn't wait for you." He glanced at Thor. "That's all I know."

"What was his name?" Cinnamon asked.

"I don't know. Blue-striped uniform, black boots. Not the regular guy." His gaze was trained on Thor, who was drooling all over Chip's gown.

Cin leaned into Chip. "What else?"

Chip hesitated.

Cin looked at Thor. "He hasn't eaten in two days."

"Okay, okay." Chip licked his lips. "He flipped me a hundred for it. Then I figured, since you weren't around, I could swipe some bottles, and no one would notice. I hid the case inside the Dumpster and snuck it into the basement with the rest of the stock later that night."

"Then what?" I said.

He tilted his head back and sighed. "I was at the top of the stairs and I tripped. A bottle busted, sprayed everywhere. I tried to clean it up, honest."

He looked at Cin, who shook her head.

"I'm so sorry. I didn't mean to hurt anyone," he said.

I was sure he meant it. "It was an accident," I said.

We started away, but before she opened the door, Cin turned to Chip and said, "You tell anyone about our visit, you will go to jail." Then we walked out to meet Derek.

"That explains how the fire climbed to the main floor. Maybe we just got in the way." We were buckled into Derek's car again, heading to Main Street.

Cin shook her head. "No one on my list has a uniform like that, Stacy."

"Okay, fake distributor bribes a kid to accept a liquor order. But who lit the match and why?"

"To frame me? Ruin my business? Monique is the only person who hates me that much," Cin said.

I considered this. "I don't know. I'm still leaning toward a cover-up of the murder."

"But you said yourself, the body was there for more than twenty years," Cin said. "Why now?"

"Jesus Lord, who gave that dog pepperoni!" Derek said and covered his nose. "I'll have to get this ride overhauled just to get the stank out."

I looked at Derek, and a tiny bell rang in my head.

"Derek, you're a genius," I said.

"I am?"

"He is?" asked Cin.

"Yep, because I just figured out where it all started."

Chapter 21

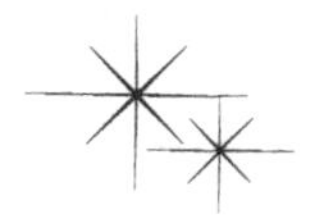

Thor grabbed a drink from the water fountain, and I went to check in with Parker.

He was reading the comics when I knocked on the open door.

"Well, if it isn't the Angel of Death," Parker said.

"Not funny."

"Heard you had an interesting morning."

"You said a mouthful." Literally. He was eating a sub.

"Any new leads on the fire?"

"No, but you have fresh copy and photos, plus I'll get you the piece on the coroner's murder."

"Any suspects?"

"Not yet. I'll have to check in with Leo."

"That reminds me. He called. Wants you to stop at the station."

Before I could take care of any other business, I had to pump out a story on the murder of the coroner. I sent it to Parker, then called Chance.

"Tony has your Jeep, but I doubt it can be resurrected," he said. "Then I think Leo wanted to scrape it for evidence."

"Thanks. Did you find my bag?"

"Nope. Sorry."

Damn. "Can you give me a ride to the DMV?"

"Anything for you, gorgeous."

The implication of his words hung in the air like spicy cologne as I dialed my credit card company. Turned out explaining a lost card wasn't as easy as it seemed. After spinning on the merry-go-round of customer service, in which they claimed I would need the account number or access code on the back of the card to request a new one, to which I countered, "But it's at the bottom of the lake, and I'm not a deep-sea fisherman," I hung up.

Chance had the motor running when I walked out.

"I'm starving. Mind if we grab a sandwich?"

"That sounds great," I said.

Over ham-and-cheese melts and green tea at Muddy Waters, Chance listened to the theory that sprang to mind when Derek mentioned overhauling his ride. Cinnamon had everything lined up to do renovations on the bar, which might have led to tuck-pointing and sealing the brick in the basement. If it looked like the structure was damaged in any way, old bricks might have needed to be replaced, and the body could have been discovered. Perhaps whoever was responsible for the arson thought it might be easier all the way around if the place just burned to the ground. But it didn't, so he or she sneaked back in and filled in the three missing bricks.

He sat back, thoughtful for a minute, and ran a napkin over his lips. "If Cinnamon filed all the paperwork to get the renovations done, there are dozens of people who could have access to that request. Contractors can freely bid on projects for historic buildings, although not all of them would get approved. Plus, the office personnel, city officials, and anyone on the historic preservation committee would have to vote on it for final approval." He bit into a pickle.

I sighed. If the renovation request was what set in motion the need to cover up the body, and therefore the reason for the arson, then I had to be getting closer to Kathy's killer. And, I suspected, Mr. Sagnoski's. The question was, how did I find out exactly who had seen the documents? And even if I gathered that information, how did I know the person didn't talk about the job? Anyone could have overheard a conversation like that anywhere in Amethyst. The rumor mill was a 24-7 operation. So even if I got my hands on the list of contractors and board members who needed to approve the work, that did not mean the person responsible for Kathy's death wouldn't have heard of it.

"Where do I start?"

"Talk to Kirk McAllister, the building inspector. He'll know every hand that touched that document."

I ran into Monique coming out of the DMV. She looked like she had run into a paint palette.

"Well, if it isn't Susie Sunshine," she said.

"Hello, Monique. I see you're learning to color inside the lines. Good for you." I brushed past her and gripped the handle when she stopped me.

"I hear you're investigating about what you found inside your cousin's bar. Planning on printing all the gory details? Not a good idea."

"Who told you that?"

Her white furry hat reminded me of a horny rabbit I had once. "A man who loves my company who is just young enough to please me, but not too young to get me arrested."

Derek. Now I had an excuse to let Cinnamon kick his ass.

"Monique, when you start sleeping with my editor, then you can tell me what to print. Seducing the photographer doesn't carry any clout. Didn't they teach you that in slut school?"

She fumed. "Stacy, tourists hate to read about dead bodies and murders while they're scarfing down burgers. Ruins their whole weekend. Don't suppose your grandmother can support herself on Social Security."

She smiled the way Lucy would before she yanked the football away from Charlie Brown.

I was too tired to think of a clever comeback, so I pulled her hat over her face and went to get my license.

Chance graciously waited for me and dropped me at city hall when I was finished. He hugged me close and said, "Please be careful."

"I will. Thanks for the ride."

A smile formed on his face as his mind minced my words into a double entendre, and he drove away.

I was about to rap on Kirk McAllister's door when I heard a loud voice drifting through the wood.

"Kirkie, no. I wanna go home now." The slow drawl belonged to Eddie, Kirk's brother.

Eddie. He won the bid for the masonry work.

If Kirk responded, I couldn't hear it.

Eddie came through again, shouting, "You can't make me! I do good work!"

A muffled tone. Then Eddie said, "You stop now! I'm going!"

The knob twisted, and I stood there facing Kirk and Eddie.

Eddie pushed past me and ran down the steps.

"Eddie!" Kirk shouted, but his brother kept going.

He sighed and turned to me. "What can I do for you, Stacy?"

"I was wondering if I might take a look at Cinnamon's proposal for the renovations she had in mind at the Opal."

"Okay." Kirk's eyes watched as Eddie shoved open the door. "Well, I can dig it out for you, but it will take a while. It's been filed already."

"I can wait," I said. "Actually, I was really interested in the bids."

"The bids? Why?"

Good question. Why would I want those? "Well, I thought I might have a patio put in at the cottage, so I could use some contacts."

"I could put a list together for you."

Of course he could. That was the kind of week I was having.

"Well, it's been my understanding that when it comes to the businesses and the historic nature of Main Street, contractors can be quite fair. For the private sector, though, I heard prices vary greatly, so I was just hoping to get an idea of what to expect someone to charge per hour."

Kirk looked at me like I was snowing him, which, of course, I was.

"The bids are confidential until the request filters through the entire approval process, and since the fire, everything has been put on hold. We're waiting for the insurance report."

"But I thought Eddie was pretty much approved to do the job?"

"Well, he was in the lead—he's the best mason worker around—but the initial request called for carpentry and metalwork as well. There was a newer construction company with subcontractors who could have done it all at a pretty fair price that I was about to show to Cinnamon before the fire."

Kirk said he would give me a call after he pulled together the contact list. I thanked him and left city hall nonplussed. But something about that brotherly exchange didn't sit well. The vision I had at the Elks Lodge—Kirk standing over a fresh grave—penetrated my mind.

I thanked Kirk and jogged across the street to meet Leo.

Could Kirk have had something to do with the fire? And who was lying in the grave site? I tried to recall the voice I had heard from the scrying session. I thought it was deeper than Kirk's, but could it have belonged to him? He would have been just past thirty in 1989. Eddie was ten years younger.

"Stacy?" Betty interrupted my thoughts. Her bouffant hairdo took up all the space in the threshold, and her lilac perfume took up all the space in my lungs. "You coming in, honey?"

"Yes, thanks."

"He's waiting for you in his office." Betty went back to her tabloid, and I pushed through the little half gate.

I sometimes wonder if, had I knocked first, things would have turned out differently.

Leo smiled when he saw me, and I barely got the door closed when I said, "You are going to be proud of me." I slithered to his desk, leaned over, and grabbed his shirt.

As I was kissing him, a voice said, "So, why is that, Miss Justice? Did you *not* find any dead bodies this afternoon?"

Son of a bitch.

I pulled back, pasted on a smile, and faced the mayor.

"That's right, Mr. Mayor. Just the one."

"Well, maybe things will pick up." He filled the folding chair in Leo's office. Legs crossed, hands steady, he had the practiced aura of a man who never lost at poker.

"So," I turned back to Leo, "what did you want to see me about? Did you find any evidence in my water-logged vehicle?"

"No. We're still working on the Jeep; it's some mess. No prints on the scalpel, either." Leo darted his eyes to his favorite uncle. "I wanted to give you this." He handed me an envelope.

I raised my eyebrows at him and opened the envelope. Inside were a brochure and a ticket for a cruise. I was flabbergasted.

"We're going on a cruise!" My voice raised an octave, and I smiled back at the mayor.

He avoided my eyes.

"Wow, Leo, this is perfect. As soon as things settle down."

Leo stuffed his hands in his pockets. "Actually. It's just for you. I thought you could use a break."

I dropped the envelope.

"Are you kidding? Leo, I'm working on a story."

"You mean interfering with an investigation," said the mayor.

I backed up so I could look at both of them. "No. I'm working on a story." I said it slow and clear so no one would be confused.

The mayor stood. "Is that what you call telling the parents of a lost girl that their daughter is dead?"

"That was an accident."

"Yes, well your accident"—he used finger quotes (I hate that)—"had me on the phone for an hour with a distraught mother. I had to promise her we would find the girl's killer."

"We will," I said.

"*We have no body*!" the mayor shouted. "Now, if it even was the Sims girl, how do I tell them they can't bury their daughter?"

No one spoke for a minute. A wave of guilt washed over me.

I spoke softly. "It was her. The clothes she was wearing, the pin. I saw the same pin in a photograph at her home."

"Gone," said Leo.

"But I saw them. I can identify her possessions," I said, aching for her parents. I knew I screwed up, but I couldn't do anything about that now.

The mayor stepped forward. "You will do no such thing, Miss Justice. I want you off this story, before you screw up this case and more people wind up with their throats slit."

"With all due respect, Mr. Mayor, you have no authority over me. You can't force me into submission."

"No"—he reached for his hat and coat—"but I do have authority in this town. Things like bed-and-breakfast licenses, building permits, and liquor ordinances are well within my reach."

I watched him leave, and then I turned to Leo. "Did he just threaten my whole freaking family?" I said.

Leo looked down and raked his hand through his hair.

"Leo?"

He sighed. "Take the cruise."

"What?" I was shocked. "Are you kidding me?"

"Stacy," Leo said sharply, "I'm afraid of what will happen to you if you keep pushing this. You have taken this thing to a whole different level. It's not your job anymore; you made it personal. You're not thinking clearly, and you need to stop and gain some perspective." He raised his voice. "Leave the investigating to me. Are we clear?"

I was so angry my hands were shaking, but my voice was low and steady. "Now, you listen to me, Leo. I nearly died in that fire. My cousin nearly died. She lost her livelihood. The business she poured blood, sweat, and tears into. Someone ran me off the road, tossed a rock through my window, and planted an explosive on my porch. It is personal, goddammit!"

I stopped talking when I realized I wasn't helping my case.

Leo put a hand on my shoulder. "Please, get out of town for a while. Let me figure out who's doing this."

I shrugged him off. I had every intention of telling him about how the fire started when I walked in there, about the mysterious deliveryman. But now something made me keep that from him.

"I can't walk away, Leo." I met his eyes and said, "And if you can't understand that, we're done here."

Leo stepped forward, his dark eyes meeting mine. "Okay," he sighed. "We won't talk about it anymore. I'll call you later."

"No"—I shook my head and pointed between us—"I mean *we* are done."

Chapter 22

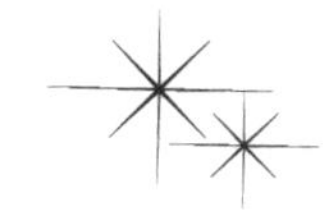

Anger has a strange way of keeping a body warm. Despite the arctic temperatures and the clouds snatching the sunshine, my blood boiled as I thought of Leo's utter gall of trying to send me on a cruise so I wouldn't impede the case.

Okay, so I slipped up with Kathy's parents and the coroner took one in the neck, but I was getting closer to the truth. Obviously, someone wanted to hide any evidence Kathy's autopsy might have revealed and poor Mr. Sagnoski got in the way. But I didn't ask for that anymore than I asked for a rock through my window or a chicken with a firework shoved up its butt.

Did he really think my leaving would make everything all better? And if he did, what did that say about his feelings for me?

My moon boots carried me up the hill to the cottage, where I was hoping to find a car. Thankfully, Gramps had come through.

It was a beast of a vehicle, with four-wheel drive and the perks you would expect from a man of wealth. The keys were on the seat, and his note said simply, *Enjoy*.

The car was warming up as I dashed inside for my checkbook, the necklaces, and the Blessed Book. I ran several errands, which included replacing my cell phone and picking up a long wool coat, Sherpa-lined boots, hats, gloves, and a canvas tote.

Then I called Derek and told him I would be around late in the day to pick up Thor. I left out my encounter with Monique. That needed to be reprimanded face-to-face. I fantasized of all the ways Cinnamon would make him cry as I drove out to the Simses' place. The chimney was puffing out smoke as I rolled into the driveway half an hour later. I sat there for a minute, working up the courage to knock. I had to find out who Carol was.

A pane of ice covered the steps leading to the bell. After a moment, the lace curtain fluttered, and Mrs. Sims's owl eyes stared through the glass.

"You go away!" she said.

"Mrs. Sims, I understand you're upset. Please. I have a few more questions for you."

"Go away!" Her face was an angry knot.

"Please, I just want to help."

She flapped her arms and screamed, "*Go*!" And her eyes said, *Haven't you done enough?*

I turned and shuffled down the steps, stabbed with guilt.

In the parking lot of a fast-food restaurant, I called information and connected to Matt Huckleberry.

"Huckleberry Tree Farm," said Matt.

"Hi, Matt, this is Stacy Justice. I was wondering if I could ask you a question."

"Sure, Stacy."

"Did you know a Carol back in high school?"

Matt didn't hesitate. "Sure. She was Kathy's best girlfriend."

"Do you know where I might find her?"

"Sure."

I guess when you own a tree farm, the tendency is to send everyone you've ever met a Christmas card in October.

Carol lived a few blocks from the Simses, and thanks to Gramps's super mobile, I found it easily through the GPS.

The house itself, a stately mini-mansion, with etched-glass windows and round pillars, overshadowed the tiny lot it sat on. Carol had done well for herself.

A tall, frazzled woman with a baby on her hip greeted me. "Come on in," she said. "The room is upstairs. I have no idea what to do with it, but I can't stand the pink."

I followed her in and said, "Um, I think—"

"Billy!" she screamed. "Stop hitting your brother!"

Billy put the bat down and pouted. His brother looked pleased. Seemed like a setup to me.

"Go on, I have to feed the baby, but I'll meet you upstairs in a minute," she said.

"Excuse me, Carol?"

"Yes?" She brushed her hair back and wiped spit off the baby's mouth at the same time.

"Hi, I think you have me confused with someone else."

"Aren't you from Defined Concepts?"

"No."

Carol looked disappointed.

"I'm Stacy Justice. I wanted to talk to you about Kathy Sims."

Carol blinked, then swayed. I grabbed the baby just before she fell onto the carpet.

"She never told me his name," she said fifteen minutes later.

We were sitting at Carol's kitchen table, me with a baby in my lap and vomit on my new coat, Carol with a glass of water.

The baby fussed, and Carol lifted him from my lap. "Sorry about your coat."

"No problem." I pulled the necklace from my pocket. "Did this belong to Kathy?"

Carol examined it and shrugged. "I've never seen it before."

I tucked it away and asked. "Do you know if she was pregnant?"

Carol nodded. "A week before she left, we took a pregnancy test together. I did it just so she wouldn't be nervous. Hers was positive."

"Did she tell anyone?"

"Not that I know of. I don't even think she told him. But she wanted the baby. She was a wild child, for sure"—Carol's eyes flicked to her own children—"but she said to me that she was going to keep it no matter what. I figured that was why she ran. Her parents never would have understood. Her dad would have killed her."

"And you have no idea who the father was?"

She shook her head. "Just that he was a cop."

I snapped to attention. "A cop? Are you sure?" Of course! The star. The star from the scrying session. It was a badge.

"Yes. That's why she wouldn't tell me who he was. He was older, and she didn't want to get him in trouble. You don't think he had something to do with her disappearance, do you?"

I wasn't about to stick my foot in my mouth again, so I just told her I didn't know.

But I did.

I knew now that a police officer was the father of Kathy's unborn child.

And she lost her life because of it.

Chapter 23

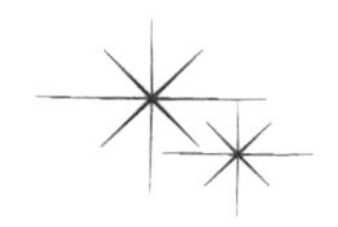

My rearview mirror got a workout as I sped toward Amethyst. I wasn't about to lose another vehicle to water damage. Thankfully, there was no sign of anyone following me.

A cop. I didn't see that coming. If a police officer got an eighteen-year-old girl pregnant, it might not ruin his career, but if that girl was underage when their relationship began, that was a whole other ball game. A statutory rape conviction would put him in prison with criminals he had sent away. He wouldn't last a second. Carol didn't know what town the guy worked in or if he was with the county sheriff's office.

Which made it harder to identify him.

I spotted Eddie McAllister patching a wall along the river as I coasted into town. I still didn't understand what the conversation meant between him and his brother, but I was certain I could squeeze more out of Eddie than Kirk.

I pulled over and trotted to Eddie. His breath sliced the air in short bursts, and his gloves were covered in wet cement.

"Hi, Eddie. Got a minute?"

He didn't look up. "Very busy. Need to work."

"Well, that's okay. Maybe I could buy you a cup of coffee when you're through?"

Eddie mixed up more cement, which didn't look easy given the frigid temperatures. "Why?"

"Well, because you look cold and coffee is hot."

Eddie's head was bent over his work. "Hot chocolate tastes better."

"Hot chocolate it is, then. Meet me across the street at Muddy Waters?"

"Okay." He tested the goop with a small shovel.

"What time do you think you'll be done?"

"I stop at five o'clock."

"Five o'clock it is, then."

When I got to the paper, I marched into Derek's office first and slammed the door.

Thor trotted to greet me, and I told him to lie down.

"It's about damn time, Justice," Derek said. "This dog snores, farts, and burps more than my grandpa. It's disgusting."

"Where did you go to journalism school?"

Derek gave me an odd look. "Why?"

"Because I want to know what kind of school teaches students to discuss stories with the town tramp."

Derek swigged his water and said, "I don't know what you're talking about."

I plastered my hands on his desk and said, "I had a conversation with your booty call."

Derek looked away, then met my eyes. "Let me explain."

"Explain what?" I threw my hands up.

"Monique was scared about the fire and the arson rumors, so I was just trying to ease her mind."

"That doesn't sound like Monique." I folded my arms.

"Then she got me drunk, and I didn't know what the hell I was saying."

"That sounds like Monique."

Derek was humbled for the first time in front of me. "My bad," he said.

Thor trotted to my hip. "Just don't do it again," I said. I clutched the handle and added, "In fact, don't go near that woman without protection."

"You mean a condom?"

"I was thinking more like Cinnamon."

I gave Derek my new cell number and told him to pass it on. Then I polished some copy and sent Thor to do his business before I paid a visit to Gladys.

Her nose was hidden behind a paperback book titled *A Witch in Every Woman.*

I cleared my throat, and Gladys looked up. "Oh, hello, Stacy."

"Hi, Gladys. Interesting book?"

"Oh, yes. We are all witches. Did you know?"

"I did not." Hoped not, anyway.

Gladys launched into a description of the chapter she was reading on how a woman's menstrual cycle mirrors that of the moon and how the moon controls the tides, and since the tides are water and humans are made up of mostly water, that means women control all human life.

I wondered if Gladys had ever heard of the miracle of birth before I cut her off.

"Listen, I have some work for you."

"Oh, good. What you need?" She pulled her glasses down and waited.

I explained that I wanted her to try to dig up a police roster for the whole county from 1989.

Gladys agreed, and I ducked out for my hot chocolate date.

Muddy Waters was empty when I got there, and the clock told me I had some time to kill. I ordered a cappuccino, found a table, and pulled out the Blessed Book for a cram session. I didn't find anything on hunting down a crazed maniac, but the first chapter after the history was "Calling on Your Spirit Guides." I figured I could use all the help I could get, so I sank in.

I wasn't sure how many pages I had devoured before darkness descended, but the clock on my phone read five thirty. I was just about to shut the book when a gust of wind fluttered the pages. They flipped back and forth before finally resting on this passage: *The Seeker of Justice shall cross with one who embodies the old soil, the force of which will have great impact on Geraghtys, past, present, and future. The choice she makes shall decide her fate. One path leads to unity and three become one. The other leads to destruction that shall never be repaired.*

I sat back. "One who embodies the old soil." What the hell did that mean? I read the words again. Skimmed the script with my fingertips.

Two paths.

One choice.

Why are witches so cryptic? Why couldn't she just write, *If you come to a fork in the road, take the one on the left and you won't completely screw up everyone's life?*

I read on, hoping there would be a hint as to which was the right choice. Because if the wrong path were set in motion, it didn't sound like the outcome would be favorable for anybody. And I had enough bad decisions behind me.

Suddenly, my cheeks grew hot, like someone was watching me.

Slowly, I lifted my eyes. The mustached man stared at me through the window.

Call it stupidity, call it blind faith, call it a coffee high, but I grabbed my stuff and sprinted out the door after him.

He was gone by the time I made it outside. I looked right, then left, before spotting him climbing the steps. I was about to call out when a tristate tourism bus loaded with passengers blocked my path. The driver let a carriage horse carting a young couple pass by before I could squeeze around it. By then my stalker had disappeared.

I stood for a minute, chastising myself, before I decided to backtrack to the river and catch up with Eddie.

The cement bucket was there, hardening, and it looked like the wall wasn't quite finished. I wandered the embankment, calling his name. No answer.

The viaduct was close, so I ducked in there, thinking he might have gone in to warm up.

That's when I learned a new sign. Shivers down the spine? Understood. Nausea? Nailed down.

But for the past few days, I was equating the cold in my lungs to the calendar date. Now I knew it meant something more.

Death was near.

Chapter 24

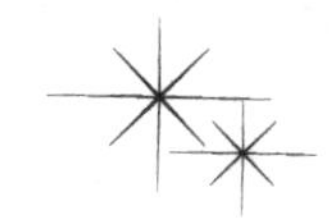

The vision of Kirk slumped over a fresh grave played in my head as I stared at Eddie, his throat pried open with a putty knife.

Is that what my vision was telling me? Kirk would bury his brother?

I decided to worry about that later, since there was a killer on the loose and I was in a dark storm drain. I ran back to my car and tried to call in an anonymous tip, wondering why anyone would murder harmless Eddie. He must have known something for certain.

The anonymous tip idea wasn't going over so well.

"Is this Stacy?" Betty asked. "You mean to tell me you found another body? Hey, Chief, you ain't gonna believe this."

My phone buzzed just after I hung up, and Derek said, "Are you going to come get this dog?"

I met Derek in the back lot behind the newspaper building and told him about Eddie. He jumped at the chance to cover the story, and I was ready to plan my next move. I needed to spring a step or two ahead of the game, but I wasn't sure how. Every person I'd thought might help me wound up with an extra orifice in his head.

Thor had some energy when we got home, having napped most of the day, so I threw the ball around the yard at the cottage. As I did, I thought about the players in this chess match and how none of them lined up properly.

Mr. Huckleberry owned the building. He was also the father of Matt, Kathy's good friend. I couldn't find any other link and couldn't decide what reason either of them would have to kill her. Did she have dirt on one of them? Was she threatening to pull Matthew from the closet?

Then there was Mario. The necklace. The cigar ring. Seemed like there was a connection there, but Mario only visited Amethyst occasionally. How would he have become acquainted with a girl who didn't even live in this town?

Of course, there was always the possibility that Monique actually did pay someone to torch the bar, but that would mean the body was a coincidence, and I just didn't think she had it in her.

Then there were Eddie and Kirk. Lifelong Amethyst residents. But Eddie was dead now. And I had no proof of any connection between Kirk and Kathy.

I packed a few things in my bag and walked to Angelica's, calling Cin along the way to meet me there.

"I'm here already helping my jackass uncle enter an online dating profile."

"You're kidding."

"Do I sound like I'm kidding?" She did not. "Hey, if it gets him out of my hair, I'm all for it."

I didn't mention Eddie. I wanted to tell Cin about that in person, alone.

I knocked on the back door, and Angelica called for me to come in. Sweet fennel and caramelized onion kicked through the screen, announcing her homemade Italian sausage with roasted peppers.

"Stacy, dear, you stay for dinner, hah?"

"Sure will."

Cinnamon was sucking on a Guinness when I walked into the living room, her dark curls tangled as if she had twisted them with her fingers a hundred times.

"No, Mario," she said, keeping the beer close to the computer.

Mario was hovering over her wearing a *No Fat Chicks* T-shirt, his belly testing the elasticity of the fabric. The fabric lost.

"But why not, Cinnamon?" he whined.

"Because everyone in the free world knows what George Clooney looks like, okay? No one will take it seriously, and I'm already bending the laws of physics describing you as a"—Cin looked to a sheet of paper—"virile, young Italian with a godlike physique."

I choked out a cough, and they both looked up.

Mario smiled at me like a snake charmer. "Ah, Stacy, *mi bella*. I am on the line!"

"Online," Cin corrected.

"Good for you, Mario." Not so good for the unsuspecting cast of single females.

"I turned on the parental controls," she said.

I shook my coat off, and Cin offered me a glass of wine, which I accepted. I needed all the courage I could muster tonight.

"Ah, my necklace." Mario kissed his fingers and said, "You are a vision. One-of-a-kind necklace for a one-of-a-kind girl, hah?" Then he laughed.

Cin and I shared a curious look as Angelica walked in with a bowlful of sausage and peppers.

"*Mangia*!" she said.

I helped Cinnamon gather the salad and bread. "Did you hear that?" I asked when we were alone in the kitchen.

"What?" Cin's head was buried in the refrigerator, digging for dressing. All I could see were her Levi's.

"One of a kind? Is that true?"

She fished out a bottle of homemade Italian dressing and shut the door. "Please, Stacy, you expect honesty from that man? He would lie to the pope if he thought it would get him laid or paid."

"Guess I need to ask him about it." I twisted the cross around, and Cin cocked her head.

"Is that the necklace you just bought?" She pointed to my sweater. "It seems familiar."

"It does?" I perked up. "It matches the one I dug out from the basement. Where do you think you've seen it before?"

Cin shrugged. "I'm not really sure."

"In the bar?"

"Could be." She frowned. "Then again, Mario might have shown it to me."

"Well, let's find out," I said. I moved to get the olive oil when Cinnamon's expression stopped me.

"What? Did you think of something?" I asked.

"Yes. Why are you dressed like a ninja?"

I bent my head down at my black jeans, black sweatshirt, and black boots. "I'll tell you later," I said.

"Can't wait," Cin said.

We carted everything to the dining room table and settled in. Cinnamon explained to her mother that Tony was at a friend's house watching a basketball game, and Angelica seemed to accept that, darting her eyes toward Mario, who was lining sausages on his plate like soldiers preparing for battle.

"So, Mario," I started, "where do you get your jewelry from?"

"From Italy," Mario said. He stabbed at a sausage and piled it into his mouth. "Good price, eh?" he said with his mouth full.

"Mario, you make her pay?" Angelica asked, and her tone indicated she didn't approve.

"I give her good price. Right, Stacy?" He reached for a slice of bread, and Angelica slapped his hand and screamed something at him in Italian.

Cin got up to get another beer, and I stared at my plate, feeling bad for Mario.

"Mama, stop," Cin said when she came back. "Let's not fight, okay?"

Angelica shot Mario a menacing look and helped herself to some salad.

The Seeker of Justice shall cross with one who embodies the old soil.

Old soil. Mario? But that wasn't my old soil.

Okay, let's try this again.

"So, you said the necklaces are one of a kind?" I asked Cin's uncle.

Mario said, "*Si,*" and Angelica said, "Hah!" Then they started bickering again and flashing each other hand signals.

I hoped Cin could decipher what they were saying, because I had no clue and I felt dangerously close to starting a family war.

Cinnamon and I pretended to talk about recent movies and books we'd seen or read as Mario and Angelica ate in silence.

"Well, that got me nowhere," I said later as I helped Cinnamon with the dishes. Angelica had gone down to the bakery to start the dough for the morning's pastries.

"Mama was just mad at Mario for charging you for that necklace you bought. She called his jewelry cheap, and that made him mad. Then he said something about other people here appreciate art, and she said he wouldn't know art if it smacked him on the head. Then she threatened to smack him on the head."

Wow. She knows her Italian. "What else?"

"I don't know. I tuned out after that."

"Okay, well, Angelica's gone. So I'll show Mario the other necklace and ask him who he sold it to."

"Good luck." She smirked.

"What's that supposed to mean?"

"It means the man can't remember to wear pants half the time. He won't remember who he swindled into buying a cheap necklace two years ago."

"Well, what if it wasn't that long ago?"

Cin squirted more soap into the sink. "It still had to be at least five years ago. That was the last time Mario was in town. Before that, I don't recall and I didn't own the bar."

Either way, it didn't matter. Mario was passed out with his mouth open in a Sicilian food coma when I went back into the living room.

Cinnamon came up behind me. "Now what?" she asked.

I turned to her. "You up for playing ninja?"

"*The Seeker of Justice shall cross with one who embodies the old soil, the force of which will have great impact on Geraghtys, past, present, and future. The choice she makes shall decide her fate. One path leads to unity and three become one. The other leads to destruction that shall never be repaired,*" Cinnamon read.

"What do you think?" I asked.

"I think you're losing it," Cin said.

I snatched the page from her hand. I had copied the passage from the book before I left home that night. "I'm not losing it." I stuffed it away in the bag.

"Stacy, we are crouched between Dumpsters behind city hall at eleven o'clock wearing ski masks. I think that's the definition of losing it."

She did have a point. What the hell was I doing? Two stints in jail in less than a week, and here I was again, about to break the law. I had to get to those damn papers, though. I wanted this to be over before I stumbled across another corpse. Maybe when Maegan mentioned the old soil she meant Kirk. He was Irish, right? McAllister? That would be my family's old soil. Unless he was Scottish. I wasn't sure.

"Do you really think Kirk McAllister killed his own brother?" Cinnamon whispered.

"I don't know, Cin. But the vision, then the argument I overheard. I make plans to meet with Eddie and an hour later he's dead? Something stinks. Maybe the answer is in Kirk's office."

"And you think this piece of paper is proof?"

"Of course not. But I bet there's something in his office that ties him to Kathy. Maybe Kirk was a cop."

"Why can't we wait for Gladys to find that out? You told me on the way over here she was working on that for you."

I shook my head. "That could take a long time, Cin. In case you hadn't noticed, we've got two strikes, two outs, and three balls."

"What does that mean?"

"It means two people are dead."

"Okay, so that's two strikes. What about the outs?"

"I'm out of ideas."

"Well, where do three balls come in?"

"Oh yeah. Three people are dead. Those are the balls. I don't want to be the fourth ball."

"That doesn't make sense. Then what are the strikes?"

"Forget the metaphor."

"That was a metaphor? I thought it was an analogy."

"Can we get on with it?"

"Yeah, I'm not too thrilled about sitting next to you right now," she said.

"Quit complaining. As many fights as I've gotten you out of, you can sit here with me while I plan a breaking and entering."

"What about Leo? Why can't you just ask him to get a search warrant or something?"

I scratched my nose. "Um, no. That might, um, tip him off. Kirk, I mean."

Cin lifted her mask and studied my face. "Why are you lying to me?"

"I'm not. Come on. Let's get on with it."

"Oh, I don't think so." She waved her hand at me. "What are you not telling me?"

Geez, I really didn't want to get into this right now, but I knew Cin would not relent. "I broke up with Leo, okay?"

"What?"

Her voice was too loud, and I covered her mouth with my hand. "Shh."

"Why the hell did you do that?"

"Can we please discuss this later?" My nose hairs were frozen solid, but thanks to several flexible layers, I was warm and comfortable everywhere else.

"Fine. Boost me up," Cin said.

When Cinnamon was a teenager, she made Lindsay Lohan look like a Camp Fire Girl. Mostly, her temper got her in trouble, but she was also skilled at sneaking into places she didn't belong, which was about to come in handy.

City hall is a historic building, so the integrity of the original structure has been preserved for the most part. The upstairs windows are the small, old-fashioned kind that jut out from the building on warm days, secured only with an eyehook.

Cin carefully popped the screen out with a flathead screwdriver and glanced down. I extended my arms and caught it.

Then I tossed her the crowbar, and she didn't so much as flake the paint as she eased the window open.

I hopped up on the Dumpster and we climbed into Kirk's office, shutting the window behind us.

"Cin, I'll take the desk. You see if you can open the file cabinet."

She gave me a thumbs-up.

I shuffled through drawers filled with stacks of invoices, work approvals, and city planning maps.

Cin picked the lock on the file cabinet as I opened the bookcase. The tiny flashlight in my hand revealed volumes of building codes, city ordinances, and past projects.

"I think I have something," Cinnamon said.

"What is it?"

"It's a picture. I can't see the guy's face, but he's wearing a uniform. Could be military. Toss me that flashlight."

I lobbed it to her, and it rolled underneath a door inside Kirk's office. Bathroom? Closet? I tiptoed toward it and twisted the knob.

Then the phone rang and I jumped.

Cin and I stared at the phone. After the fourth ring, the answering machine clicked on.

"Yeah, hi, Kirk? Are you there? Because we got a call down at the station about a light on in your office. I just wanted to be sure, is all." It was Gus. "Anyway, call me back if you get this." Gus paused. "Sorry about what happened to your brother, but we're on it. We'll find out who did it."

After he disconnected, Cinnamon said, "I am not going to jail tonight. We have to get out of here."

I agreed and we started back toward the window before the sound of footsteps stopped us.

"The closet," I whispered.

Cin closed the file drawer, darted for the door, and gave the handle a tug.

"Damn!" she said.

"What?"

"Locked."

"Damn."

We scanned the room. The options were to hide beneath the desk or in the filing cabinet.

I dragged Cin to the left of the door and smashed her against the wall with my body right before Kirk walked in.

We each held our breath as he crossed to the cabinet, unlocked a drawer in the dark, and said, "Where the hell is it?"

He must have hit the answering machine then, because I heard Gus's voice. When Gus said, "We'll find out who did it," Kirk grunted and said, "Sure you will."

I caught my own reflection in the windowpane just as Kirk lifted his head and looked right at me.

Chapter 25

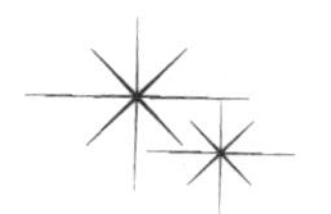

Kirk screamed and rubbed his eyes. I hit the floor and Cin wiggled closer to the doorjamb. I managed to crawl around and crouched behind there with her.

When Kirk braved another view through the window, the floating head he had seen (me) was gone.

"Jesus," he panted, clutching his chest. "I have to get the hell out of here." He searched a bit longer before he gave up and mumbled, "Must be at home."

I wondered what "it" was as he shut the door behind him.

Cinnamon and I both held our breath longer than we needed to.

"You think he's gone?" she asked.

"I hope so."

We slipped out the same way we came in and ran down the alley.

"Did you grab the photo?" I asked when we were on our way back home.

"In my pocket." Cinnamon stopped walking and grabbed my arm. "Oh my God, Stacy," she said.

"What, what? Are you okay?" I searched her face.

Her eyes lit up. "I just remembered where I saw that necklace!"

"Where?" Cin's enthusiasm spilled over to me.

"The Opal. There's a photo collage of events and various customers from over the years. It's tacked up behind the bar. I don't know who was wearing it, but I just remember thinking I thought the design was unusual, so it stuck in my mind." She nodded. "I'm certain of it now. You know how it is when you see the same thing every day so you just don't pay any attention to it? I think that's why I couldn't place it before."

"Let's go," I said to Cinnamon.

All of Amethyst was asleep. The bars and restaurants were closed. Shop windows dark, businesses tucked in for the night. Except for the wind that occasionally swept the sidewalks, the streets were bare and quiet. We hurried past the lamplights, crossed Main Street, and started for the rear of the Black Opal.

Cinnamon approached the door as I scanned the street. No sign of life.

"Dammit!"

"What's wrong, Cin?"

"Look." She stepped aside, and I saw the problem.

The back door was boarded up.

I glanced at the crowbar in my hand and looked at Cin.

"First you want me to bust into city hall. Now I'm supposed to break into my own bar? Is that it?" She jutted out her hip and rested her hand on it.

I shrugged. "Pretty much."

Cin sighed and took the crowbar from me. The first nail pop was loud, but the others extracted smoothly and we were inside within minutes. The back door hung from the hinges, the lock destroyed when the firefighters barreled through.

I paused.

"Stacy, come on."

"I just thought of something."

"What?"

"We could have checked to see if the front door was unlocked."

Cin lifted her ski mask and said, "I'll pretend you didn't just say that."

We crept through the maze of tables and chairs, making our way to the front of the building. Cinnamon had yet to hire a cleanup crew since the insurance company had delayed her claim. I suspected, after Fiona's encouragement, Smalls would come through soon.

The photo collage was displayed to the right of the mirror behind the bar. Cinnamon gave me the photo from Kirk's office, and I went to check out the ones on the wall.

Cin muttered, "Damn door is open." She leaned the crowbar near it.

I quickly scanned the pictures and removed my sweatshirt and the necklace, setting it on the bar next to the photo of Kirk. It was an old picture, and it looked to be cut. There was definitely something around his neck.

The photo collage didn't appear to be arranged in any particular order. They were jumbled all together on a large, white poster board, and from the looks of some of the faded prints, it had been a work in progress as long as Mr. Huckleberry had run the place. There were shots of Scully, Cinnamon, Uncle Deck, Tommy, some tourists, and various other familiar faces. In the center was Leo, in uniform. I leaned in for a closer look. He too was wearing something around his neck. I gasped and yanked the photo from the wall.

"You got it?"

"Maybe. I need a magnifying glass."

"I think there's one in the register," she said.

Upon closer inspection, there was the distinct shape of a black cross in both pictures. The same kind that now lay on the Black Opal bar. Was this a costume party? Policemen's ball? I flipped the pictures over. No dates.

I looked up to ask Cin a question and saw a silhouette.

"Cinnamon, lock the door!"

"I'm on it," she said just as Kirk walked in.

My mind was racing, trying to connect all the dots. Kirk, Leo, Kathy—none of it made sense.

Kirk gave a little chuckle and said, "So, I guess it was the two of you in my office." He crossed his arms.

Cinnamon took a step backward. "I don't know what you're talking about."

"Me either," I said.

He pointed toward both of us. "So the ski masks, then, just a coincidence?"

We nodded.

"Look, ladies, I have had a helluva a day, so just hand it over and I'll be on my way."

"Hand what over?" I asked.

"Don't play games. I know you were snooping for the bids, but I think you snatched something else by mistake, so just give it back to me and we'll forget all about the B and E."

"We didn't take anything," I said.

Kirk rubbed his forehead. "Okay, I'll play. It has four sharp edges and a date on it."

What had a date on it? Was he talking about the necklace?

"Where's my cruise ticket?" Kirk walked up to the bar and looked at the necklace.

Did he just say cruise ticket? Leo bought a cruise ticket. Did Leo know Kathy? But he would have just been a kid.

Kirk touched the cross and said, "Wow. I haven't seen this since..." He halted his words and met my stare. "Where did you get this?"

He recognized it. So it was his!

My eyes landed on Cinnamon. She tensed, sensing the danger. *Crap. Crap. Crap.* I flicked my gaze to the crowbar in the corner and back to Cinnamon. She creased her brow, not understanding. I concentrated, trying to send her a telepathic message. Which really only works in the movies.

Kirk slammed his hand down and said, "Tell me where you found this."

People don't always make the smartest choices under duress. Looking back, I suppose I could have handled things differently, and perhaps that night Cin and I would have both slept in our own beds.

Of course, I'll never know for sure.

"I found it in the basement here. After the fire," I said.

Cin shot me a look that said, *Now is not the time for honesty.*

Kirk looked from Cinnamon back to me. No one moved. I made a quick phone signal to Cin, and she shook her head. She didn't have it. I had left mine at Angelica's house. *Perfect.* I wondered if the phone in the bar was working.

Then again, who would I call—Leo?

"Well, it's a very nice necklace," Kirk said and stepped back. "Now, about my ticket?"

"Sorry, Kirk, we don't have your ticket," I said. "But don't you need to make arrangements for Eddie? Seems like an odd time to leave town."

Cin groaned and put her head in her hands.

Kirk shifted his stance. "People deal with grief in different ways. Lots of people get away after the loss of loved one." He stared at me hard. "You of all people should know that, Stacy."

That stung to my very core. "We don't have your ticket. You can leave now," I said. "Unless you want to finish off what you started. You know, burn the rest of the place down."

"Stacy…" Cin said, her voice on edge.

"Excuse me?" Kirk said.

"I know all about it, Kirk. The kid, the bribe."

"Have you lost your mind?"

I continued. "Chip was here on Thursday, planning to sneak in and steal some booze before Cinnamon opened up. No one was supposed to be here." I paused to let that sink in and to organize my lie. "He saw the guy's face before the match was ever lit. He was pretty scared this afternoon when he told us the story, but we finally convinced him to tell the investigators what he saw. He's giving a statement as we speak."

Kirk looked at me, my expression solid. Then he turned to Cin, who nodded.

Kirk bowed his head and whispered, "Eddie."

Eddie? Cinnamon shot a curious look in Kirk's direction.

So Kirk sent his little brother to do his dirty work? I couldn't think of a more disgusting betrayal. How dare he take advantage of his brother?

To my amazement, Kirk slumped onto a bar stool and a small sob escaped him.

"It's all my fault." He stared at the floor as the words poured from him. "It was supposed to look like an electrical fire. After the inspection, I was going to do it." A tear sloped down his cheek. "But Tommy never left the room, so I couldn't. Then I went to plan B. I sent Eddie because I was running out of time. It had to be done, but I couldn't get in here to do the job." He looked up. "No one was supposed to be here." He looked up at me, his eyes bloodshot. "Neither of you were supposed to be here. Leo mentioned some family celebration." He wiped his arms on his sleeve. "No one was supposed to get hurt."

Leo. How could he? Why would he?

"So the fire, the arson—it was all to cover up the body buried in the wall and Kathy's murder?" Cinnamon said.

He lifted his gaze. "What? No! There was no murder. Kathy's death was an accident." He shook his head as if that would convince us.

"No. It wasn't, Kirk," I said. "She had ligature marks on her neck."

Kirk sat back and stared in the mirror. "No." His words were careful, thoughtful. "That's not true." His jaw cracked, and his voice grew steady, tears drying up. He stood, angry. "It was an accident, but we had to hide her."

"Listen to me, Kirk. It was no accident. The girl was strangled, and she was pregnant at the time of her death."

"What?" Kirk stood up and shook his head. "You're nuts. It was an accident, that's all. She fell and hit her head. But no one would have believed it. What good would it have done to ruin two lives? The girl was already dead."

My anger broke, and I didn't think before I blurted out, "I suppose Mr. Sagnoski was an accident? And your brother? Was he an accident too?"

Before I could react, Kirk lunged at me across the bar, both hands squeezing my throat, cutting off my airway.

Cinnamon jumped on Kirk's back, and I struggled to reach for a booze bottle to hit him with. I pointed behind Cinnamon, to remind her of the crowbar in the corner.

She understood that time and turned to retrieve it.

The world grew hazy as my lungs lost oxygen. This was it. Now I would die the same way Kathy had. I briefly wondered if my father would meet me before my legs lifted off the floor.

Somewhere between this world and the other, shots cracked through the night. The coppery taste of blood filled my mouth as my head slammed on the hard wood.

Chapter 26

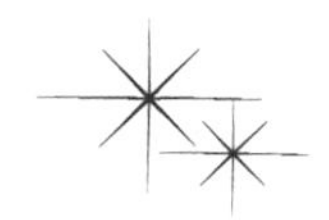

I blinked twice, just to make sure I was still alive.

Kirk's hands were no longer roped around my neck. My head felt like a hundred pounds as I peeled it off the hard oak.

The mayor stood in the doorframe, a gun in his hand. "You all right, Miss Justice?"

"Yes. I think so." I rubbed my neck and inhaled all the air I could.

From the amount of blood oozing from his head, I suspected Kirk wasn't going to make his cruise.

"Cinnamon? Cin?" I croaked.

She gave no response.

I ran around the bar to find my cousin, my best friend, motionless on the floor, a liquid red fanning out from her hair. Either she fell on a shard of glass, which still lay everywhere from the fire, or a bullet hit her.

"Oh my God. Cinnamon!" I dropped to my knees, panic elevating my heartbeat.

"Don't touch her! Go call for help." The mayor rushed forward as I dashed back behind the bar and reached for the phone, reciting under my breath the lesson I had read that afternoon about calling forth the spirit guides from the Blessed Book.

"To all who have gone before, once loved, now lost, heed my call."

I picked up the receiver.

"Spirits of the Summerland, one and all."

There was no dial tone.

My voice grew in intensity. "To those that left us too soon and lost souls of the departed."

I clicked the receiver a few times, my voice getting louder. "The watchtowers come forth, help me finish what I started."

"Put the phone down, Miss Justice," the mayor said. "It appears to not be working."

I hung up and said, "Do you have a cell phone?"

When I turned, I was staring into the barrel of a gun.

"What are you doing?" I asked.

He had flipped over both photographs. His hand was on the photograph of Leo. That's when I noticed it was cut too. And the pair seemed to fit together as if it had been one photo, cut in two.

The mayor's face twitched for a moment, then relaxed.

The photos fit together, but that was a much younger Kirk, and Leo looked to be the same age.

But how was that possible. Unless…

God, how could I have been so stupid?

Before he even said it, I knew.

"You thought that was Leo in the photograph, didn't you?"

Oops. They really looked eerily alike.

He laughed.

"It's not that funny," I said.

"Well, it is, but no matter. You would have looked at it in a better light and realized that it was me in that old picture. I noticed the necklace around your neck when you popped into my nephew's office. I thought you might connect the dots sooner or later." He clicked his tongue. "So, where did you find it? I looked all over for it when Kirk said he had lost his."

I didn't answer him. Instead, I said, "Please, Cinnamon is hurt. She had no part in this, I promise you. You can't just let my cousin lay there and die."

"I'll call for help as soon as I take care of you."

That was less than comforting.

"Like you took care of Kathy?"

"I made Kathy happy. But she got greedy. Careless."

"So you killed her."

"It was an accident."

"Sure it was. That's what you told your friend, wasn't it? That's how you got Kirk to agree to help you."

The mayor smiled at me with disgust. "A partner would do anything for a fellow officer. Men are like that."

Partner? Kirk was the mayor's partner on the force?

"Watchtowers of the north, come forth," I said.

"Stop that. No one can help you now, Miss Justice. Although, I must admit, I've tried every method of scaring you into submission. But nothing frightens you."

"Actually, that gun in your hand has me a little jumpy."

"Really?"

I nodded.

The Mayor made a tsk-tsk sound. "You should have just taken that trip. I knew Kirk wouldn't need the ticket."

"I freckle."

The mayor frowned. "And what was it you told my nephew? You couldn't just walk away?"

"That too."

"Yes, Kathy had the same attitude. Didn't get her far, did it?"

"Watchtowers of the south, come out," I said.

"Okay, that's giving me a headache now."

"Watchtowers of the east, come meet."

"You honestly think this chanting will save you?"

It was worth a shot.

"Come out from behind that bar," he said.

"No way, you psycho sewer rat."

The mayor's jaw went hard. "Fine. I'll shoot you where you stand."

"And how will you explain that?"

He thought a minute. "My good friend Kirk pulled the trigger on you, then turned the gun on himself. The guilt was too much."

I considered the angle of the trajectory and where Kirk had been hit. That might actually work.

"That won't work," I said.

"Of course it will."

"Watchtowers of the west, confess."

"I have had enough of you."

The mayor aimed his weapon, and I yanked the soda gun out and fired a stream of Coke in his face. It threw him off balance and landed square in his eye. Then the liquid slowed and trickled to a halt. I looked at the handle.

Damn! There must have been only a little left in the hose. The firefighters probably disconnected the CO_2.

"Goddammit!" the mayor said as he wiped his face. He pointed the gun at me again. This time I knew he wouldn't miss. I hunted for something to throw at him, but a lot of the bottles were already smashed.

My fingers found a mixing tin, and I fired that off. It bounced off his chest as he squeezed off another shot. I bobbed and weaved, but the bullet punctured my shoulder, ripping my flesh. I scrambled for more ammunition as the mayor positioned for a clean shot. I tossed everything I could get my hands on. Napkin holder. Straws. Salt and pepper shakers. Pour spouts. My last hope was a giant jar of brandied cherries at the end of the bar.

Before I could nail him with it, the mayor turned his gun away from me.

I stopped. I knew what he was pointing at.

"She can live. Or she can die," he said casually.

Cinnamon.

Chapter 27

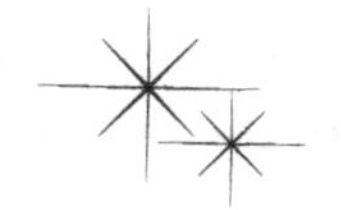

My arms were jelly as I set the fruit down.

"Good choice. Come out from behind there," he said.

When faced with the knowledge that your life will soon end, you either move incredibly slowly or maniacally fast. My legs carried me as if they'd been on the job for ninety years.

The mayor was considering his options. I already had one wound. Which was throbbing at that point. He would have to kill me carefully to construct a believable story.

For Cinnamon's sake, I hoped he got it right.

I waited for instruction.

"Move to the left of Kirk."

I did. Where were my spirit guides?

"No"—he waved the gun—"over there."

Again, I followed his directions. Did I miss something? Didn't I cast the spell correctly?

"Yes. That's it."

The goddess. I forgot to call the goddess.

"By the power of Brighid, I release thee!" I said.

"Too late," said the mayor.

He pointed the gun at my head.

I closed my eyes.

Nothing happened.

He drew a breath. "K…Kathy?" I heard him say.

I opened one eye. The mayor was staring over my head into the mirror behind me, transfixed on something.

He was distracted enough for me take a split second to crash a barstool into his skull. The gun flew from his hand, firing a phantom shot in the air before skating beneath the old jukebox.

I belly flopped toward it and crammed my torn arm underneath, but I couldn't see the weapon. I felt frantically for it. Then I remembered there was a crowbar nearby.

Flopping like a fish, I tried to wiggle free, but the hole in my shirt was snagged on something and it wouldn't let go.

Behind me, something made a sound.

I sneaked a peek. His face bloody, the mayor was towering over me, crowbar high above his head.

I flipped over, my arm still lodged, and I saw him bring it down. A sickening thud echoed in my ear as pain ripped through my shoulder. Again.

I thrashed in place, my arm clearly not cooperating, still conjoined to some unidentifiable piece of the jukebox. The second blow came and sliced through my jeans. The cut was deep, and blood gushed from it immediately. Before I could worry about the damage, I helicoptered my legs around and landed one good roundhouse kick, taking the mayor's feet out from under him. He landed on his back. Hard.

For a second, I was sure he had broken it, thanks to the crunching sound that punctuated his fall.

Then I looked up.

The overhead beam had split wide. The last bolt dangled, hardly holding the huge Gothic chandelier with the pointy spikes.

Apparently, the gunshot had made a direct hit.

The mayor was gasping for air, the wind knocked from him, it seemed.

And behind him, a moonbeam reflecting off her head like a halo, stood Kathy in her pink sweater and poodle skirt, a scarf neatly tied around her neck. She smiled at me, then looked at her former lover and shook her head, haunting eyes revealing a trace of peace.

I looked away before the fixture plummeted, impaling the mayor. I heard him scream in agony before I squeezed my eyes shut.

Chapter 28

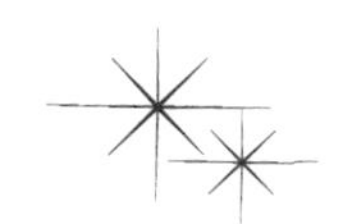

The essential oils of lavender and myrrh coaxed me awake. Lolly was working on my leg, which burned like hell. Her copper head bobbed up and down like a buoy. Birdie leaned over me, adjusting something, her shawl feathered around her shoulders. She stopped and looked at me. My head felt heavy as the stark white of the room penetrated my eyes.

"Welcome back, Anastasia," Birdie said.

"Hi," I croaked. My mouth was dry.

Behind Birdie, Fiona was arranging flowers, her face painted to perfection. "Oh, sweetheart, thank Brighid you're all right," she said.

Something was off. No capes. No lectures on how I am not fit to be a witch. My pulse quickened a bit, and I heard a machine beep.

"Lolly, the frankincense." Lolly produced a small brown bottle, and Birdie waved it under my nose.

"Stop it, Birdie. That stuff stinks."

The machine stopped beeping.

"Well, I want you to stay calm. Can't have those nurses poking their heads in while we work on you."

A hospital. I am in a hospital.

"That's right and you're going to be just fine," Lolly said.

How did she do that? I didn't say that out loud, did I?

"Cinnamon," I said and sat up, crystals raining around me.

Birdie pushed me back down. "She's fine, Anastasia. A mere flesh wound where the bullet grazed her skull. She just needed a little cleaning up and a few stitches."

I smiled at that, thanking the spirits.

"And Mr. Huckleberry is going to help her rebuild the Black Opal," Fiona informed me.

"Now, just lie still and let the crystals work," Birdie said. One by one, she picked them up and put them back on my head, a crown of smooth rocks.

"So, what's wrong with me?" I asked. My arm was stiff, and I felt like I was wearing a baseball mitt.

Birdie's bracelets jingled as she folded her hands in her lap. "Your right wrist is sprained, and the bullet was removed from your shoulder. The gash on your left leg cut to the bone, but that will heal nicely, thanks to your aunt Lolly."

"What time is it?"

"It's nearly eight o'clock on Tuesday."

"What? I've been out for a whole day?" That was impossible. How could I have slept that long? "Thor..."

"Taken care of," Birdie dismissed my concern with a sweep of her arm.

Lolly smiled, and I caught a whiff of Jameson.

"These beautiful roses are from Leo," Fiona said, cupping the flower heads. Then she moved to the window. "This arrangement is from Chance." She winked. "And of course there are plants from the office and cards and letters from half the town over here." She motioned to a counter beneath the window. "Would you like me to read you Leo's note?"

"No, thank you."

"Now, shall we talk about the lessons you've learned?" Birdie said, getting down to business.

"I'll pass on that too, Birdie."

"Nonsense." She waited.

I drew in a deep breath and thought about the events that had transpired over the last four days. The fire. The murders. Poor Kathy, buried in darkness for all those years.

And then she came to my rescue.

Birdie tapped my knee. "Well?"

"A picture is worth a thousand words," I said. I would have figured it all out sooner, had I known that photo was on the wall. Well, maybe.

Birdie pursed her lips. She motioned to Lolly.

Lolly reached behind her and pulled out the Blessed Book. She handed it to Birdie, who placed it on the cart next to my bed.

"Trust in your power. The rest will come," Birdie said and patted the cover.

There was a knock at the door, and Leo poked his head in. "Is it okay?" he asked to no one in particular.

Birdie rose, walked to the door, and whispered something in Leo's ear. He looked at her briefly, then nodded and smiled at Fiona and Lolly. The three of them waltzed from the room, and Leo stepped in.

His leather jacket was open, a white shirt offsetting his olive skin. I watched as he chose a chair near the foot of the bed. He clasped, then unclasped his hands. He crossed his legs. He uncrossed them. Then he stood and faced the window.

Geez, did I look that bad? I smoothed my hair out.

"Stacy, I'm so sorry. About everything." His voice was hoarse, but his shoulders were solid, and the view reminded me of why I had fallen for him in the first place. A heat trailed up my toes and through my legs.

I didn't say anything, because I wasn't sure what I was supposed to say. Relationships are not my area of expertise.

He reached into his pocket for something and held it in his hands, still facing the window.

"I feel like my heart's been ripped out. What my uncle did…it's…unbelievable." He shook his head. "I guess you know now the cruise wasn't my idea. He had me convinced that something terrible would happen to you. I can't believe I didn't see what he was doing. For that, I will always be sorry." He swore softly.

That's why he was sorry? I was expecting this conversation to go a little differently. Like, *Sorry I didn't believe in you, Stacy. I'm a schmuck and you deserve better.*

I sighed. I thought about the conversation with Birdie at the inn, the fact that the women in my family seem destined to remain single, and how Leo's eye twitches every time magic is mentioned. If I were to continue on this path, Leo couldn't be a part of it.

But this wasn't the time to tell him that.

"It wasn't your fault, Leo. You couldn't have known." Then I thought of something else. "Did you find Kathy?"

"Her body was stuffed in a freezer in my uncle's garage, along with a string of love letters. They're searching his place for evidence now. The theory we have is that Eddie and Kirk helped him bury the body in the wall, and that's why he killed them. Only they could link him to her. Mr. Huckleberry had hired Eddie at one time to stabilize the foundation. Eddie suggested that he rebuild the entire wall instead. We figured that was when they buried her there. The dates match up to Kathy's disappearance. We won't know for sure until we do some more investigating, but those were good guys. They couldn't have known her death was intentional."

He pulled an envelope from his pocket. "I didn't understand...things, Stacy, I know that now, but I think I'm starting to. I want to anyway."

He crossed to me and put the envelope on the nightstand. Then he looked at me for the first time, so much emotion in his eyes that my heart cracked.

He cocked his head. "What's in your hair?"

I felt the crown of my head and bumped into the crystals Birdie had put there. I pulled them out, one by one, and examined them.

Gemstones have spiritual properties as well as healing capabilities, so I gave Leo his first lesson in magic. "Amethyst, for rest; argonite, to heal bones; bloodstone, for wound repair." Bloodstone—the warrior stone and a symbol of justice, Birdie once told me.

Leo smiled. "Guess I have a lot to learn."

He leaned over the bed and softly kissed me. "Get some rest. If you decide you want to try again, you know where to find me."

My gaze followed as he started for the door. I ached to call him back.

Leo stopped and turned around. "Stacy?"

I waited, hoping he wouldn't say what he looked like he wanted to say. He didn't have to. I could feel it.

His lips parted, then paused. "Get better."

A knot formed in my throat, and I rolled onto my side. The door clicked, and he was gone.

After a moment, I reached for the envelope.

Inside were two tickets to Ireland and a brochure of a castle. Leo's note read, *I've heard this place is magical. I thought you two should meet, and I wanted to be the one to introduce you.*

I smiled and sank into sleep, dreaming of ivy-blanketed countryside, lapping waves, and knights in leather armor.

But dreams, as I have learned, can be deceiving.

I left the hospital the next evening with my arm in a sling, Vicodin, crutches, my book, and the crystals.

Gramps drove me home safely, and I begged him to tell Birdie and the aunts that I wasn't up for dinner or company. I just wanted to snuggle with my dog, read a book, and eat macaroni and cheese.

Thor acted like he hadn't seen me in a month as Gramps set my things on the counter. He hopped around me, nuzzling my free hand and talking in that way that Great Danes do. I kissed his big nose, and he wiggled.

Gramps hugged me gingerly and told me to call if I needed anything. Then he left.

In the living room sat a box filled with things from my office that Derek had delivered while I was in the hospital. His note read, *Parker thought you'd be more comfortable working at home until you recover. Take some time off. Call when you can.*

The note was taped to the three muses sword that I threatened Derek with earlier in the week. I laughed at the recollection and propped it against the counter. Maybe Cinnamon would help me hang it up later.

I set about organizing my desk. Plugged in my laptop, sorted through files, tossed office supplies in the top drawer. Then I put the Blessed Book next to all of it and fumbled with the bloodstone.

I supposed I would have to build my own supply kit if I was going to start practicing the craft—candles, oil, stones, a scrying mirror. I needed the whole shebang. Then perhaps my own spells would find their way between the pages of the Blessed Book. Maybe I would finally become a Geraghty Girl.

The thought made me shiver. I wasn't sure if that was what I truly wanted, but I owed it to myself to find out.

Thor scratched at the front door, telling me he had to go out, and I hobbled over to open it. The leg didn't hurt as much as I thought it would, so I doubted I would use the crutches much. The real bitch was carrying my arm in a sling. How was I going to work? Dress? Pee?

I shuffled into the bathroom, clipped my hair up, and crawled into sweatpants. I took a long, hard look at the mirror that had disrupted my life. Thankfully, it had no messages for me today except that I was tired. A yawn escaped, and I went in search of food.

While I was in the hospital, Chance had replaced the glass in the backdoor window, and Gramps had ordered me a new refrigerator. It was a sleek stainless model that I could never afford. I didn't like to take advantage of his wealth and generosity, but I needed a refrigerator and he needed to pamper someone, so it was a win-win.

I snagged an apple from the counter and bit into it. Then I went to check Chance's handiwork. As usual, it looked great. I walked toward the back door, marveling at my fortune of knowing such talented people.

Then I halted.

When trouble comes knocking, most of us ignore the signs. I have been guilty of it myself more times than I care to count. In hindsight, people will often admit that, yes, their creepy neighbor seemed a bit off, or the minute they walked down the alley, they knew it was a mistake.

But right then—after all that had happened—I knew when I saw the spiderweb I had an uninvited guest.

An intruder.

I swear to the gods, if my bedroom saw as much action as the back door of my cottage, I would be a much happier woman.

The door was locked, so I didn't bother trying to figure out how someone could have gotten inside. The question was who?

And more importantly, when?

Was someone here now? I centered myself, drawing on the power within me, but the Vicodin cast a haze over my intuition, and my senses were duller than usual.

I took a deep breath. No chills. No nausea. Just…fuzz. A buzzing in my ear like a bell.

I picked up the sword, not taking any chances.

Chance. Maybe that was it. Chance wasn't invited to fix the window. He just did it.

Or maybe the painkillers were causing hallucinations.

The cottage was calm. Thor was outside. I was safe.

I limped over to the window, the sword my cane, and watched my dog romp in the yard. I stood there, letting the tension slip away and peace take over. It felt good. My lungs filled with air, and I let my eyes slide shut.

When I opened them, a face flashed in the bay window.

Only it wasn't outside.

It was behind me.

And it wore a mustache.

Chapter 29

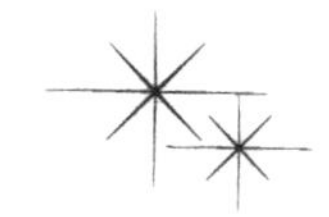

I kicked my uninjured leg behind me and whirled around, stabbing the wall perpendicular to the window with the sword. The three muses bobbed up and down, as if laughing.

At him or me, I wasn't sure.

Bull's-eye. He was tacked up by his overcoat.

I had a few advantages over the little guy. I was taller, there was a huge Great Dane outside, and I had a really cool sword in my hand.

He, however, had one huge advantage over me. Anonymity.

"Who the hell are you, and why have you been following me?" I demanded.

He refused to speak. He just shook in his boots, rattling against the blade; then he swallowed hard, and something about it struck me as odd. I looked at his neck, his features, his frame. All…dainty. My chest tightened.

The words of Maegan penetrated my head as we stared at each other: *The Seeker of Justice shall cross with one who embodies the old soil, the force of which will have great impact on Geraghtys, past, present, and future. The choice she makes shall decide her fate. One path leads to unity and three become one. The other leads to destruction that shall never be repaired.*

This was it. This was the moment Maegan warned about.

"Why won't you speak?" I asked.

He looked down, his toes barely touching the carpet. I don't know why, but I plucked the sword from the drywall and lowered it to my side.

He seemed vulnerable, not threatening, standing there in the shadow of the sun.

I sighed, losing patience. "Okay, as you can see, I've had a pretty screwed-up week. So off with the hat and glasses and let's talk about what it is you want so you can leave my house and I can get on with my life. And if the sword isn't a big enough incentive not to try anything that might get your arm lopped off, then take a gander at my boy, Thor." I pointed out the window.

He peeked, then faced me again.

He looked at the carpet, contemplating his next move. Wisely, he chose the right one.

The sunglasses floated down first. Then the mustache and gloves.

He lifted his head up and slowly removed his hat.

I gasped as a pool of long red hair, the same color as the setting sun, spilled around the shoulders of a female.

I stepped back, staring. Disbelief overwhelmed me.

Her green eyes.

Her red hair.

But it couldn't be. It was impossible.

I have only seen that shade of hair on one other person.

But how was this possible?

She removed her coat, exposing a cape.

And before she said a word, bells were ringing, and somehow my heart knew. Just *knew.*

Geraghtys past, present, and future, Maegan whispered in my mind.

But I would have known. I would have felt it these last few days. All these years.

“Who are you?” I demanded.

The words reached out at me, knotted around me.

“My name is Ivy. I’m your sister.”

The snow was knee-deep, my leg hurt, and my sweats were soaked, but I was hopped up on painkillers and a huge dose of pissed off, so I didn’t care.

“Stacy, wait!” Ivy said behind me, her voice desperate.

I ignored her as I marched into the Geraghty Girls’ house, slammed the door behind me, and screamed into the foyer. “Birdie! I need to talk to you right now!”

How could they keep her from me? Why would they keep her from me? A million questions swirled in my head. *How old is she? Did my mother know she was pregnant when she left?*

“Stacy, don’t, please.” Ivy spoke in a hushed tone. “Listen to me.”

“This is not about you, Ivy. Just back off,” I said.

“No, wait. You don’t understand. They can’t see me,” she squealed in that high-pitched voice that only teenagers can manufacture.

I stopped and turned to her. “What do you mean they can’t see you? Are you invisible? Are you a hallucination?”

At this point, anything was possible.

"Please," she begged, "come outside."

"Tell me one good reason right now, Ivy."

"Mom's in trouble," she said quickly. "And Birdie doesn't know about me."

I wasn't sure I believed that. Birdie knows everything.

"Please," she said again.

We locked eyes, and as I read her young face, I knew my life was about to change forever.

~END~

Author's Note

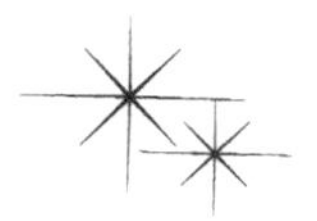

The Imbolc festival recognizes that time of year when one can just begin to feel a spark of spring. It is a celebration of spiritual awakening, renewal, abundance, and the return of the fire goddess, Brighid, who breathes life into the dead of winter. In Ireland today, Brighid (St. Brigit in Christianity) is still highly revered, and her perpetual flame—guarded by a group of nineteen priestesses for centuries—is now tended by the Brigidine Sisters of County Kildare. You can learn more about them here: http://www.solasbhride.ie/.

I decided to set *Opal Fire* around this Sabbat for several reasons. First, and perhaps most obvious, is that the book opens at the scene of a malicious fire. The threat of death and destruction starkly contrasts with the symbolism of rebirth and hope that is Brighid's eternal flame, much like the cycles we face every day of our lives. Also, Brighid is Birdie's namesake, and her character has an inner fire that fuels Stacy's journey. Lastly, because Stacy herself is on a path to spiritual enlightenment and Imbolc is a favorite dedication day for new witches, it was the obvious jumping-off point for this series.

If you want to create your own celebration in honor of Brighid, wear colors that attract the sun, like white, green, yellow, or gold. Do a bit of spring cleaning. Indulge in a purification bath scented with rose oil. Make fresh lemon–poppy seed cake or a batch of vegetable soup. Then sit back and imagine the snow melting and the trees budding.

Lemon–Poppy Seed Cake

Ingredients

1 cup butter
2 cups powdered sugar, sifted
3 eggs
1½ cups cake flour
2 teaspoons lemon extract
½ cup poppy seeds

Glaze (optional)

1 cup powdered sugar, sifted
1 fresh lemon

Directions

Grease a Bundt or tube pan and preheat the oven to 325°F. In a large bowl, cream butter and sugar. Beat in eggs one at a time. Add flour and lemon extract. Stir in poppy seeds. Fold batter into pan. Bake for 40 to 45 minutes, or until done. Allow to cool. Invert pan onto serving plate. Make glaze by mixing 1 cup sifted powdered sugar with fresh lemon juice. Drizzle over cake.

Also by Barbra Annino

Bloodstone: Stacy Justice Book Two

Tiger's Eye: Stacy Justice Book Three

Gnome Wars: a Short Story

Doppelganger: A Novella

Every Witch Way But Wicked: An Anthology

(includes a Stacy Justice story)

Acknowledgments

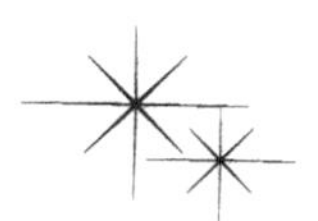

To the folks at Amazon Publishing who have helped countless authors reach numerous readers and especially Terry Goodman, for taking a chance on me. To Ashley McDonald for a superb editing job. To the town of Galena, on which Amethyst is loosely based. My mother, for the Irish. My aunt for the marriage retreat story.

And finally, to George, for the magic.

About the Author

Photo by GeorgeAnnino, 2011

Barbra Annino is a native of Chicago, a book junkie, and a Springsteen addict. She's worked as a bartender and humor columnist, and currently lives in picturesque Galena, Illinois, where she ran a bed-and-breakfast for five years. She now writes fiction full time—when she's not walking her three Great Danes.